Torn

Karen Moore

www.darkstroke.com

Discover us online:
www.darkstroke.com

Find us on instagram:
www.instagram.com/darkstrokebooks

Include **#darkstroke** in a photo of yourself
holding his book on Instagram and
something nice will happen.

*For my mum and dad
who would have been so proud.*

Acknowledgements

I would like to thank Laurence and Stephanie Patterson at Crooked Cat/Darkstroke for their belief in me as a writer and for all their guidance and support in bringing *Torn* to publication. Thanks also to my editor Christine McPherson for her keen eye and patience and for making the editing process so smooth and painless. And my additional thanks to the Crooked Cat writing community for their warm welcome and helpful insight into their world.

Thanks to all my fellow writers at Manchester Scribes for their invaluable advice which helped shape *Torn*, especially to Sue Barnard, Joe Fenton and Louise Jones who read early versions of the book. Your continued encouragement is much appreciated. My gratitude also to the Stockport Writers critique group for their honest feedback on my emerging chapters and developing writing skills. I couldn't have done this without any of you.

Thanks to my good friends Janet Finucane and Nathan Lee for their entertaining company, delicious meals, and endless patience over the years, listening and responding to my ideas for the book and putting up with continual updates. Their Welsh cottage helped inspire the North Wales setting of *Torn* and from which I have shamelessly borrowed. My apologies and thanks!

To Italy for being such an inspiring, exuberant and vibrant place and to all the people I've met there over the years who've contributed unwittingly to the *Torn* storyline. *Grazie mille.*

About the Author

Karen Moore is a British writer based in Cheshire. She lived in Italy for ten years and worked as a tour guide in Europe, the USA and Canada, followed by a career in PR and marketing. *Torn* is her debut novel.

Find her online:

www.facebook.com/karenmooreauthor
www.twitter.com/KarenMo35731701

Torn

Chapter One

The weather was getting worse as the storm drew nearer. Visibility had been reduced to a minimum by the driving rain battering the windscreen of the little Fiat 500, the incessant drumbeat of the windscreen wipers almost hypnotic.

In the passenger seat, Hanna looked again at her watch, fearful that they weren't going to arrive in time.

"Don't worry, we should be nearly there now," said her friend Ceri as she struggled to keep the car on course along the dimly-lit waterlogged road.

"Even if we get there in time, there's every chance that the flight will be cancelled," Hanna pointed out, her attempts at staying positive eroded by the stress of the last few weeks. "It would have been so much easier to fly from Rome, but we couldn't take the risk."

Huddled in the back seat, Hanna's daughter Eva lay half asleep, still in her fleecy pink pyjamas, topped by a thick down jacket in a deeper shade of pink. Wedged in by her side sat an enormous scarred suitcase crammed with their most treasured belongings.

"There's the airport sign now," said Ceri, straining to see through the windscreen. "We should just about make it."

Hanna glanced at her watch again. It was just after 7pm. Check-in was due to close at 7.45pm. It had turned 7.30pm when they finally pulled up outside the terminal building.

"Let me go and check everything's OK with the flight first," said Hanna, opening the passenger door. Ceri nodded.

She scurried over to the departures board. Only a handful of flights were scheduled to leave that evening, most of

3

which had already been cancelled. Her heart sank. But scrutinising the board more closely, she noticed that the Bristol flight was still open. Over the tannoy came the last call for passengers to Bristol.

Hanna dashed back to the car. Ceri helped her drag the bulky suitcase from the back seat, followed by a very drowsy Eva, and loaded them both onto a nearby trolley.

"Thanks for everything, Ceri," said Hanna, hugging her friend, tears welling in her eyes. "We couldn't have done it without you. I just hope…"

"Rhys will look after you both," replied Ceri firmly. "You couldn't be in safer hands."

"I'm counting on it."

"Look after yourselves. Keep in touch and let me know how you get on," said Ceri.

"Will do. I'll call when we get there," said Hanna with a tight smile, and she turned to hurry towards check-in with a brief backwards wave.

"You're in luck, *signora*. The Bristol flight is the last one out tonight and you've just made it in time," said the desk attendant, taking their tickets and passports. "Boarding has already started so you'll have to hurry. Gate 5. I'll let them know you're on your way."

Hanna smiled appreciatively as she hauled the suitcase onto the waiting conveyor belt while their documents were checked.

"*Buon viaggio!* Have a good trip!" said the attendant, returning their passports along with their boarding passes.

Hanna picked Eva up and rushed off across the concourse towards the departure gates. Security was quiet and they passed through quickly, arriving at the gate with a few other latecomers. Hanna noticed to her dismay that there was no shuttle bus or covered walkway so they would have to brave the elements to reach the waiting plane which was sitting several hundred metres away on the main apron. She set Eva down, unable to carry the three-year-old any longer.

The biting wind howled around them as they fought their way across the tarmac, the rain turning to a mixture of hail

4

and sleet, a constant stream of icy pellets striking their faces. Hanna prayed silently to a God that she didn't really believe in that the weather wouldn't stand in their way at this late stage.

She grabbed her daughter's hand tightly. "Come on, Eva, we have to hurry," she urged, as the little girl looked up at her with puzzled eyes. "*Sbrigati!*" she added in Italian, trying to make the sleepy child understand the urgency of the situation.

Clutching her battered old teddy Orsina, Eva clumsily tried to do as Hanna asked. They bowed their heads against the driving gale and hailstones that attacked them like little bullets as they struggled over towards the waiting plane. The plane that would take them far away from the country they'd come to regard as home.

Her heart thumping, Hanna cast an anxious glance behind her. She could barely make out the blurred mass of the terminal building fading into the darkness, and the last few stragglers bent almost double in their efforts to reach the plane. Nothing seemed amiss.

At last they reached the steps leading up to the open door of the plane where the welcoming smile of the waiting flight attendant had frozen into a frown. *Not the best omen*, thought Hanna as she swept Eva up into her arms for the last few steps.

A few almost inaudible words of Italian came from her offspring, clearly agitated and bewildered by being parted from her warm bed and bundled into the car for a long bumpy journey to the little provincial airport on the coast.

"*Che succede*? What's going on? Where are we going?" Eva wailed. "Isn't *Babbo* coming, too? And where's *Nonna*?"

"Don't worry, *piccola,*" said Hanna, kissing the top of her daughter's head lightly as she stepped inside the plane with her precious cargo. "We're going on a surprise trip, an adventure, just you and me. Daddy and Gran couldn't come. You'll enjoy it, you'll see."

The flight attendant forced a tired smile as she showed them to their seats. Eva yawned, hardly able to keep her eyes open. Hanna settled her down, fastening the seatbelt around her sleepy daughter before attending to her own.

Almost immediately, the engines started up, bringing the plane slowly to life. Through the window, Hanna could see the fading lights from the airport building as the plane taxied down the runway and started its gradual but difficult ascent, buffeted by the strong wind. The plane finally escaped from its grasp and settled to a steady cruising speed.

Eva had already fallen into a deep and seemingly untroubled sleep, her lips curved into a slight smile, her appearance angelic in stark contrast to the harsh artificial light and brash décor of the budget airline. Hanna stole a look around at her fellow passengers. No one seemed to be paying them any attention and she didn't recognise anyone. Reassured, she settled back in her narrow seat and heaved an enormous sigh of relief.

We've done it, she thought triumphantly, *we've managed to get away.* But this was tempered by a feeling of overwhelming despondency and dread of what lay ahead. Not only did she have to create a new life for the two of them, but she needed to make sure that they stayed safe and well away from Luciano's clutches.

She had to decide what to do about Luciano. But for now, that would have to wait. All that mattered was that their old life was behind them. Hanna felt drained; she laid her head back and closed her eyes, falling into a light but troubled sleep. Half an hour later, she woke with a start, her head pulsing from the dark remnants of her nap. She felt wearier than before. Eva was still fast sleep, a faint enigmatic smile on her face. Hanna's heart lurched as she watched the little girl's chest rising softly as she slept.

For the first time in ages, Hanna started to relax. *We're safe*, she thought.

At least for now.

Chapter Two

Sicily, Friday 16th August, 2013

"It's been ages since we've had a chance to catch up," said Ceri in her soft melodic Welsh lilt. "How're things going with Luciano?"

The two friends were sitting at one of Taormina's popular pavement cafés, the late morning sun caressing their faces, the light sea breeze taking the edge off the heat. The terrace boasted a magnificent picture-postcard view of the lofty peak of Mount Etna to the south and the shimmering waters of the Gulf of Naxos off to the east.

"Really well, couldn't be better," replied Hanna happily, sipping her iced coffee, "A bit scary really — the chemistry, I mean. It sort-of takes over. Everything else pales almost into insignificance. Sorry I've been neglecting you a bit of late."

"I'm just concerned for you. It can't be that easy trying to spend time with him when you're only here for a couple of days at a time and you've always got your group to look after."

Hanna and Ceri both worked as tour guides but for different companies. They had met the previous season when they kept running into each other at the various historic sites across the island. The two young women found they had a lot in common and became good friends. They would meet up whenever Hanna was in Sicily, which was usually about once a month now that she was alternating her tours with another around Tuscany and the isle of Elba.

"We manage okay but you're right, it *is* difficult when you've always got one eye on the clock," replied Hanna.

"Sure it's not just a holiday romance that will dwindle out at the end of the season?" Ceri asked.

"Who knows? It's doubtful, but we'll have to see. Whatever it is, I'm not going to pass it up, even if it's short-lived."

"Have you met any of his family?" pressed Ceri.

"Only his younger sister, Paola."

"And how was she with you?"

"What's with all the questions, Ceri?" Hanna frowned.

"It's just that…"

"Come on, Ceri, out with it."

"Well, there's talk… that Luciano might not be all he seems."

"Meaning what exactly?"

"I'm not sure," stammered Ceri apologetically. "It's just gossip, it's nothing. I shouldn't have mentioned it."

"Well, you haven't really said anything yet," said Hanna, a touch of annoyance creeping into her voice.

Just what was bothering Ceri? Maybe she was a little envious of her whirlwind relationship with Luciano? He was, after all, an amazingly attractive and successful local businessman. Hanna had met him at the opening of a swish new bar in the lively coastal resort of Giardini Naxos, about six kilometres south of Taormina.

She remembered the moment vividly. Both girls had dressed with care for the occasion – Hanna in a designer abstract-print linen dress, and Ceri in flamboyant burnt orange georgette. The guests' attention at the launch party focused on one man, who appeared to lap it up like a Hollywood actor before his adoring fans. He was easily the most attractive man there, the epitome of tall, dark, and handsome in a very Sicilian way. His face was particularly striking, with high cheekbones and a prominent aquiline nose.

As Hanna and Ceri accepted a flute of *spumante* and made their way through the crowded bar to the terrace overlooking the sea, the man glanced their way, fixing Hanna with his flashing coal-black eyes and intense mesmerising gaze.

Smiling, he extricated himself from his acolytes and headed towards them, his gaze fixed relentlessly on Hanna. She remembered feeling helpless and rooted to the spot, like an animal in a snare, spellbound.

When he spoke, his voice was deep and velvety just as she'd imagined it would be. She struggled to understand his thick dialect but could make out his name and the word "*bedda*", the local dialect word for beautiful; enough for her to understand that he was paying her a compliment. And when he smiled, it seemed to light up the whole bar. All the guests and the chatter and clinking of glasses faded into the background – it was as if only the two of them were in the room. This was Luciano; the effect he had on her was something that she had never experienced before. Hanna was smitten from that very first moment.

That had been at the beginning of the season, and they'd been inseparable ever since. Whenever she was in Sicily, Hanna and Luciano would meet up and spend every minute of their free time together. This often didn't amount to much; although she spent a few days on the island every month, she still had her tour group to look after.

The language didn't present a problem. Hanna's Italian was pretty fluent by now, although Luciano's was usually peppered with local words, some of which she was starting to recognise. It was a different story when he spoke to his friends. Then it was in a thick, guttural dialect spoken at machine-gun speed that she couldn't decipher.

Luciano told her that his family had a wine production business and although he didn't elaborate, it was obviously pretty lucrative. He had a small, stylish apartment overlooking the sea in Cefalu on the northern coast of the island, but seemed to spend little time there, preferring the company of friends and family. Whenever they met up, the apartment became a handy hideaway, their own private love nest where they could take time out from their busy lives. It was a luxury that neither of them had the chance to enjoy that often.

Her reverie was broken by the appearance of a waiter at

her side, asking if they wanted anything else. The two friends ordered two non-alcoholic aperitifs.

"What are you getting at?" asked Hanna, picking up the conversation where it had left off.

"It's just that… well, haven't you noticed anything unusual about him?"

"In what way?"

"Well, the fact that everyone's so… what's the word? Deferential, I suppose."

"He certainly seems to have a fair amount of influence, but that's just the circles he moves in, you know that," replied Hanna, unruffled.

"How are we doing for time?"

"Twenty minutes to go."

They finished their drinks, paid the bill, and left the café to walk through the narrow winding streets crowded with holidaymakers, towards the coach park to join their respective groups.

On the way back to the hotel, Hanna thought again about their conversation. What had Ceri been trying to tell her? Hanna had often wondered about the way people behaved in Luciano's presence, but she put it down to a mixture of respect for his family's business, their standing in the community, and his considerable personal charisma. Things were different here; there was still a strong sense of family and community. Religion also played its part. Families were close-knit; business transactions rarely involved people from beyond the island.

Although Hanna hadn't experienced any problems in her work, she wondered if she would ever be accepted if she were to settle down here permanently. Or would she forever be considered an outsider, a *straniera*?

Maybe Ceri was slightly envious. She'd just discovered that the coach driver she'd been seeing off and on since the start of the season was married with three small children living on the mainland. A touch of sour grapes, perhaps?

There was no more time to think about that now as the coach was pulling up at the hotel. Hanna announced the arrangements for the following day: an early departure from the hotel; a quick stop in Messina before the short ferry trip to the mainland; and then the long journey north through Calabria.

She planned to spend the afternoon completing the tour paperwork and accounts before meeting up with Luciano for dinner, followed by an early night. She smiled in anticipation of the evening to come.

Chapter Three

UK, Sunday 22nd – Monday 23rd October, 2017

It was gone ten when they finally touched down at Bristol Airport. Eva had dozed on and off throughout the flight once they'd left the storm behind. Hanna felt exhausted, the stress of the last few days taking their toll. Thoughts raced through her head, about the past and what lay ahead. The flight passed uneventfully, and in no time at all the plane started its descent before landing on the tarmac with a thud.

Eva was still asleep. Hanna shook her gently, noticing how like her father she was, with her dark curls and olive skin. "Come on, sleepy-head, *svegliati!* Wakey, wakey!"

Grumpy and dishevelled, Eva slowly came to life, rubbing her eyes sleepily. She seemed annoyed at having been disturbed so suddenly from her slumbers. Hanna began to sing softly, a favourite lullaby, as she unfastened the seatbelt around the toddler, running a hand through her mop of curls. It had the desired effect and Eva started to smile at the old familiar song. Hanna collected up their hand luggage and grasped her daughter by the hand as they joined the throng of passengers making their way off the plane.

The terminal building was deserted except for a few airline and passport staff waiting with bored expressions to process them. Theirs was the last arrival of the day. At the luggage carousel, Hanna glanced around anxiously to see if anyone was taking more than a passing interest in them. For a few seconds, she thought she saw a familiar face, an old associate of Luciano's, and she immediately went cold. But she must have been mistaken, for when she looked again, the image was nowhere to be seen.

But when Hanna turned round, neither was Eva. There was no sign of her anywhere. Panic coursed through Hanna's veins, making her feel nauseous and lightheaded. She forced herself to think rationally: it had only been a minute, Eva couldn't have got far. How could she have been so lax? She dashed round to the other side of the carousel, in panic. Nothing. Then suddenly, through the crowd of people moving towards the exit, Hanna spied Eva clutching Orsina, her teddy bear. Her anxiety turning to relief, she ran over and threw her arms around the little girl.

"Eva, where've you been? I was so worried! What happened? Don't ever leave me like that again!" Hanna chastised her.

Eva's eyes brimmed with tears. "Sorry, *Mammina,* but Orsina got lost. I had to save her."

Orsina was Eva's favourite toy and the two were inseparable. Eva refused to go anywhere without her. She must have dropped the teddy and wandered back to look for her.

"Well, never mind, you've found her now. Everything's fine," Hanna said, hugging her daughter tightly. "But please don't ever wander off again. Just let me know if there's a problem and Mummy will sort it out." She lightly kissed the top of Eva's head and wiped away the few tears trickling down the toddler's cheeks. "Come on, we're both tired. We need some sleep 'cos we've got another long journey tomorrow."

Grabbing Eva firmly by the hand, Hanna collected their battered suitcase from the carousel, loaded it onto a trolley, and together they headed for the exit. An icy blast greeted them as they stepped outside, Hanna battling with the reluctant luggage trolley and the equally reluctant toddler.

The hotel shuttle bus was waiting for them, its engine running, the driver keen to end his shift and return home. They were the only passengers and the bus left as soon as they had boarded. Within twenty minutes or so, they reached the hotel and checked in. The room was large, clean, impersonal, and cold. Hanna shivered and turned up the thermostat.

She gave Eva a carton of apple juice from the mini bar which the youngster slurped noisily through a straw before allowing herself to be undressed and tucked up in bed. The toddler drifted off to sleep almost as soon as her head hit the pillow, clutching Orsina tightly to her chest.

Feeling drained, Hanna quickly undressed and slipped gratefully between the cool sheets. She too fell asleep almost immediately, only to wake up an hour later, her head buzzing with the events of the last few days and the plans that she and Ceri had hatched together. The rest of the night followed a similar pattern, with Hanna sleeping in fits and starts which did little to relieve her tiredness.

The next day dawned bright and cold. Hanna woke early with a muzzy head, full of the million and one things that lay ahead. *One step at a time*, she thought. Eva was still sleeping peacefully, curled into a tight little ball. After a long, hot shower, Hanna was changing into a fresh pair of jeans and a shaggy multi-coloured sweater when she heard Eva's voice. Turning round, she found the little girl sitting up in bed, a puzzled expression on her face.

"Where are we?" she asked, looking round the unfamiliar surroundings.

"We're back home," explained Hanna, "or rather, we soon will be."

"But this isn't home. I want to see *Babbo*. Where is he?" Eva's voice wobbled, rising in pitch, the tell-tale signs of an imminent tantrum.

Hanna gave her a reassuring cuddle. "We're on a special adventure, just us two girls. It'll be exciting, you'll see! We're going to have lots of fun while Daddy's working."

Eva's eyes widened as she let out a conspiratorial giggle. "Goody, goody!" she said, throwing her arms wide for Hanna to undress her. Then she frowned. "Orsina, she's gone again!"

"No, she hasn't, sweetheart. Here she is, still tucked up in bed," said Hanna, pointing to the little bear peeping out from under the duvet. "Bring her along and she can watch you having your bath. Then we can get some breakfast and go and see our new house and meet our new friends."

Eva seemed satisfied with this response and let Hanna bathe and dress her without any fuss. Leaving the room, she skipped along the corridor to the breakfast room at Hanna's side, Orsina grasped tightly in one hand.

Breakfast took a little longer than expected as Eva was captivated by the crackling noise that her cereal made and kept insisting on adding more milk to prolong the experience. She wasn't happy until it ended up as an inedible sloppy mess which she then pushed to one side.

It was nearly ten by the time Hanna picked up their luggage and went to the reception desk to check out, and collected the keys for the hire car that had been arranged in advance. She had no trouble in finding the little black Vauxhall Corsa at the far side of the car park. Eva jumped up and down with excitement at the prospect of another car journey. Hanna felt relieved; she'd been so sure that Eva had been on the verge of a tantrum. Instead, she seemed to be enjoying it. She loved going to new places. Maybe it was turning into an adventure, after all, just like Mummy had promised. Even if Daddy was missing.

Once Hanna had finished loading their luggage into the small but perfectly functional car, she rummaged through her handbag for Ceri's old UK pay-as-you-go mobile phone. She sent her friend a quick text to let her know everything had gone to plan and that they'd arrived safely. Then she punched in a speed dial number and waited for a response.

"We're just leaving. Should be with you early evening, depending how it goes and how often we stop. Where's best to meet?"

She paused as she listened to the response. Seemingly content with what she heard, Hanna ended the conversation and started the car.

Chapter Four

Sicily, Thursday 12th September, 2013

Hanna was sitting on the balcony of her hotel room, enjoying the views of the sea shimmering out in the bay, when her mobile phone rang.

"*Pronto*," she answered.

"*Ciao amore,* it's Luciano. How's it going? Are you still okay for lunch?"

"Just got to finish off these accounts, then I'm all yours," said Hanna.

"*Va bene.* Pick you up about one then?"

"Perfect."

"Wear something impressive – we're going to that new restaurant I've been promising to take you to."

"Can't wait," she said, her voice suddenly shrill with excitement and anticipation. "See you in a bit."

She looked at her watch. Just over an hour before Luciano would pick her up at the hotel. Just enough time to finish off the paperwork and shower. It was getting towards the end of the season but the temperatures showed no sign of letting up. Even sitting on the balcony had left her feeling hot and sweaty.

Her thoughts turned to what she would wear. She didn't want to let Luciano down. Hanna had always taken care with her appearance. Being in Italy was a joy – she felt like a child in a sweet shop. So many beautiful clothes, as long as you observed the strict colour code that changed from season to season, and the fabulous array of handbags and shoes and the stunning jewellery. Shopping, even window shopping, was sheer bliss.

She sometimes wondered whether Luciano simply wanted a trophy companion, someone attractive and well presented to be seen out and about with. Appearances mattered in Italy. It was so important to put on a good show and make the right impression; they even had a special phrase for it, *fare la bella figura*. But she quickly dismissed this thought – she knew there was far more to their relationship than that.

After a quick shower, she dried her long, curly chestnut locks with the hairdryer on cool and added a touch of mascara and lipstick, which was all the make-up that this heat would allow. She put on the new lemon linen dress that Luciano had bought on his last business trip to Rome, and a pair of elegant bronze wedge sandals that complimented her tanned legs. A spray of her favourite *eau de toilette* and she was ready. A final inspection in the full-length mirror. *Not at all bad* – she hoped Luciano would be pleased.

Another ring from her mobile. "I'm here. You ready?"

"Just coming down. I'll be with you in two ticks."

As Hanna hurried down the steps to the bright red Alfa Romeo sports car waiting outside the hotel, Luciano appraised her coolly from behind the wheel.

"You look stunning," he said with an appreciative glance, before taking her in his arms in a long, lingering embrace.

"Don't I always?" she laughed in response. "You don't look too bad yourself!"

Luciano was always immaculate, never a hair out of place. Today, he was dressed in pale blue linen trousers and a fitted white shirt that was partially unbuttoned, revealing a mat of dark chest hair. As ever, he smelt heavenly. Her heart lurched as she succumbed to her usual reaction to him, a relentless throb in her loins that was difficult to ignore.

"I hope you're hungry?"

"Ravenous!" Hanna confirmed. Food was another facet of life in Italy that she loved. The delicious range of cuisine was always made using the freshest ingredients that differed from region to region. Luciano had a voracious appetite, and hers wasn't far behind. When she wasn't with him, she tried to watch what she ate to keep her weight in check.

Luciano drove with one hand casually guiding the steering wheel, the other caressing her thigh through the thin material of her dress. His touch sparked an electric charge that surged through her body, and as the throb intensified Hanna did her best to ignore it. He expertly negotiated the narrow winding roads, swinging the car round the bends as they climbed up towards the little village in the hills. Hanna was used to the landscape now and could handle the twists and turns that at first had made her feel nervous and nauseous.

In no time at all, Luciano pulled up outside the restaurant which was buzzing and packed to the brim with hungry diners. The owner of the restaurant – a middle-aged man, a little rotund but still handsome – made a dramatic exit from the dark interior of the restaurant, greeting Luciano like a long-lost friend, embracing him and kissing him on both cheeks before turning his attentions to Hanna.

"At last, Signor Cortazzo. I'm so glad you've finally been able to make it to my humble little restaurant in the hills. Welcome, welcome to you and your lovely lady friend!" he boomed theatrically. "One moment, please, and I'll find you a table."

Moving deftly between the crowded tables, he stopped at one positioned in the corner of the terrace. It was already occupied by an older couple who were waiting to be served. In an instant, the table was vacated and he beckoned Luciano and Hanna over: "Come this way, *signori*! Your table awaits!"

The table boasted a commanding view over the arid countryside in the valley below and out to the sea beyond. The setting was picture-postcard perfect.

"*Prego*, make yourselves at home," the restaurant owner, whose name was Sandro, continued. "I'll get you some drinks. What would you like to eat?"

"What do you recommend?" asked Luciano.

"Personally, I'd go for the *pasta con le sarde* – it's a house speciality – followed by grilled swordfish and a little green salad."

Luciano looked over at Hanna who smiled happily in agreement.

"*Perfetto*!" Luciano declared.

Sandro scurried off, only to return a few minutes later with a bottle of robust local white wine, suitably chilled, and a large bottle of sparkling mineral water. He filled their glasses before disappearing once again into the kitchen.

Hanna settled back in her comfortable padded chair and quickly drained the icy mineral water in her glass as she admired the panoramic view and the dramatic landscape laid out before her. Sometimes she couldn't believe that this was her life – it seemed more like a dream, a fairy tale that had come true. *How long would it last?* she wondered. Luciano smiled back at her, his eyes as dark as hardened lava fixed on her from across the table. He stretched out and took her hand in his and started to stroke it gently. Hanna trembled at his touch.

Their reverie was broken by the shrill ring tone of Luciano's mobile. Glancing at the screen, he frowned and stood up, saying, "Sorry, I need to take this – it's business that won't wait."

Without waiting for a response, he quickly made his way through the tables and left the restaurant to take the call in privacy. He returned to the table a few minutes later just as Sandro reappeared, bearing two bowls of the typical Sicilian pasta dish. The chef had excelled himself – it was truly delicious: fresh sardines, wild fennel, and raisins – a strange combination that somehow worked so well. They attacked the pasta with relish, chatting between mouthfuls.

Halfway through, Luciano asked casually, "Any idea what you'll do at the end of the season?"

"Not really," she replied. The truth was that the mere idea of being apart from Luciano for any period of time was like a physical pain, a knife in the stomach, and she couldn't bear to think of their relationship ending. "Why do you ask?"

"Would you want to go back to the UK?"

"Not really, but I need to work."

"Well, I may have a solution. Rosalia, a friend of my sister Paola, runs a language school for adults in Palermo and she'd kill for a native speaker to teach English. What do you think? That way you could work *and* stay here with me."

"That might be just the thing," answered Hanna, a shiver running through her body, feeling relieved that he wanted her to stay. Luciano seemed to have a knack for fixing things, whatever the problem was. "Maybe I can meet Rosalia and talk it through?"

"No problem, I'll arrange it for the next time you're here."

With that, the conversation turned to other issues as they continued to devour their food. Luciano was a lively conversationalist and had a keen interest in politics and current affairs as well as being a patron of local arts and crafts. He had developed a keen interest in ceramics when he was younger, before he was diverted into the family wine business. Lulled by the wine, Hanna relaxed and listened to his every word. He really was the perfect companion in every way.

Chapter Five

UK, Monday 23rd October, 2017

Just as Hanna predicted, the journey took all day. She'd chosen to go cross country, staying away from the motorways. It was shorter in mileage but longer timewise. Eva seemed content to look out the window for much of the way as the little Corsa ate up the miles. When she got bored, they sang silly songs and played I-Spy.

They stopped off in Hereford for lunch, taking advantage of the fine autumnal day to go down to the River Wye for a makeshift picnic despite the chilly wind. To Eva's delight, the riverbank was full of dozing ducks that didn't take too kindly to her efforts to force feed them their leftovers from lunch. Eva jumped up and down in excitement, making quacking noises as she chased after them until they escaped one by one, taking refuge in the gurgling river.

An elderly couple out for a stroll laughed at her antics and stopped, the wife bending down to say something to her. Eva looked at her blankly and with some alarm, not understanding the stranger's words, before running away to resume her pursuit of the ducks.

She eventually let herself be herded back to the car for the next leg of the journey. The soothing music from the car radio quickly lulled her to sleep, her arms clasped tightly around Orsina, leaving Hanna alone with her thoughts. There was little traffic and she had studied the route in advance, so it was easy enough to follow the road signs with just an occasional glance at the sat-nav for back-up.

So many practical issues to be resolved despite all the

earlier planning and Ceri's help, Hanna thought. And did she really think that this was the answer to their predicament? Not that she was having second thoughts – she really didn't have any choice in the circumstances. The memories started to come flooding back and she shuddered, fighting to keep them at bay, trying to focus on the present rather than the past. She had enough to deal with for now.

Glancing in the rear-view mirror, Hanna noticed with a growing feel of unease the silver Mercedes, one of the slick smaller sporty models, was still there. The car had been on the same road for the last half hour or so, keeping a steady pace some way behind, the driver a dark, sexless silhouette. Eventually, it turned off, much to her relief, but she kept a watchful eye out for the rest of the journey.

After making another couple of short stops, they reached North Wales a little after six. Hanna had arranged to meet Rhys, Ceri's brother, outside Conwy Castle, phoning ahead to let him know what time they'd arrive. She felt pretty sure that she'd easily be able to find such a significant landmark even without the sat-nav, but was a little overawed when it finally came into view. *Pretty impressive*, she thought, tired though she was. The car park behind the castle was almost empty at this hour and it was easy enough to spot Rhys's battered old Land Rover parked at the far end. She drew up alongside him, got out, and went over to greet him.

"Hi, you must be Rhys," she said, offering her hand. "I'm Hanna and my daughter Eva's in the back asleep. Great to meet you at last! I'm really grateful for all the help you're giving us. We're really putting you to a lot of trouble."

Rhys shook her hand warmly. "Hi, Hanna. Nice to meet you, too. It's no trouble – just glad I can help out. Did the journey go okay? You must be tired and hungry. Let's get you both to your new home. You can leave the car here and we'll arrange for the rental company to pick it up tomorrow. Let me help you with your stuff."

He quickly transferred the luggage and the car seat containing the still sleeping Eva into the Land Rover, and they set off on the last leg of their journey. As Hanna relaxed in the passenger seat, tiredness hit her, and she was grateful that she didn't have to drive any further. The roads were becoming narrow and tortuous as they climbed out of the town into the hills in the fading light. Storm clouds were gathering on the horizon, dark and threatening. The temperature was dropping, and Hanna reached over to the dashboard and turned up the heater.

She studied Rhys's profile in the fading light, comparing it to the photos of the brother that Ceri often talked about. She couldn't ever remember him coming out to see his sister, but it was clear that they remained close despite the distance that separated them. With rugged features and a wild mop of thick, dark hair that bounced in rhythm with each bump in the road, he exuded an air of quiet self-confidence, a self-absorbed man happy in his own company. He wore a thick fleece bearing the logo of Snowdonia National Park.

Turning towards her, Rhys looked at Hanna expectantly, unaware of her scrutiny.

"Sorry, did you say something?" she asked. "I was lost in my thoughts. Must be tired. It's a while since I got a proper night's sleep."

"No problem." He smiled. "You've been through a lot. Nearly there now. See those lights over to the right? That's us."

Hanna could make out a few faint lights glimmering against the dark shadow of the hill looming up ahead.

"The cottage is pretty much ready. We'll get your stuff in and have something to eat. Then I'll leave you to get settled in. We can talk more tomorrow about where we go from here."

She felt relieved that he seemed to understand without her having to go into lengthy explanations. They continued to wend their way through the hills towards the flickering lights in the distance. As they drew nearer, Hanna could see that the lights were more dispersed than she'd first thought and were coming from a small number of buildings some way away from each other.

"This little hamlet is called Heulog, which means sunny in

Welsh. It was named by the New Age travellers who settled near here, but they preferred their tents to the cottages. There's still the odd one living round here but the cottages are owned by the National Park now and are let out to artists or holidaymakers looking to get away from it all. I thought it'd be ideal for you, but we'll need to get you some transport otherwise you'll be stuck," said Rhys.

"But you're not completely isolated," he added quickly, seeing Hanna's crestfallen expression. "You do have a couple of neighbours who live here all year round. You'll meet them soon."

He pulled up with a jolt outside a solid stone cottage that must have stood there for centuries. Eva woke with a start and stared at the stranger in the front seat. Hanna quickly explained that Rhys was Mummy's new friend and was giving them a lift to their new home.

A stiff breeze greeted them as they got out of the Land Rover, whipping up the newly fallen leaves. Hanna shivered. She wasn't used to the cold and was dreading the wet. Both the climate and the landscape felt alien, so different to their previous life. But at least they were safe for the time being.

Rhys unlocked the front door and showed them inside. In the lounge, a fire blazed in a wood burning stove, warming the damp air and welcoming its new residents. Two over-stuffed cranberry sofas faced the fire, an enormous shaggy rug covered the stone floor, and pretty floral curtains in tones of cranberry, pistachio, and cream adorned the windows, matching the cushions on the sofa. The décor was simple but tasteful, giving the cottage a cosy and comfortable feel. Hanna looked around appreciatively.

"What do you think? I had a bit of help in making it more homely," said Rhys. "It was pretty basic before."

Hanna smiled. "It's lovely. You've done a good job. I'm sure we'll be happy here, won't we, Eva?"

Eva's eyes widened in surprise – she had never seen a country cottage quite like this before – and muttered, "*Una favola!*"

"What's that?" asked Rhys.

"It's Italian for fairy tale – take that as a compliment!" Hanna replied.

"Okay, will do," he laughed. "I'll give you the guided tour of the rest of the place in a minute. Just let me put this casserole in the oven first to heat up. Then I'll get your luggage in before the rain starts."

"You seem to have thought of everything!" Hanna smiled. "The casserole will go down a treat. It seems ages since we had lunch. I could eat a horse!"

"Well, we don't eat horse in these parts," joked Rhys. "I know they do in some parts of Europe. But you'll find our lamb and beef none too shabby. The casserole is chicken. You do eat meat, I hope?" he asked, almost as an afterthought.

Hanna reassured him that she did. After disappearing into the kitchen for a few minutes, he emerged with an open bottle of wine, a carton of apple juice, and three glasses. "Only got red, I'm afraid. Will that do?"

Hanna gratefully accepted a glass of wine and gave some juice to Eva. But her small daughter had other things on her mind. Tugging Hanna's arm, she tried to propel her out of the lounge, saying, "Where's my room, Mummy? I want to see my room. Now!"

Hanna laughed. "We better do the tour straight away before this young lady has a tantrum!"

Rhys smiled. "Right you are. First stop, little Miss Eva's room!"

Chapter Six

Sicily, Wednesday 9th October, 2013

Hanna's mobile rang as the tour bus was pulling into a service station on the motorway between Rome and Naples.

"*Ciao, amore*. It's Luciano. I've arranged the meeting with Rosalia."

"Sorry, can't talk right now. Call me back in ten minutes," she answered. Luciano rang off with a cheery 'No problem, will do.'

Hanna had picked up a new group at the airport that morning. She knew from experience that if she didn't explain the system of paying first at the cash till before ordering at the counter, they'd end up in a muddle and the stop would take forever. She'd just finished and was about to get herself a coffee when Luciano called back.

"Rosalia's agreed to meet you on Friday morning at ten at the language school in Palermo. I thought that'd be okay as your group's usually on their city tour then, aren't they?" he said. "That way, we can avoid making the long drive from Giardini Naxos."

Giardini Naxos was the resort on the east coast of the island, the only place where Hanna stayed several nights and had some free time. Otherwise, the tour was a packed itinerary of overnight stays, with long days of early departures and late arrivals.

"That's perfect, thanks so much," she answered, feeling a little frisson of joy. He was obviously serious about making plans for her to stay at the end of the season.

"Oh, and she may even be interested in taking on your friend Ceri if she wants to stay, too. The school's just landed a new contract with one of the local ferry companies and a major research centre based in the outskirts of town. The principal is looking for native speakers for conversation classes. Apparently, being English is enough – you don't need any teaching experience."

"Sounds good. I'll let Ceri know. She might be interested, particularly as things seem to be getting serious with her new man, Sergio."

"You'll have to sort out the hours and salary directly with her. Sorry, I'll have to go. I'm needed on the other line. Can't wait to see you at the weekend."

"Me too, *amore*. See you then. Speak soon."

A warm sensation spread across her stomach. Now all she needed was for the meeting with Rosalia to go well.

Hanna found the school easily enough. It was set back from the coast in an elegant old building in a quiet side street, with intricate wrought iron balconies. A small number of rooms clustered round an inner courtyard crammed with gigantic terracotta pots brimming over with scarlet geraniums and enormous white daisies with bright yellow centres, bees humming as they hovered round them in the sunlight.

Rosalia, the owner of the school, greeted her effusively and led the way to a first-floor office where a tray of coffee and freshly-baked cannoli, the sweet ricotta-filled pastries that were a local speciality, awaited them.

"*Prego, signorina*, make yourself at home," said Rosalia, sinking into one of the white leather sofas carefully positioned around a glass and steel coffee table to secure a view of the sea.

Hanna took a seat on the sofa facing the principal, and accepted a cup of freshly-brewed coffee and one of the rich pastries. The hospitality gave her an opportunity to weigh up her potential new boss. Rosalia was a short, self-assured woman in her forties, with dyed blonde, shoulder-length hair that had been expertly styled. Her skin was the colour of a pecan nut and her face was heavily made up despite the heat. She wore a deep orange linen trouser suit that must have cost a fortune, with a white camisole that showed off her ample breasts. Heavy silver jewellery completed the look.

Rosalia surveyed Hanna, looking her up and down, before nodding slightly as if she'd just passed some unknown test. She conducted the meeting in expert English, marred only by a thick accent which sometimes masked her words. Hanna had long ago learnt that there was a certain ritual to doing business in Italy that required an exchange of personal niceties. Cutting to the chase would be considered disrespectful, even offensive. She played along until Rosalia was ready to talk shop.

"You see, *cara*," Rosalia said, smiling and gesticulating wildly with her arms, "you two young ladies will be my trump card. It would be quite a coup for my little language school to have native speakers of English, particularly with your background in tourism. That would be ideal for the new contract with the ferry company. My clients are corporate businesspeople who need to be able to speak excellent conversational English. Do you have any experience of teaching English as a foreign language?"

Hanna's only teaching experience was from her days as a language student when she had spent her vacations working abroad, but nothing like this. She wondered whether she was up to the task of teaching businesspeople and researchers. The prospect seemed more than a little daunting.

"I've done some, but only informally with schoolchildren," she answered. "Nothing as demanding as businesspeople. Luciano gave me to understand that you weren't looking for teaching experience."

As if sensing Hanna's uncertainty, Rosalia responded quickly. "It's not essential but it would obviously be useful. We use a structured course for beginners and intermediates to take them through the fundamentals of the grammar, but it's the application and colloquial English that's missing. That's where you and Ceri come in – you can help to develop and deliver the conversational classes. Do you think that you'll be able to handle that?"

Hanna gulped nervously and felt her face flush. She felt unsure but was desperate to stay on the island for the winter and didn't want to let Luciano down. It would be so different to anything she'd done before, but it was worth a try. She would make a go of it somehow.

"To start off with, I could probably offer you 3-4 days' work a week," continued Rosalia. "I think you'll find the salary more than adequate…"

She quoted a figure that was much more than Hanna was expecting. *Could teaching English as a foreign language be so lucrative, even without experience?* she wondered.

"What do you think, and how soon can you start?" The conversation lapsed back into Italian.

"That sounds fine, but I'd need to check with Ceri first, of course," Hanna replied, conscious that Rosalia seemed to have made up her mind. "We should both be available by the end of October. I would imagine you'll want to meet Ceri, too, before we start?"

"Don't worry, any friend of Luciano's…" Rosalia let the phrase hang mid-sentence. "That would suit me perfectly. Please get back to me and confirm a convenient starting date so I can get on with planning the courses."

Hanna promised she would, and the two women shook hands before parting company. She felt a warm glow as she set off to rejoin her tour group. The meeting seemed more like a done deal than an interview. Luciano had obviously put in a good word. Relieved everything had gone so well and pleased with Rosalia's offer and the thought of being able to spend the winter in Sicily, she reached for her phone to call Luciano to tell him the good news.

Chapter Seven

North Wales, Tuesday 24th October, 2017

Hanna woke with a thumping headache. She opened her eyes to the sun streaming through the sheer curtains and for a minute imagined herself back on the island that she'd come to regard as home. Slowly, she became aware of her surroundings and the reality of the situation dawned on her: it was the first day of their new life.

Pushing back the covers, Hanna swung her legs out of bed and shivered when her bare feet made contact with the stone floor. She fished her shoes out from under the bed, threw on the previous day's sweater over her nightie, and went in search of Eva in the little bedroom next door.

But the bed was empty, and Hanna felt her stomach lurch as she recalled the recent incident at the airport. Then she spotted the toddler on the other side of the room, kneeling on the window seat, elbows propped on the sill, intent on watching something outside.

Relieved, she went over and kissed Eva lightly on the top of her head. "Morning, sweetheart. What are you doing up so early?"

Eva squealed with delight at the sound of her mother's voice and turned, throwing her arms round Hanna's neck. "Ciao, *Mammina* – the birds, they woke me up." Eva pointed at the offenders – a small group of starlings that were foraging for their breakfast, squawking and squabbling over the feast of worms and slugs left by the heavy overnight dew. She rubbed her eyes sleepily; she obviously hadn't been up long.

"Never mind, let's go and get some breakfast. Then we can go and explore. That'll be fun, won't it?"

Eva's face dissolved into an angelic grin. "Yes, yes, yes!" she nodded enthusiastically, her voice rising to emphasise each word. "Let's go!" She made a clumsy descent from the window seat, half falling to the floor before grabbing Hanna's hand, trying to propel her into the kitchen. Hanna joined in the game, laughing as she went, spurred on by her daughter's eagerness.

In the compact kitchen at the back of the cottage, Hanna began opening cupboards to see what was there. She needn't have worried. A plentiful supply of basic foodstuffs greeted her: milk, butter, cheese, and eggs in the fridge; ground coffee, cereal, bread, and marmalade in the cupboards, together with a variety of dried and tinned produce, and a bowl of fresh fruit.

After making a pot of coffee, she prepared two bowls of cereal with slices of banana and strawberries. Eva devoured hers quickly, making loud slurping noises which made Hanna frown, followed by an amused smile, pleased that the toddler could adapt to their new circumstances so easily. The food made her feel better and the headache was easing.

Breakfast over, Eva began tearing round the cottage, pleading with Hanna to let her go outside in her pyjamas.

Hanna gingerly opened the double bolt on the back door. It led out into a small courtyard, warmed by shafts of sunlight and sheltered by high stone walls from which small plants sprouted at intervals. It was only when they ventured into the back garden beyond that the brisk wind hit them, a stark reminder that it was autumn.

"C'mon, Eva, let's go back inside and get dressed. We don't want to catch a cold and be ill, do we? Then we'll go for a walk. You'd like that, wouldn't you?"

The little girl nodded in agreement. Hanna hastily pulled some warm clothes out of the suitcase, gave Eva a quick wash, and dressed her in dungarees and a fluffy pink sweater before trying to restore some order to her tousled locks with a hairbrush. She pulled on jeans and a claret-coloured sweatshirt, making a mental note that they both needed some warmer clothes if they were to survive the Welsh winter.

Outside, the wind whipped up the fallen leaves in their myriad hues, shimmering in the autumnal sun. Its energy was intoxicating, filling Hanna with a vigour and positivity that she'd not felt for some time and transforming Eva into a whirling dervish, hurtling through the countryside like someone possessed.

"Eva, not so fast! You'll fall over and hurt yourself," Hanna shouted after her.

But the little girl kept on running until she became so breathless that she ground to a halt, flinging herself on the grass, arms and legs outstretched like a starfish, giggling uncontrollably. Hanna did likewise, the pair of them lying on their backs, looking up at an almost cloudless sky, happy and relaxed. It was as if neither of them had a care in the world.

The spell was broken by Hanna's mobile. It was Rhys ringing to see if they were okay and needed anything. He confirmed that the rental company had picked up the car, and suggested he came over in the afternoon to show them around the area. They arranged to meet early afternoon, once Rhys finished work.

Returning to the cottage across the fields, Eva was more subdued now after her initial burst of energy. They held hands, swinging their arms, singing at the top of their voices *Se sei felice*, the Italian version of *If You're Happy and You Know It*.

The beauty of the landscape took Hanna's breath away. She had no recollection of the Welsh countryside being so spectacular, but then she only had childhood memories to go on. Green hillsides flecked with purple heather surrounded them, punctuated by the occasional sheep or cow. Of humans, there was little trace, apart from the curls of smoke coming from the chimney of the neighbouring cottage. Hanna imagined it could be quite lonely and isolated, especially in winter, and wondered what they'd do for company. She vowed to call her friend Ceri when they got back to the cottage and check on the situation she'd left behind.

Chapter Eight

Sicily, Sunday 3rd November, 2013

Luciano came into the bedroom, jangling his car keys impatiently. "Are you nearly ready?" he asked. "We need to stop at the florist's to pick up the flowers first, and they'll be shutting soon. And we don't want to keep *Mamma* waiting."

"Nearly there," said Hanna as she finished applying her lipstick. In her haste, she caught the edge of her make-up bag with her elbow, spilling the entire contents across the floor. She cursed inwardly as she gathered up the numerous items and stuffed them back in the bag. "What d'you think? Will I pass the test?" she asked, giving a little twirl.

"*Ammazza, come sei bella*! You look amazing! My family will wonder what I did to deserve you!" Luciano came over and planted a kiss on her nose so as not to spoil her make-up.

Hanna had applied what she hoped was just enough to make a good impression. Her hair and nails had been given some expert attention the previous day. Her chosen outfit was a wide-necked, eau-de-nil sweater and matching scarf, a slim-fitting black skirt, semi-opaque tights, and a pair of mid-heeled, mock croc shoes. Stylish but not too showy, she hoped, slipping an ornate silver cuff on her wrist – a present from Luciano.

He had sprung the surprise invitation to Sunday lunch at his family's house a few weeks into Hanna's new job. Apparently, it was his idea rather than his family's. "Don't worry, it's not a vetting process. They may as well get used to us being together sooner or later. It'll be fine, you'll see –

they're really easy-going," were his words.

Although she took this as a sign that he was serious about her, Hanna worried whether his family would take to her. She was a foreigner, after all, and Sicilian family life seemed so steeped in traditions that were quite alien to her. Being involved in the family business, Luciano had a close relationship with both his father Michele and younger brother Giulio, and spent a lot of time with them. Hanna resigned herself to the fact that she had to meet them eventually so it might as well be now.

But now the nerves were starting to show, despite her own curiosity about his family and their business interests. Giving her hair a final brush and checking her appearance once more in the full-length mirror, Hanna declared, "Okay, I'm ready. Let's go!"

Once in the car, she gave Luciano an appreciative glance. He looked pristine as usual, in a light blue shirt that offset his dark hair and olive skin, a sweater thrown casually around his shoulders.

After a quick stop at the local florist's to pick up their order, they soon left the pretty little coastal town behind. The Cortazzo family lived between Enna and Caltanissetta, about an hour's drive from Cefalu.

Passing through groves of olive and lemon trees as they headed inland, Hanna marvelled at the November weather. It was still warm enough to go out without a jacket, the sun shining brightly in a cloudless hazy blue sky. She couldn't remember the last time it had rained. *So unlike the grizzly grey Novembers back in Britain*, she thought, settling back in the leather seat, taking in the changing panorama of the countryside.

With mounting trepidation, her thoughts turned to the coming meeting and how it would go. Humming along to the CD playing in the background, Luciano shot her a reassuring smile and squeezed her hand. Before long, they started to pull away from the interior plains and climbed slightly to a heavily-gated estate. Fishing a remote control out of the glove box, Luciano pointed it at the entrance and the gates whirred into action and began to part slowly. Beyond, a driveway led a further kilometre or so over the crest of a hill to an extensive *masseria,* an old farmhouse that had been lovingly restored and extended.

As they approached the entrance, Hanna flinched when a pack of lean, long-legged, chestnut-coloured hounds hurtled out from behind the house, barking frantically and surrounding the car. Luciano laughed at her reaction and called out to them, using dialect words that Hanna couldn't decipher. They calmed down and greeted the newcomers with wagging tails.

"Don't mind them, they're harmless enough," he said, getting out of the car and patting them. "They're bred for hunting and make excellent watchdogs, as you can see, but they're soft and gentle really."

Before Hanna could reply, the old wooden double-fronted doors of the farmhouse swung open and the four family members spilled out, talking incessantly, making almost as much noise and fuss as the dogs had done. They embraced Luciano while Hanna looked on, clutching the bouquet of flowers with sweaty palms, a nervous smile touching her lips. Luciano stepped in and introduced her to his father, mother, and younger brother in a formal manner. Hanna had already met his sister Paola at the language school where she was working.

Arazia, Luciano's mother, appraised her coolly, accepting the flowers graciously after glancing at her watch. "It's a pleasure to meet you at last. Welcome to our home. Lunch is about to be served so let's go through to the dining room."

"We're not late, are we?" asked Luciano.

"When are you ever on time?" she teased, smiling.

Luciano shrugged off the comment with a grin, taking Hanna by the hand. "As long as we're not too late for lunch, it doesn't matter!"

His father Michele led them inside to the spacious dining room that sat at the back of the house overlooking an expanse of neat terraces sculpted into the hillside. He handed out glasses of sparkling *prosecco* which were raised in a toast to the young couple, as if they had just announced their engagement.

A sumptuous feast of assorted *antipasti* awaited them on a heavy wooden table: roast peppers and grilled aubergines; slices of salami and various cold cuts, together with a range of local fresh cheeses; delicate ricotta-filled courgette flowers; *arancini* – fragrant rice balls stuffed with minced meat and cheese; marinated anchovies, and a cold seafood salad.

"I warned you that there'd be enough food to feed a whole town!" Luciano whispered in Hanna's ear as they took their seats. She smiled as he handed her a plate piled high with delicious-looking food.

No sooner had they finished the starters, steaming plates of *pasta alla Norma,* a local pasta dish made with a sauce of tomatoes, fried aubergines, and salted ricotta cheese arrived, followed by the main course of succulent lamb, served with a fresh orange and fennel salad. To finish, Paola had brought a tray of exquisite delicacies from the local *pasticceria*.

Throughout the meal, the conversation flowed as freely as the wine – a hearty red Nero d'Avola – but Hanna had a hard time keeping up. For one thing, they all spoke at once in an Italian heavily peppered with dialect, a thick Sicilian accent adding a further hurdle. Every so often, Hanna would feel the weight of Arazia's gaze on her, summing her up critically as if she were the subject of an ongoing interview process. She wondered how she was measuring up to the scrutiny. It promised to be a long and lively afternoon.

Chapter Nine

North Wales, Wednesday 25th October, 2017

The clanking of the battered old Land Rover warned of its approach long before it came into view. With a screech of brakes, Rhys pulled up outside the stone cottage. Hanna opened the front door and went to greet him, closely followed by Eva. He wasn't alone. In the back of the vehicle stood a bundle of fur, its tail wagging wildly, eager to escape and make friends with the newcomers.

"Come and meet my best pal, Bryn," said Rhys. "Watch him, mind – he can be a bit boisterous."

Eva squealed with delight; she loved all animals regardless of size, and showed no fear in their company, much to her mother's dismay. This time was no different. Hanna's face fell when the dog jumped down from the Land Rover. She was struck by its powerful build and indeterminate breed, although Border Collie seemed to account for a large part.

"He's just starting to calm down and learn a few manners now he's out of the puppy stage. I'll put him on a lead until he gets used to you both," said Rhys.

Eva seemed to get the gist of his words without understanding them fully and sensed that Bryn wouldn't hurt her. Hanna breathed a sigh of relief. Her worries about the dog knocking Eva over, or worse, were short-lived. Bryn strained on the lead, eager to greet them. Eva was already toddling towards him, arms outstretched, collapsing in a heap and giggling happily as he smothered her with wet kisses. Rhys laughed at her reaction.

"Eva seems really taken with Bryn," said Rhys. "Is she used to dogs?"

"We didn't have any, but she's used to being around them at her grandparents'," Hanna replied, realising that she still hadn't called Ceri. It would have to wait until later when she was alone and could talk freely.

"We'd better get a move on if you want to see some of the place. We don't have too long, what with the days starting to draw in already," said Rhys, steering Bryn back to the Land Rover with some difficulty.

Hanna collected jackets from the cottage, with Eva reminding her to bring Orsina along too, then helped her daughter into the car seat. At Eva's insistence, she ensured that the little bear had pride of place and an excellent view of her new surroundings before getting in the front. Bryn gave Orsina a lick for good measure before being relegated to the rear of the vehicle.

As Rhys pointed the Land Rover along the track heading further into the hills, Hanna wondered where they were going and looked at him questioningly.

"Thought we'd do the grand tour of Heulog first before we head for civilisation, or what passes for it in North Wales," he joked.

"That's fine," said Hanna, glancing back at Eva who was having a one-sided conversation with Bryn. Lapping up the attention, the young dog looked wistfully through the caged-off area in the back which prevented him from jumping over and joining his human companions.

They bumped along the dirt track until they reached another stone cottage, from where Hanna had noticed a trail of smoke earlier in the day.

"Nerys and Lars are your closest neighbours and live here all year round," explained Rhys, coming to a halt outside the cottage. "They've been here a couple of years now, moved up from London though she's originally from these parts. He's Norwegian. I'm not sure how they met. I don't know them that well. Apparently, they're both creative types: she's a potter and he paints."

Just then, a tousled redhead in an old pair of jeans and sweatshirt, both spattered with paint of various hues, came out of a nearby outbuilding. Rhys wound down the window and leant out as the woman approached the stationary vehicle.

"Hi, I heard you coming up the track. We don't get many visitors in these parts so thought I'd come and investigate," she said with a warm smile.

"Morning, Nerys, long time, no see. Just thought I'd bring Hanna and her daughter Eva over to say hello. They're staying at the next cottage for a while, so you guys are going to be neighbours."

"That's great news!" said Nerys. "Once you've settled in, you'll have to come over for lunch and meet Lars. We'll show you around the studios. We've got lots of animals that Eva might be interested in," she added, noticing that Eva's attention had turned to the hens roaming round the cottage, clucking contentedly.

"We'd like that very much, wouldn't we, Eva?" Hanna replied. Eva gurgled as if in agreement.

They arranged to meet the following Tuesday, then Rhys reversed and headed back down the track towards the coast. As he drove, he pointed out a number of dwellings and farm buildings, some in ruins, others abandoned, while others awaited their seasonal visitors seeking a temporary refuge from city life.

Hanna marvelled at the lush green hillsides dotted with sheep and trees sculpted by the winds. Its raw yet gentle beauty filled her with a sense of serenity. She hoped that she'd made the right decision and that she and Eva would be able to carve out a life for themselves in this peaceful valley.

For the next few hours, Rhys gave her a guided tour of the local area – not only the countryside but also the nearest towns and villages, and even the coast less than an hour away. They stopped for coffee in a small resort full of lofty Victorian terraces overlooking a wide sandy bay. Despite being tired and restless, Eva insisted on paddling in the sea, yelling out when the icy water curled round her toes. Bryn frolicked in the spray beside her, relishing the freedom after being cooped up in the back of the Land Rover for so long. To the casual onlooker, they could have been on a carefree family outing.

It was getting dark as they returned to the Land Rover and started the climb back up through the hills to Hanna and Eva's new home.

It was gone six when Rhys dropped them off at the cottage and by now pitch black, save for the odd glimmer from neighbouring farms and cottages. Hanna waited until he drove off before rummaging through her handbag for her mobile. She dialled the familiar number.

Ceri picked up straight away. "Are you both okay? When I didn't hear from you, I thought something might have gone wrong."

"My fault, we're both fine. How are things with you? Any news of Luciano and how he's reacted?

"Apparently, he's frantic and has been pulling out all the stops to track you down. He's got people on the lookout all over the island and on the mainland, too. He's bound to wonder if you've gone back to the UK, but I'm not sure if his influence goes that far. You'll have to lie low for quite a while."

"Yes, you're right," said Hanna. "I'm going to have to tread carefully. Has he said anything to you?"

"Not directly, but he must know that I was away when it happened. He can't really question me too closely, in the circumstances. But it all feels pretty tense as if something major's about to happen," replied Ceri. "Sergio's been offered a job in Rome, but he doesn't know whether to take it or not. He wants to see this thing through. Personally, I'd leave tomorrow, after everything that's happened. How's Eva doing?"

"Oh, she seems fine – just needs to get used to English. Either that or Rhys's dog will have to learn Italian!"

Hanna explained what had happened earlier in the day, which helped to lighten the mood. They drew the conversation to a close, promising to speak again soon.

As she switched off her mobile, Hanna's mind turned once again to their dilemma. Who was she trying to kid? Luciano would move heaven and earth to find them. Eva was his only child and Hanna had left without warning. Her actions would have reduced his pride and reputation to tatters. That was bad enough, but would have been worse if he'd been aware of the full story. Even so, he was likely to pursue them relentlessly. *Would they ever be free from his grasp?* she wondered.

Chapter Ten

Sicily, Friday 22nd November, 2013

Hanna's life on the island soon settled into a new rhythm. During the week, she shared a small apartment in a shabby chic part of Cefalu with her friend Ceri. Luciano had found it for them at a ludicrously low rent, partially but tastefully furnished. The two girls lost no time in shopping for the remaining bits they needed to make it feel like home. Hanna would spend evenings and weekends at Luciano's place when he wasn't away on business.

She was beginning to enjoy the teaching and found her mature students lively and eager to learn. Even the hour on the train to and from Palermo was a pleasure, with its views of the Mediterranean basking in the pallid sun on one side and the rich cultivated inclines of the hinterland on the other.

Although both girls worked at the language school, they usually did different hours and at different venues. Hanna did most of her teaching at the headquarters of the ferry company while Ceri covered the new contract with the research centre on the outskirts of Palermo. One morning, they both happened to be at the school at the same time and took the opportunity to get a bite to eat before they headed off in different directions. They decided to go to the little bar round the corner – a favourite haunt of their colleagues, owing its popularity not only to its proximity and the friendly staff but also to its wonderful array of delicate ricotta-filled *cannoli* pastries that were baked fresh on the premises every day.

A blast of warm air, the aroma of fresh coffee, and the

loud chatter of the other customers hit the two girls as they pushed open the door to the bar. The coffee machines continually worked their magic, glugging and hissing happily, dancing to the tune of the baristas' endless orders.

"*Ciao, Claudio*," Hanna called over to one of the young baristas who was busy filling a row of cups with frothy steaming milk. He responded with a smile and nod of his head, indicating a free table by the window in the back room. Hanna waved her thanks and Ceri went to grab it while she ordered coffee and toasted *panini*. She followed Ceri to the table and flopped down onto a padded chair.

"Thank God it's quieter in here, at least we can talk. It seems ages since we've managed to catch up. For two people who share an apartment, we don't get the chance to talk very often. How are things going with Sergio?"

"Couldn't be better," Ceri replied. "He's always on some major story or another which he never goes into any great detail about – it's usually organised crime, corruption, that sort of thing. Sounds pretty endemic, but collecting enough hard evidence to make any charges stick and go public with the story seems pretty difficult to do, from what I gather. Mind you, it can't harm having a father so high up in the police. What about you two?"

"Oh, it's all great, but sometimes it feels a bit overwhelming, as if I'm not in control of what's happening," replied Hanna with a slight frown, taking a bite of her melted cheese and grilled aubergine *panino* which the waiter had just brought over.

"Maybe you should try taking it more slowly?" Ceri suggested.

"Maybe I should but it's not that easy. It's like being caught up in a whirlwind. It's exhilarating, compulsive, and completely addictive, all at the same time. I've never known anything like it. I certainly don't want to do anything to spoil things."

"It must be love! Next thing you know, I'll have to buy a hat!" joked Ceri.

"Steady on, it's not come to that yet! We've got some

celebrating of our own to do first, your big 3-0! Any idea what you fancy doing? Something special?"

"Sergio's being all mysterious – I think he's got something in mind, if he can tear himself away from that damn newspaper office long enough! I don't suppose he's mentioned anything to you?"

"Well, he did say something about one idea he had but I don't know if it came to anything. I guess we'll both find out soon enough. Whatever it is, we really must use it as an opportunity for the four of us to get together. I can't believe that the boys still haven't met."

"It's not for want of trying," said Ceri. "Every time we arrange something, Luciano always pulls out at the last minute. It's almost as if they're destined never to meet. Have you managed to find out any more about his business interests?"

"Well, he seems to have a finger in a lot of pies. As well as playing a key role in the family wine business, he also acts as a consultant and advisor for other companies on import/export issues," explained Hanna, rising to Luciano's defence. "He's often called away on some urgent matter or another. He used to get so many calls and messages coming through at all hours that he's had to put his phone on silent, otherwise we wouldn't get any sleep."

"Not so different to Sergio, then. I'm sure they'd get on well – they've certainly got lots in common!"

The two girls laughed, easing any temporary tension between them. They quickly finished their lunch, leaving a handful of euros on the table before stepping out into the still warm autumnal sunshine and going their separate ways.

"I've got some bad news, I'm afraid," said Luciano, reaching across the table to take Hanna's hand. They'd just finished dinner at the little *trattoria* around the corner from the apartment, which was becoming a regular haunt of theirs.

"What is it?" asked Hanna, a note of alarm in her voice.

"Ceri's birthday party. I'm not going to be able to make it, after all. I've got to go to Rome with my father on business," he explained, stroking her hand gently. "I'm really sorry, *amore*, I know how much it means to you, but it can't be helped. You probably won't even miss me." He smiled and kissed her lightly on the cheek.

Hanna turned away slightly, her expression and mood darkening. Of course, she'd miss him – Ceri might be her closest friend, but Luciano was her world. Without him at her side, it was as if a part of her was missing. "Can't you go some other time? We've been planning this for ages," she pleaded, a crestfallen expression on her face.

"There's nothing I can do, I'm afraid. It's an opportunity that's too good to miss and it's now or never. You know how family business is…" he replied with a shrug of his shoulders.

No, she didn't. Surely, she was the most important thing to him, as he was to her? She reprimanded herself at the thought, realising she was behaving like a spoilt child. It wasn't even *her* birthday. It certainly wasn't the end of the world. She forced a smile.

"Well, if you must. It won't be the same without you, but I understand."

The truth was that she didn't understand. She'd have liked to wrap Luciano up and keep him to herself, cocooned in their love nest, happy and far from the demands of the real world. Realising how fanciful and nonsensical this was, she dismissed the thought and tried to push it to the back of her mind. Nevertheless, the news shattered the mood of their evening. They walked down the dimly-lit narrow street back to the apartment without another word, Luciano's arm slung casually across her shoulders.

Later that night, as she snuggled next to him in bed, Hanna wondered for the umpteenth time how important she was to Luciano. It took some time for her to get to sleep, her head buzzing with doubts and anxieties. She had just drifted off when Luciano's mobile rang briefly before he killed the sound and responded in muffled tones, going into the bathroom and closing the door so as not to disturb her. *He must have forgotten to switch it off,* she thought. For a few moments, she wondered what could be so urgent for someone to call at this hour, before sleep took its hold on her once again.

Chapter Eleven

North Wales, Tuesday 31st October, 2017

Hanna woke with a start, drenched in a cold sweat after yet another night of tossing and turning. Sleep inevitably carried her back to Sicily, sometimes to the idyll of her early years there, but more often to the nightmare of the recent past.

Over a week had gone by since their departure. Eva seemed happy enough in her new surroundings, despite finding everything so different to what she was used to. *Lucky her*, thought Hanna wryly. Left alone with her thoughts, Hanna found her fears could surface freely. Only Ceri was aware of the full extent of the threats.

Hanna was careful not to use her mobile any more than she had to, so their contact was limited. It was as if she had stepped out of one world into another. She still harboured doubts about whether she'd made the right decision, but they certainly couldn't have stayed, in the circumstances. Although she didn't feel totally safe now, at least she didn't feel in constant fear for Eva.

If only she had internet access, she would feel more in touch with the outside world, although the whole point of coming to Wales was to distance herself from it. But they couldn't stay hidden away for ever, not if they were to make a new life for themselves.

Her thoughts turned to her finances. She'd kept her UK bank account open while she'd been in Sicily. All her earnings as a tour guide had been paid into this and she had simply lived off her tips. She'd also inherited a modest sum of money when her parents died which would keep them going for a while, but not for ever. She needed to make longer term plans.

Cabin fever, or rather cottage fever, was setting in despite Rhys popping round as often as he could. Fortunately, the cottage was comfortable and provided all they needed, apart from Wi-Fi and transport, and the need to top up their food supplies. Rhys had managed to find an old Peugeot that she could use and was bringing it over at the weekend, so that would solve one problem.

Lost in her thoughts, at first she didn't notice the bedroom door opening. A sleepy Eva appeared in her pyjamas, clutching Orsina in one hand and rubbing her eyes with the other, a glum expression on her face.

"Hi, sweetie, are you ok? Did you have a bad dream?"

"Where's *Babbo?* When's he coming?"

"He'll be with us as soon as he can, *cara.* He sends his love and says he misses you," said Hanna, quick to reassure the youngster with a ready lie. She really had to come up with a plan to explain Luciano's continued absence. "But he wants you to have fun without him. Today, we're going to see Nerys – remember her, the nice lady we met the other day with all the animals? If you're very good, she might even let you help her make some pots. You'll like that, won't you?"

A smile crept over Eva's face and she skipped over, struggling to climb on the bed to join her mum. Amused, Hanna watched her determined little daughter's efforts, scooping her up when they started to fail. She held the toddler high up in the air, pretending to drop her before catching her again until Eva was so overcome with giggles that she developed hiccups and Hanna had to set her down on the bed.

"Come on, little Miss Giggles, let's get you washed and dressed. Then we can have some breakfast and be off," she said, taking Eva's hand and leading her into the bathroom.

Wrapped up as much as possible against the blustery wind, Hanna vowed to make a shopping trip soon to get some warm winter clothes. They followed the stony track up the valley towards the studio, the same route that they'd taken in the Land Rover with Rhys the previous week. Velvety green slopes rose gently on either side, dotted with sturdy sheep with white faces and matching woolly coats. Further up the valley, the inclines grew steeper, developing into a rocky ridge that led into the heart of Snowdonia. They made their way over an old stone bridge, crossing a stream where a pair of wagtails bobbed up and down in the shallow water.

Hanna pointed out items of interest as they walked along, making it into a game for Eva to learn the English words for them. Eva happily joined in, repeating them back in a parrot-like fashion. After about half an hour, the stone cottage and its adjoining outbuildings came into view. By the time they finally arrived at the cottage, Eva's pace had slowed right down and she'd started to get bored of the game.

As Hanna opened the garden gate, the heavy wooden front door opened and Nerys appeared with a cheery smile. It was as if she'd been monitoring their approach.

"Hi, come in, both of you. Enjoy the walk up?"

"It was lovely, the scenery's quite stunning and it's so peaceful. We're not late, are we?"

Nerys laughed. "No, of course not. Lars has just had a great idea for a new project and is busy getting it down on paper while it's still fresh in his mind. He won't be long. I thought we could have lunch first and then I'll show you around. Here, let me take your coats."

Hanna helped Eva out of her light quilted jacket, once again realising how ill-equipped they were for their new life, but nothing that couldn't be resolved. A wood fire burned in the hearth, giving a welcome warmth and glow to the living room, adding to the muted jewel shades of aubergine, cinnamon, amber and claret of the furnishings, more reminiscent of Morocco than Wales. A tabby cat was curled up asleep on the rug in the front of the fire, but not for long as Eva went over to make friends.

Every available space on the walls was taken up with some form of artwork or another – abstracts, landscapes, ceramics, textiles. Nerys followed her gaze.

"You can't tell that the place belongs to artists, can you?" she joked. "We'll have to move to something bigger or start on the outbuildings when we run out of space!"

It was like a living art gallery, thought Hanna as she went to take a closer look.

"Is this any of yours or Lars' work?

"Yes, some of it," said Nerys, indicating several large ceramic pots in an alcove by the stove and a number of colourful canvases on the walls. "But others are by artists that we particularly like, some local, some not. Are you interested in art?"

"I've had friends who were artists or were involved in restoration work, and I know what I like but I'm no expert."

As if summoned by the theme of their conversation, a tall, fair-haired man with an athletic build opened what must have been the kitchen door, judging by the delicious aroma that wafted in with him. This evidently was Lars who, once the introductions were over, led them into a spacious kitchen where an old oak table was laid out for four, with a makeshift high-chair for Eva.

Lars brought over a heavy pot from the stove and Nerys ladled out portions of beef stew and dumplings, packed with vegetables and pulses. Hanna cut a small portion into pieces for Eva and helped her to eat, although the toddler's attention and affections had now found a new home in the shape of the couple's chocolate Labrador, Brady, who had wandered in from the back garden.

Nerys and Lars chatted about their work. They'd fallen in love with Wales during a short break from the city, and realised that moving here would provide the space and stress-free existence that they'd both craved for, as well as inspiration for their work. They'd bought the cottage and the outbuildings at a reasonable price as they were in a bad state of repair and needed a lot of work. This had suited them as they'd only been renting in London so didn't have a large amount of money to invest up front.

Once they'd polished off their dessert of gooseberry fool,

with berries from the back garden, the conversation inevitably turned to Hanna and Eva.

"So, what about you, Hanna?" asked Nerys. "We've told you our life story, but we still don't know anything about you. Heulog's a pretty isolated part of Wales at the best of times and October's not exactly the holiday season. And Rhys implied that you might be staying a while…"

Hanna had anticipated their curiosity and delivered her prepared answer, confident that Eva wouldn't be able to understand her words.

"My marriage broke up and it all got pretty nasty. I just had to get away for a while to take stock and decide on how best to create a future for the two of us. If you don't mind, I'd rather not talk about it in more detail at the moment – it's still rather recent and raw."

Nerys nodded sympathetically, but Lars' face remained stony and unconvinced. *Tough*, thought Hanna, *that's his problem. I'm not being drawn into any revelations about my personal life.*

"So, how long do you think you'll be staying?" Nerys continued.

"A few months at least, while I get my head together."

"It can get pretty lonely up here, even for us at times."

"I can imagine. It's still early days, though. I'll have to see how it goes." Hanna wasn't being pushed into a more precise answer. She did, however, explain that Rhys was the brother of a good friend of hers who had suggested Wales as a temporary refuge and offered his services to help her locate a suitable place to rent.

The subject was left at that and the rest of the visit was taken up with a tour of their two studios in separate outbuildings. The potter's studio was quite small, filled with pots at various stages of their life, with a separate room for glazing and firing. Nerys gave them a quick demonstration of using a potter's wheel, although her preferred technique was to hand-build many of her creations. Eva got to make a little clay pot of her own, which she surveyed proudly despite its wobbly stance. Her face lit up even more when Nerys promised that she could paint it on her next visit.

Lars' studio in comparison was spacious, with a window that overlooked the valley in place of one of the walls.

"What a fabulous view! It must be an amazing place to work," said Hanna.

"It's really inspiring, particularly in my line of work as I specialise in abstract landscapes, usually for large-scale corporate commissions," he explained, indicating a number of sizeable canvases lying propped up against the walls. They too were at different stages of development – some in soft mute tones and others in bright hues, more reminiscent of the Mediterranean.

Lars must have caught Hanna's confused expression as he explained, "The colour palette is down to the client. My preference is to work in colours that are more in keeping with the landscape here. These are a couple of my favourites that I couldn't bear to part with," he added, indicating two smaller pieces hanging either side of the window.

"Yes, I see what you mean," said Hanna. "I tend to agree with you."

Lars smiled and went on to explain that there was a significant market for this type of work and, although only in his late thirties, he had managed to establish a name for himself and could command not insignificant fees.

Attention turned to Eva who was starting to get restless.

"C'mon, Eva, let's go and look at the animals," said Nerys.

Hanna translated this for Eva who chortled with delight. The couple kept pigs and chickens, as well as various ducks and geese on the sizeable pond at the bottom of the garden. In her excitement and to her mother's horror, as Eva hurtled towards the pond, she tripped and fell on her knees. This resulted in bursts of anguished wails until Brady wandered over and licked her face and grazed knees better. The wails transformed into peals of laughter as the dog's rough tongue made contact with her flesh. Hanna smiled, the danger and anxiety averted.

The temperature was dropping and the light fading as they

returned to the warmth of the cottage. Nerys made a large cafetière of coffee which she laced with brandy as a parting gesture before Lars bundled them up into his Nissan Qashqai for the short journey home.

Chapter Twelve

Sicily, Saturday 7th December, 2013

Ceri's 30th birthday dawned so mild and sunny with the lightest of breezes that it was difficult to believe it was early December. Nothing like the icy, blustery conditions back in the UK. Hanna shivered at the thought.

"Come on, birthday girl, we're going to miss the train if you don't get a move on," said Hanna, going into Ceri's room. "What the…?" She didn't finish the sentence as she surveyed the mess of half-opened shoe boxes and a mountain of handbags that littered the floor.

Ceri grinned sheepishly. "I'm just trying to find my best shoes and matching handbag. I've set my heart on wearing them but… ah-ha, here they are, at last," she proclaimed triumphantly, opening what seemed to be the last box dragged from the wardrobe. Both were made in the same shade of soft, buttery suede.

"Wow, they look fabulous," said Hanna. "Is that it? Can we go now?"

"Ready, how do I look?" said Ceri, slipping on the shoes.

"Not bad for a 30-year-old!" joked Hanna, propelling her friend towards the front door.

All the way to the station, Ceri chatted incessantly about how she was looking forward to her big day. First stop was the trip to Palermo, where they'd been invited to the lunchtime opening of a new gallery featuring local crafts. It belonged to Aurora, an old friend of Luciano's. Ceri had jumped at the chance of going when Hanna told her that

Luciano would be away on business on the day of her birthday. It was a source of continued frustration between them that Luciano hadn't yet met Ceri's boyfriend, Sergio. He always had some excuse or another, usually business-related. It was as if he wanted to keep Hanna to himself, sharing her with his own family and friends from time to time but not wanting to get involved with hers.

Just thinking of Luciano and his excuses for not being there threatened to dampen the euphoria that emanated from her friend. Hanna pushed it to the back of her mind, determined that it wouldn't spoil their day.

It was late morning by the time they arrived in Palermo. The gallery was in a side street in the old Arab La Kalsa district, not far from the station. Once seedy, this area had seen a reversal of fortune thanks to considerable investment and regeneration of its dilapidated *palazzi,* and was now desirable once more. They found it easily enough, the soft strains of Sicilian singer-songwriter Carmen Consoli floating down the narrow street towards them, accompanied by babbling voices and the odd peal of laughter.

Stepping off the street into a long, narrow room of exposed stone walls and soft spotlights, the two women joined the throng of people gathered there. A tall, willowy blonde in a simple designer dress in neutral tones and antique gold jewellery, tottered over in vertiginous heels, working the room with the ease of a practised politician as she made her way towards them. *Distinctly un-Sicilian in looks*, thought Hanna, until she remembered that the island's Norman history had left its legacy of fair genes behind.

"Welcome, Hanna, so glad you could make it. And this must be Ceri," said Aurora in heavily-accented English, all beaming smile and flashing teeth, kissing them on both cheeks. "Come on in and take a look around. Let me get you a drink."

Hanna had met Aurora fleetingly at a couple of posh social events she'd attended with Luciano. A former model, she recalled. Hanna envied her poise and exuberant confidence, qualities she felt lacking in. She felt a twinge of jealousy as she had on previous occasions, wondering what the true nature of the relationship had been between this woman and Luciano. Was Aurora just a friend, one of Luciano's business associates, or something more than that? Hanna felt inadequate and gauche in comparison. What did he see in her when he could have any woman he wanted? How could she compete with his circle of stylish, well-connected friends?

Waves of self-doubt were threatening to drown her buoyant mood when the effusive and bubbly Aurora interrupted in perfect hostess fashion.

"You're just in time for my little opening speech. Feel free to look around – there's bound to be something that catches your eye. There's so much beautiful stuff and it's all made locally. You won't mind if I leave you? We can catch up later…"

As if by magic, a handsome young man, more model than waiter, appeared with two glasses of sparkling *prosecco* and a tray crammed full of delicious-looking canapés. It had been a long time since breakfast and Hanna was suddenly conscious of her appetite. Both girls helped themselves to a generous portion and tucked in.

Aurora turned on her heel, not giving her two guests time to reply. Hanna smiled and murmured her thanks through a mouthful of smoked swordfish. Their hostess disappeared into the crowd, reappearing a few minutes later on a small podium at the far end of the room. The chatter died down a little in anticipation.

Hanna and Ceri found it difficult to hear what was being said and only caught the odd word or two. Aurora seemed to be delivering her speech in dialect rather than Italian, perhaps in keeping with the name and nature of the gallery: *L'Artigianato della Sicilia – Sicilian Arts and Crafts.* She kept it short, and the gallery soon filled with applause from the assembled guests.

Gradually, they started to disperse, providing an opportunity for Hanna and Ceri to take a look around at the eclectic mix of wares ranging from ceramics to wall hangings. All had a distinctly modern feel, a far cry from the traditional or tourist products that were widely available. Aurora certainly had a keen eye and a flair for this sort of thing, Hanna had to admit. She lost sight of Ceri for a few minutes until a squeal of delight revealed her whereabouts.

"I'd know that squeal anywhere! What have you seen?"

Ceri was looking at a glass cabinet filled with delicate silver jewellery. Her eyes were focused on a filigree dragonfly necklace with wings made up of tiny stones of different hues.

"Look at that necklace, the way it catches the light! It's so beautiful, really unusual but quite expensive, I'm afraid."

"Why don't you try it on and see how it looks?" Hanna slipped the necklace round her friend's neck. "There, it really suits you. What do you think?"

"I really love it! It's just that…"

"I'll buy it for you. It *is* your birthday after all, and a special one at that…"

"Oh, I didn't mean… I wasn't hinting or anything…" Ceri's voice trailed off, her face flushed.

"I know you weren't. I was planning on getting you something here anyway. I wanted to make sure that it was something that you'd really like," said Hanna, reassuring her.

"Oh, okay then," Ceri brightened and smiled weakly, "but only if you're sure…"

"Come on, let's get it before I change my mind." Seeing the look of consternation on Ceri's face, Hanna added, "Only joking, you daft thing. I love it, too – it's just your thing."

"Well, if you insist, I can't possibly refuse!" said Ceri. "It'll be the best present ever!"

Hanna went off to the discreet cash desk in the far corner of the gallery to pay. As Aurora carefully gift wrapped the present in black paper with a gold ribbon, she said, "Of course, I can offer you a substantial discount. Any friend of Luciano's…"

Chapter Thirteen

North Wales, Friday 3rd November, 2017

Humming along to the radio, Hanna busied herself preparing dinner in the kitchen. Rhys had called earlier, promising good news but wanting to talk to her about it in person. Curious, Hanna wondered what it could be and had invited him round for dinner that evening, eager to know more.

Every so often, she popped her head round the lounge door to make sure Eva was okay. A cat with unusual black, white, and grey markings had taken to visiting on a regular basis, much to Eva's delight. She was sitting on the rug in front of the roaring wood burner playing with her new friend who was lapping up the attention. The cat seemed quite tame, not a feral or farm cat. Hanna had asked Nerys about the animal, but it didn't belong to them and there were no other close neighbours. Only a couple of weeks here and already they had a lodger. Hanna could hear Eva chattering away incessantly to the poor old moggy.

Outside, the wind was getting up and had started to howl around the cottage like an unwelcome predator. Hanna gave an involuntary shiver and wondered how they'd cope through the winter, which was likely to be harsh. She hoped they wouldn't get cut off; it was isolated enough even in good weather. At least they had some warm clothes now. One of their first expeditions in the old Peugeot Rhys had acquired for her had been to the nearest shopping outlet. There, Hanna bought warm waterproof jackets for both of them plus several sweaters and thick trousers, as well as scarves and gloves.

After checking the lamb shanks in the oven, she finished off the *tiramisu* with a light dusting of cocoa powder, hoping that Rhys would like her choice of dishes. Taking off her apron, she called out, "C'mon, little Miss Mucky, there's just time for your bath before Rhys and Bryn get here!"

Eva chortled with delight at the mention of Bryn. "But what about Cosmo?" she asked, referring to her new feline friend who she'd named after a character in one of her favourite TV programmes back in Sicily.

"Don't worry about him. I'm sure Bryn is used to cats, and Cosmo will just run off if he's not happy."

Hanna wiped her hands on a tea towel and went to run the bath. "Let's have those clothes off and get you into these bubbles. Then you'll be all nice and clean and in your pyjamas for when the boys get here," she called to Eva.

Tiny footsteps pattered up to the door of the bathroom and Eva appeared. She'd been trying unsuccessfully to undress herself en route, and had ended up in a muddle with her head and arms stuck in her half-off jumper.

Hanna laughed. "What a pickle you've got yourself into. Here, let me help." She finished off the job, then tested the temperature of the bath water before lifting the toddler in.

She glanced at her watch. Rhys would be here in less than an hour. She'd have to hurry to get both of them ready in time and prepare the table, too.

"So, what's this news, then?" asked Hanna, unable to contain herself any longer. They were already halfway through the main course and still Rhys hadn't mentioned anything. Eva had fallen asleep on the sofa after a frantic half hour of kissing Bryn and chasing him round the cottage. Hanna had gathered her up and put her to bed.

"I'd almost forgotten," said Rhys, with a teasing twinkle in his eye. "Well, I was down at the council offices about the new volunteer scheme we've launched. They were talking about next year's annual walking festival and that they could do with help organising it, especially on the PR and marketing side. The person who used to do it has moved down south. Thought it would be perfect for you with your background, so I put in a good word. Hope you don't mind…"

Hanna's immediate reaction was one of horror, that she'd be exposed to the outside world so soon, then quickly realised that this might be an overreaction, particularly when she noticed Rhys's face fall. Her expression must have given away her initial emotions, but these were quickly followed by a wave of relief and gratitude. After all, she couldn't cut herself off from people for ever and Rhys had only been acting in her best interest.

"D'you know what would be involved?" she asked in a slightly shaky voice.

"Not really, but they'd be keen to talk to you about it. What do you think?" Rhys looked a little sheepish, as if realising his *faux pas*. "The council offices are in Llangefni on Anglesey, which is a bit of a drive, but you could probably do some work from home once the internet connection is set up."

"Worth giving it a go, I expect. Save me climbing the walls here, and I could do with a bit of extra money. And I need to do something about Eva. She needs to mix with other children. My only concern is that it may be a bit soon. I don't know if I'm quite ready yet."

"I'm sorry if I acted out of turn. It just seemed like a really good opportunity. I'm afraid I dived right in."

"It's fine, don't worry. I'll go and talk to them – it can't do any harm. In fact, it could be exactly what both Eva and I need," Hanna said, smiling to reassure him.

"Okay. I'll make the arrangements and we can go together, if you want?" said Rhys, brightening up. "How about next Wednesday afternoon? I'm not working and it's market day so we could have a look around, do some shopping, and get a bite to eat?"

"Let me think about it first. Can you get me some background information on the event, though? I really could do with having the internet here."

"No problem, I'll print you off the details of last year's

festival, so you've got a better idea of what's involved, and bring them over."

Talk turned to the food which Rhys was devouring with gusto.

"I'm starving," he said apologetically. "Been on the hills all day. You work up quite an appetite with all that hard work and fresh air. I just love lamb, and these shanks are amazing, so tender and full of flavour! How did you cook them?"

"They've been in the oven for ages on a low heat, done in red wine, with garlic, rosemary and anchovies."

"Anchovies?"

"Yes, it's how the Italians often cook lamb. Their saltiness seems to complement the meat somehow, without leaving a fishy taste."

"Well, you can cook that for me anytime," said Rhys, slightly flushed, warmed by the fire and the red wine.

"Hope you've got room for some pud? It's my own take on *tiramisu* – no eggs but lots of strong coffee and booze."

"Sounds perfect," said Rhys, as Hanna collected the empty plates and took them out to the kitchen, returning with a large bowl of the dessert. "Soon polish that off!"

The rest of the evening passed pleasantly enough as the conversation turned to other topics. Rhys had brought over several books after Hanna had said that she'd like to catch up on some of the more modern classics that she'd never got around to reading, such as Hemingway and D H Lawrence. They chattered amicably over coffee and into the small hours until Rhys caught sight of the time and made his excuses, saying he had an early start in the morning. He kissed Hanna a hasty goodbye on the cheek and took his leave, Bryn bounding at his heels.

As she closed the front door on the inky, starless night and blustery wind, Hanna froze as she felt something brush past her and rush into the house. She was relieved to see it was only Cosmo, seeking refuge from the stormy weather. Her startled reaction to such a small event made her wonder whether it was wise to be venturing back into the real world quite so soon.

Chapter Fourteen

Sicily, Wednesday 18th December, 2013

Hanna had been mulling over the news for a couple of days, dreading the moment she would have to tell him, unsure of his reaction. Her opportunity came one Sunday as they were taking a rare stroll together along the beach, Luciano's arm slung casually round her shoulders.

"Luce, I've got something to tell you," said Hanna, in a low faltering voice. "I think I might be pregnant."

Luciano's face registered surprise, horror, and delight in quick succession.

"Really, but how…?"

Hanna shrugged her shoulders. "It can happen sometimes even with the most effective contraception. What do you think?"

He stopped abruptly and drew her to him in a tight embrace, smiling broadly.

"This is wonderful news, *amore!* You're happy about it, too, aren't you? You're not thinking about…?"

"I wasn't sure how you'd take it. I didn't want you to think that it was some sort of ploy to…"

"To what?"

"Well, you know – force things to the next stage between us."

"Don't be ridiculous. You know I'm mad about you. I couldn't be happier. Can't wait to tell the family."

Hanna gulped. "Won't they expect us to… you know, formalise things?"

He tipped her chin upwards with his fingertips and looked at her, their faces close.

"Probably, but would that be so bad?" Luciano teased, his eyes laughing at her discomfort. "Okay, so we hadn't planned it this way, but it could be a sign that we have a future together, the three of us. That is, unless you think otherwise?"

"You know there's nothing I'd like more," said Hanna, hastening to reassure him.

"Matter settled then. We'll announce it to them over Christmas and take it from there." He kissed her gently, glancing down at her tummy as if expecting some tell-tale sign to show already.

A warm glow spread through Hanna's body, starting from that very place.

"Are you sure you're pregnant, and do you definitely want to keep it?" asked Ceri, the alarm rising in her voice as she broke off from packing her suitcase, ready for the short trip back home to see her family. Hanna was sprawled across the bed watching her. She had rehearsed this conversation over and over in her head and was prepared for the inevitable challenge.

"Yes, and yes," responded Hanna patiently. "Is that so bad? Do you think I shouldn't?"

"I'm just concerned for both of you. You and your child, that is. You haven't known Luciano that long, and it may be rushing into things. But it's up to you – you know your feelings for him. It's your decision."

"It's not a situation that we'd planned or even thought about. It just happened. But now that it has and I've had a chance to think about it, I couldn't be happier. And Luciano seems to feel the same way, too."

"Well, as long as you're sure. You realise it's a commitment to living here in Sicily, too?"

Hanna hadn't really given this much thought but as she loved the island, it didn't seem to be a problem. She had no immediate family of her own, so where she chose to live her life and bring up a family wasn't an issue.

"Anyway, you can talk," said Hanna, changing the focus of the conversation. "Rushing home for a few days to see your folks so you can be back with Sergio for New Year. It'll be your turn next!"

"Unlikely, but who knows?" said Ceri, catching Hanna's eye. The two friends laughed in relief as the tension in the room subsided momentarily.

"The problem with Sergio is that I feel I only know one side of him. He keeps his work issues to himself, saying that being an investigative journalist is like being in the police. Says he can't talk about things until they're published, and even then he's loath to do it. Maybe it's better I don't know any of the details."

"Maybe it is,'" said Hanna. "Less to argue about!"

She knew how Ceri felt as Luciano was exactly the same with his business dealings and still spent a lot of time away from her. But this only meant that the time they were together was even more precious. The chemistry between them couldn't be denied and showed no signs of waning.

The warm glow returned. *A good omen*, thought Hanna, sure that she was making the right decision and that everything would work out for the best.

The shrill, piercing horn from Sergio's Fiat 500 announced his arrival in the narrow street outside the girls' apartment.

Ceri opened the lounge window and called down to him: "*Ciao,* Sergio. Wait there, we're on our way down." And to Hanna: "I'll take the case if you can give me a hand with the rest."

"No problem. Are you sure you're only going for a few days?" asked Hanna, surveying the sizeable suitcase sitting ready in the hall.

Ceri laughed. "I'd intended just to take a carry-on bag, but I couldn't fit all the presents in," she said, struggling to manoeuvre the suitcase down the narrow staircase. "I've never been one for travelling light."

"As long as you're coming back!" said Hanna. She

followed with the rucksack she'd seen Ceri stuff full of Christmas goodies, including a king-sized chocolate *panettone* and boxes of the local *buccellati* biscuits filled with nuts and dried fruits.

"Eh, *ragazze,* let me take those bags off you," said Sergio, meeting them halfway up the stairs. "I hope this little lot will all fit in the car!"

Fortunately, the car was one of the larger Fiat 500 models that fitted it all in with ease. Sergio pulled out into the traffic which was building as last-minute shoppers descended on the town centre. Festive lights adorned the streets, and shop windows tried to outshine each other with their seasonal displays. Families thronged the streets, more jovial and noisy than usual, stopping to buy roasted chestnuts from the outdoor vendors. Soon, the three friends left the town behind as the car headed towards Palermo airport.

The journey took about 45 minutes. The roads were quiet, only getting busy as they drew near the city and on the approach to the airport. Chaos reigned at International Departures, it seemed as if half the city had chosen to spend the Christmas vacation abroad.

Sergio managed to find a slot in the drop-off area outside the terminal building. No sooner had he pulled in than a taxi and two other cars blocked his exit. He swore quietly in dialect at their dilemma.

"Don't worry about seeing me off," said Ceri. "You won't be able to stay here, and it'll be a nightmare finding a parking space in this scrum. Just leave me here, I'll be fine."

"*Sicura?* Are you sure? I don't like leaving you like this, but I don't know what else we can do. As you say, it could take ages to find a parking space," said Sergio, opening the car door and getting Ceri's luggage out of the boot.

"Yes, I need to check in pretty smartly anyhow," said Ceri, giving Sergio a hug. "I'll miss you loads. Have a good Christmas. Not long until New Year!"

Sergio murmured something in Ceri's ear.

Hanna slipped out of the back seat and hugged her friend.

"Have a good flight and have fun. Give my love to your family and don't forget to keep in touch!"

"Will do, if I ever get a moment to myself! It'll be great to see everyone again. Just wish that you could come, too, Sergio. That damned job of yours again!"

"Someone has to be here to report on what Sicily's up to, even over the festive period!" Sergio replied with a grin.

"Never mind, it's not for long and we can see the New Year in together," said Ceri, pausing to give Sergio a long, lingering kiss before collecting her luggage and waving merrily, then she disappeared into the throng of people in the terminal building.

Hanna and Sergio returned to the car. She climbed into the passenger seat, looking forward to seeing the newspaper offices where Sergio worked. She'd expressed an interest in the paper and Sergio had offered to show her round. The stance of *La Gazzetta della Sicilia* was that the island had to change and turn its back on some of the accepted traditions such as the *pizzo* – protection money paid to the Mafia by many businesses just to be able to trade. That and the bribes paid to officials in return for lucrative contracts. She'd jumped at the chance when he suggested that they could do it on the way back from the airport after dropping Ceri off, as offices would be less frantic than usual.

"Fancy a quick *aperitivo* first before we hit the office? There's something I want to talk to you about," said Sergio, as he pulled away from the airport.

Chapter Fifteen

A sense of foreboding remained with Hanna despite everything. Washing up the breakfast things, she kept a watchful eye on Eva through the kitchen window. It was a blustery day and Eva was chasing leaves round the back garden, observed lazily by Cosmo, their adopted cat. He had taken to spending more and more time with them but still disappeared for days on end. Now, he was lying on his side in a sheltered spot next to the privet hedge, grooming himself in slow motion. Bursting with toddler energy, Eva ran around in circles, shrieking in delight every time a fresh gust whipped up the leaves.

"Look at me, *Mammina*!" she cried, her arms held wide at her sides. "They're running away from me!"

Hanna watched Eva's antics in a distracted way, her thoughts elsewhere. She had been mulling over Rhys's proposition. Although there was no longer any immediate threat, she knew that the more they resumed some semblance of normal life, the more exposed they would be. But they couldn't always live in isolation. Eva needed friends of her own age and Hanna's finances wouldn't last forever.

And she might be able to work from home if they could get the phone line installed and the broadband connection set up. Rhys had promised to check this out.

She wiped her hands on a tea towel and picked up the leaflet again to look at the details of the previous year's festival. It seemed to be a major event – two weeks in late

May/early June, packed full of organised walks and cycle rides, something for all ages and all the family. It wouldn't harm to talk to the organisers about what would be involved. Decision made, she picked up her mobile from the kitchen worktop and sent Rhys a text to confirm the meeting.

At the top of the old town hall steps, Hanna looked around in vain for Rhys and Eva. They'd dropped her off in good time for her appointment and had arranged to come back and meet her there afterwards. A sea of people greeted her. It was market day in Llangefni, the chief town of Anglesey, and the main square heaved with stall holders selling local produce and shoppers jostling to buy their wares.

As if from nowhere, she suddenly heard a prolonged cry of "*Mamm…a*!" and saw Eva slip away from Rhys's grip and rushed towards the steps as if her life depended on it. Rhys looked mortified. He called after her, Bryn straining on his lead to follow. Eva clambered up the steps to join Hanna, joined shortly afterwards by a slightly out of breath Rhys and a panting Bryn.

"I'm so sorry, she just bolted as soon as she saw you," he said.

Hanna picked up her daughter and hugged her. "Don't worry, no harm done. Just as well there's no traffic around. You're not to do that when you're with Uncle Rhys," she said, turning her attention to Eva. "You have to keep hold of his hand and be a good girl."

Eva's face fell. "Sorry, *Mamma*," she mumbled. "I won't do it again."

"She's not used to being without me. Probably just a natural reaction. Has she been okay otherwise?" asked Hanna.

"She's been fine, except for making me buy her an ice cream, despite the fact it's freezing! And she's even taught me how to ask for one in Italian: *un gelato, per favore.*"

Hanna laughed and tousled Eva's hair. She tried to picture the scene with some difficulty. Rhys was more used to looking after livestock than children, after all. He even seemed to be having a hard time controlling Bryn at the moment. The dog wasn't used to being on a lead and was trying to jump up, eager to join in the reunion.

"So, how did it go?" he asked.

"Really well," replied Hanna. "More like a done deal than an interview. You must have put in a good word for me. It was more about agreeing the working arrangements. They want me to do three days a week between now and the festival, putting together the brochure and doing PR to promote the event. The only stumbling block was my lack of Welsh."

Rhys's face brightened. "Well, I can help you with that. It's not a deal-breaker though, is it?"

"No, they seem to think my experience more than makes up for my lack of Welsh-ness!"

"That's great news. I'm really pleased for you." Rhys smiled.

"I'll be able to do some work from home once we get the broadband sorted out. When I need to come into the office, there's a crèche nearby that will look after Eva. All sorted."

"Well, the phone company has promised to come next week, so that won't be a problem. This calls for a celebratory lunch. I know a quaint little pub on the coast that serves up the best freshly caught fish for miles around. What d'you say?" Bryn started to bark excitedly before Hanna could reply. "Yes, and it's even dog-friendly so you're allowed, too!"

Dark storm clouds were gathering over their heads and the first hailstones started to fall, little white bullets striking their faces. Hanna shivered. She'd left off her usual layers and plumped for a burnt-orange sweater dress and knee-high mocha suede boots, topped off with a shaggy chocolate angora-mix coat, all from her Sicilian wardrobe. Smart for her meeting but no match for this weather.

"Brrrr, I'm freezing!" she said, taking Eva's hand and setting off at a gallop. "C'mon, gang. Let's find the car and head for that lunch!"

Out of the corner of her eye, Hanna caught what she

thought was an appreciative glance from Rhys. It was probably just a reaction to her enthusiastic response to his idea of lunch.

Lunch was everything Rhys had promised. Massive pieces of cod in light, crispy beer batter, served with chunky chips and minted mushy peas, washed down with a strong Scrumpy-like cider. Rhys stuck to an alcohol-free beer as he was driving. Sitting at a corner table in the little pub, warmed by a roaring log fire, they tucked in heartily, talking little as they ate. Eva had a kiddies' portion which she struggled to finish. Bryn came to the rescue and polished off the remains, licking his lips and wagging his tail contentedly.

By the time they'd finished and left the pub, darkness was already setting in. The wind had strengthened, the hail now interspersed with sleet. Rhys's brow furrowed.

"C'mon, we need to get home before it gets any worse," he shouted above the howling wind. "If it's like this here on Anglesey, it'll be worse up in the hills…" His voice trailed off. He must have seen the look of concern on Hanna's face. "Don't worry, it'll be fine. We're used to it."

They made a dash across the car park to Hanna's old Peugeot and piled in.

The drive home took about forty-five minutes. Eva and the dog both fell asleep in the back of the car. Rhys concentrated on the road ahead while Hanna sat in silence in the passenger seat, mesmerised by the driving snowflakes battering the windscreen. She felt uneasy, as if the weather was conspiring against them, trying to prevent them from getting home. She shivered and turned the heater up, but it seemed to make little difference.

At last, they drew up at the small stone cottage which lay in darkness. A sprinkling of powdery snow covered the ground. Hanna felt relieved as she unlocked the front door and switched on the lights. Rhys carried a still-sleeping Eva inside and Hanna put her to bed while Rhys busied himself lighting a fire in the wood-burning stove.

"Can I make you some coffee or hot chocolate before you

go?" she offered.

"Thanks, but I'd better get home," he said. "I've got a few things to check on and an early start tomorrow. Bad weather usually means we're busier. Stranded animals, stranded people, that sort of thing. It's been a great day, though. I'll give you a ring to confirm when they're coming to install the phone line and broadband. I can always drop by with provisions if conditions get worse and you're getting short. That's the only problem with the cottage. It's a bit isolated and you haven't got a four-wheel drive."

"We should be able to manage. Anything we haven't got, we'll either do without or improvise," said Hanna. "I haven't got much bread but I've got flour so I can always make some. Is the weather likely to get worse?"

"Well, it wasn't actually forecast. The predictions we get at work are usually much more accurate than the general ones on TV. I'll check tomorrow and let you know. C'mon, Bryn, let's get going!"

Bryn rose reluctantly from where he was stretched out in front of the fire. Rhys kissed Hanna on the cheek and opened the front door to be met by a gust of wind and a flurry of snowflakes which settled on the stone floor. From the window, Hanna watched the tail-lights of his Land Rover disappear into the distance. The only sound was the intense howling of the wind which now seemed to have reached gale force.

She turned on the early evening television news to blot out the sound. Images of tearful women and children in lifejackets being helped ashore by aid workers flashed across the screen. Hanna turned up the volume to hear the reporter say:

"...In yet another rescue attempt in stormy conditions in the Mediterranean Sea earlier today, a number of women and children have been found in in the water a long way from land. It is believed that they are the lucky ones and that as many as fifty others may have drowned following their boats capsizing off the east coast of Sicily. They are believed to be

71

the latest wave of migrants from the Middle East and Africa trying to reach Europe. Investigations are underway into the organised networks responsible for this continuing trafficking."

Hanna watched the images with growing dismay, her blood turning to ice. So, these atrocities were continuing. Now that she and Eva were relatively safe, she had to do something. She couldn't just ignore what was happening; her conscience wouldn't let her. She had to make a decision quickly before more people perished. But it had to be one that wouldn't compromise or bring harm to either themselves or their friends.

Chapter Sixteen

Sicily, Wednesday 18th December, 2013

Sergio pulled off the *autostrada* at the slip road for Capaci just outside Palermo. Hanna looked at him questioningly.

"It'll be quieter here and we'll be able to talk more freely," he explained.

Hanna wondered why he was going to such lengths. No doubt she'd find out soon enough.

Having parked the car in a side street, Sergio led the way to an unassuming bar with a striped awning situated on the main road through the little town. The interior of the bar was cool and dark, illuminated by rows of glass shelves groaning with cakes of all shapes and sizes, some glazed with fruit, others with a minimalist shiny ganache, each one a mini work of art.

"Wow, these cakes are incredible! Are they all made here on the premises?" asked Hanna, staring at the enormous range in amazement.

"Yes, the bar was taken over by a friend of mine about eighteen months ago and he's been building himself a bit of a reputation ever since. People come here from miles around to buy his cakes, especially at the weekend. Ah, talk of the devil, here he is. *Ciao, Fabio, come va?*"

A stocky, middle-aged man wearing a turquoise T-shirt that barely covered his ample stomach, appeared from the back of the bar. He hugged Sergio warmly as they exchanged pleasantries in thick dialect. Reverting to more mainstream Italian, Sergio introduced him to Hanna.

"So, *ragazzi,* what can I get you? Anything you like – it's on the house," said Fabio.

"Maybe you'd prefer coffee and a cake to an aperitif?" Sergio asked Hanna.

"No, an aperitif will be fine. I'm not actually very hungry but I'll certainly buy a cake to take to Luciano's family tomorrow. It'd be rude not to – they all look so exquisite," Hanna replied with a smile.

Sergio ordered two Aperols and they moved to a table at the far end of the bar, away from the few remaining customers.

"So, what are you doing for Christmas, Sergio? Ceri said you might be working as normal."

"Well, I'll be pretty much working right through. That's what prompted Ceri to go home. She'd have been on her own otherwise, with you at Luciano's family place. There's a lot going on right now; you'll have heard how bad…" His voice trailed off as Fabio approached, bearing a tray.

"Here we are, friends. *Due aperitivi* and a few nibbles to whet the appetite. Enjoy!"

Fabio set the drinks down on the table with a flourish, along with a little bowl of juicy black olives in a herb, garlic, and chilli marinade, and another full of salted almonds and pistachios. Hanna marvelled yet again at the Italian obsession with food and drink.

Sergio waited until Fabio was out of earshot before continuing. "As I was saying, you'll have heard how bad the situation is getting with regards to the refugees who keep landing in Sicily in ever-increasing numbers?"

Hanna nodded, helping herself to an olive.

"Well, it's not by chance that it's happening. It looks as if there are organised networks behind it all, though it's difficult to pin them down. There are enormous profits to be made from this people trafficking. The problem is it's not just about the illegal transport of migrants. There's so much more at stake."

Hanna listened attentively, wondering where this was going and what it had to do with her.

"Some of the men are recruited into extremist groups, others are used as cheap casual labour, and others, alarmingly, are starting to form their own gangs to rival our own home-grown variety. Many of the women, and even children, end up in prostitution or are used as drug mules. That's if they arrive here alive. Many die en route, especially now the weather's bad. The boats are overcrowded and badly maintained so they often capsize. If it wasn't for the patrols, many more would perish."

Images of dead bodies washed up on the island's shores, children and babies in orange life jackets being plucked from small overcrowded fishing boats, and dark-skinned men, their faces twisted with torment, flashed through Hanna's mind.

"It's a massive problem, not just for Sicily and the rest of the country but for the whole of Europe and the West. It poses a massive security threat as well as being an economic and political problem, to say nothing of the wide-scale human suffering," he continued.

"From what I've seen on the news, the situation certainly seems to be getting worse," Hanna remarked. "And no-one seems to have a grip on it – the politicians, the charities, they all seem powerless."

"It's not for want of trying, but there are vested interests out there. Obviously, it's of interest to the Sicilian media who cover it from a news angle, but my paper's adopting a more investigative stance and is committed to looking at the root cause. We've been working with the police for some time and pooling information to try to get to the bottom of who's behind it, with a view to cracking down on it once and for all. At least, the Sicilian connection, that is."

"And how does this affect me? Why are you telling me this?" asked Hanna, trying to keep the alarm out of her voice.

Sergio shifted uncomfortably on his chair before responding. "Well, a number of our leads suggest that Luciano's brother may be connected or tied up in it in some way. It may even extend to the whole family. I just wanted to warn you to be on your guard."

"What? Are you accusing me of getting myself involved with a people trafficker?" asked Hanna indignantly, her eyes flashing angrily and her cheeks burning. "What do you take me for?"

"No, it's just that… Well, sometimes love is blind. People are often led by their heart rather than their head. I wasn't suggesting that you're mixed up in this, but you might know something unwittingly."

"By association, you're suggesting exactly that. I can assure you that I have no reason to suspect that Luciano's family is involved in anything of the sort. They seem like a family with a perfectly respectable business. What makes you think they might be?" she asked, her heart thumping and goose bumps crawling up her arms.

"We've a number of leads that suggest a small group of influential individuals are behind the Sicilian operation," said Sergio. "We're looking into people who have lucrative business interests or positions of power on the island. It could be that some people are involved in some way without even realising it."

"You'd have to be pretty stupid not to realise—" Hanna began.

"Listen, Hanna," said Sergio, impatiently. "We've been dealing with this sort of thing in Sicily for centuries and have never managed to wipe it out. Things have improved in recent years, but corruption and crime are still rife. This is merely a new channel that's being exploited for all its worth by the unscrupulous in our society. Our newspaper is determined to help smash the networks behind this, once and for all."

"And how do you think I can help?" she asked cautiously.

"I don't want to compromise you or put you in any danger, but it'd be useful if you could let me know if anything strikes you as suspicious or strange."

"I think you're mistaken. I've never noticed anything that's given me any reason for concern, and I've never been treated with anything but respect by both Luciano and his family."

"But in business, they might be different," said Sergio. "These connections are passed down through the generations. For some people here, it's their way of life – they've never known anything else but they're secretive about their dealings. I just wanted to let you know and warn you to be on your guard."

"Thanks, I appreciate that," said Hanna, still shaken and reeling from this insinuation.

"If you ever need to contact me," he added, "call my mobile, as my office phone's probably being monitored."

Hanna shivered to think that criminal activity could be so near to home. *Luciano couldn't be implicated in anything so devastating and disastrous, could he?* She suddenly remembered the phone calls at all hours of the day and night, muffled conversations, the frantic meetings and last-minute business trips. The implications of Sergio's words began to sink in, shattering Hanna's idyllic view of island life. Although she had to accept that this trafficking was going on, she had no doubt that Sergio's fears were unfounded. Luciano and his family couldn't possibly be mixed up in such a horrific business.

Chapter Seventeen

While Eva was taking a nap, Hanna took the opportunity to call Ceri. Several days had passed since they'd last spoken, as they'd agreed not to contact each other too often. Each time they spoke, Hanna was almost fearful of what she might hear.

"There's not much news, really," said Ceri, picking up on the first ring. "It's all gone relatively quiet, apart from all the migrants who keep arriving in droves. Sergio says the investigations are ongoing but every time there's a lead and someone's taken in for questioning, some hot-shot lawyer steps in to make sure they don't say more than they should. Everyone's hoping for a major breakthrough but it seems a long way off…" Her voice sounded tired and tense.

"And what about Luciano?" Hanna hardly dared ask.

"Well, the word is that he's pretty pissed off and determined to find you at all costs. Publicly, he's making out that it was all planned and you're spending some time with your family. People aren't to know that you haven't got any, apart from us. Otherwise, it would be too much of a *brutta figura,* a loss of face, for someone in his position. Apparently, he thinks you've managed…" Ceri's words faded and broke up as the line faltered.

"What was that? I lost you for a minute." Hanna wondered fleetingly if anyone could be monitoring their conversation.

"Sergio's heard through one of his contacts that Luciano thinks you've managed to get off the island somehow but are unlikely to be on the mainland, otherwise his associates would've picked it up by now," responded Ceri. "He's bound to think that you'd go back to the UK although he knows you haven't got any family or support network there."

"I'm still afraid he'll come after me."

"Well, he hasn't got the contacts there, and anyway, where would he start?"

"Yes, but he's not going to give up lightly, is he? I can't live under the radar forever."

"You won't have to. Sergio's father reckons that the net's tightening. It's just a matter of time…"

A knot formed in Hanna's stomach as she realised she could bring this whole business to a swift conclusion if she wanted. *But at what cost?* she wondered.

"How are you both, anyway? Hope Rhys is looking after you okay?"

Hanna gulped back the lump in her throat.

"We're both fine, thanks. Eva's treating it like a big adventure, but she misses her dad. Rhys has been great, really helpful. We couldn't have done it without you – we owe both of you so much." Tears welled in her eyes as she struggled with her words. "I'd better go, I've kept you long enough. I'll have Wi-Fi at the cottage soon, so we'll be able to e-mail rather than rely on mobiles."

"Okay. Well, take care and be careful. I'll let you know if there's any news."

"Will do, and you, too. Speak to you soon."

Hanna sank back on the sofa. Once again, she wondered what she should do. It felt as if she was sitting on a time bomb that she alone could activate, but it was difficult to imagine the scale of its impact. She wasn't just worried for herself and Eva, but for Ceri and Sergio and their families and colleagues and many others who'd be caught up in the crossfire. The thought of the numerous victims past and present was a dilemma; the longer she left it, the more victims would fall into the clutches of the traffickers.

How could she have been so stupid not to realise what was happening and let herself get tangled up in all of this? She felt as if she'd aged ten years or more in the last twelve months. Was speaking up too risky? And if she did, would it be traced back to her? She was torn, unsure of which direction to take. It was difficult to know what to do for the best and she couldn't really discuss it with anyone. She needed more time to think.

The trees murmured and danced in the brisk breeze as Hanna and Eva made their way up the stony track to their neighbours' cottage. They'd decided to walk as it was a bright sunny day, but the temperature remained low and Hanna was glad she'd insisted on several warm layers of clothing. Nerys had invited them over for the afternoon; Lars was away on business.

Eva skipped along, jumping over the puddles and keeping up an incessant mumbled monologue, a jumble of English and Italian words that Hanna couldn't quite make out.

"Who are you talking to, Eva?" she asked, with a wry smile.

"Orsina, of course," said Eva, pointing to the battered old teddy peeping out of her rucksack. "I'm teaching her English. She's a bit slow – but she *is* very old."

Eva was right: Orsina was getting on in years. She'd been Hanna's favourite teddy as a child, but Eva had taken to her and given her a new name. Hanna laughed at her daughter's antics, realising how bright she was and how quickly she was developing. She was ready for nursery now; it would be good for her to mix with other children. Hanna was due to start her new job the following week and had made arrangements for the nursery to look after Eva when she was in the office.

Apart from Eva's constant chatter, the only other sounds were the shrill chirping of birds and the faint bleating of sheep on the upper slopes of the valley. It was peaceful and quiet and seemed a million miles away from the cares of the outside world. If only…

The sight of her neighbour's stone cottage up ahead jolted her back to reality. *Something's wrong, it's much too quiet*, she thought. To her dismay, she suddenly realised why: she was alone. Eva was nowhere to be seen. Panic gripped her. She looked around frantically but there was no sign of her daughter.

"Eva, *dove sei?* Where are you?" she called out, her voice rising to a fever pitch. The only response was a slight mocking echo of her own voice.

Her heart thumping, she tried to focus. Where could she be? What could have happened in such a short space of time? She cursed herself for being so wrapped up in her own thoughts. Either Eva had wandered off, in which case she would probably be still in view, or she'd fallen behind. Or else… Anything else was too painful even to contemplate.

Hanna decided to retrace her steps towards the stone bridge. As she drew nearer, a faint cry could be heard, and a familiar figure lying in a crumpled heap came into view. The cries turned into wails as Hanna ran over and knelt down beside her daughter. The wails subsided, only to be replaced by wracking sobs as Eva rocked to and fro, clutching her knee.

"Whatever's happened? Are you hurt? Here, let me have a look at your knee."

Between sobs, Eva managed to explain as best she could, "I fell… *nell'acqua,* in the water… trying to save Orsina." She pointed to her beloved teddy whose fur was matted with mud and barely recognisable. "*Mi sono sbucciata il ginocchio*… my knee, I've hurt my knee." Eva's thick tights were soaking wet and a large hole had appeared in one knee, revealing a bloody gash.

"There, there," said Hanna, soothingly. "*Niente di serio*… it's only a scratch, no harm done." She planted a series of kisses on Eva's poorly knee.

"Don't do that, it hurts," Eva said crossly and began to wail again. Hanna felt sure she was overdoing it but didn't want to take any risks.

"OK, I'll call Auntie Nerys and get her to come and pick us up. We'll soon get you cleaned up and put a nice big bandage on your knee."

Hanna tried to have another look at the wound, but the

toddler wasn't having any of it and wouldn't let her near her. "I don't want you. You hurt me. I want *Babbo*... Daddy. Where is he? I want to see him now!" The tears were fast turning into a tantrum and she started to stamp her feet, despite her injury.

Hurt at the way the youngster had turned against her, Hanna rummaged through the contents of her bag until she found her phone. She quickly punched in the number.

"Hi, Nerys, it's me, Hanna. We're just down the road from you but Eva's taken a tumble and has hurt her knee. You couldn't come and pick us up, could you? I don't think she'll be able to walk and it's too far to carry her..."

"Is she okay? She's making a lot of noise."

"She'll be fine, it's only a flesh wound. You know how kids can be..."

"I'll take your word for it. Just hang on, I'll be right over."

Hanna waited for Eva to calm down a little before she went over and put her arms around her.

"You'll be fine, you'll see. We'll get you cleaned up and later, if you're feeling better, you can have some chocolate buttons or an ice cream. How does that sound?"

That did the trick, and the tantrum vanished almost immediately.

"*Va bene, Mammina,* I'll be a good girl now," Eva smiled weakly as if to apologise, her face sombre and streaked with tears.

It only took a few minutes for Nerys to reach them in the 4x4. Relieved, Hanna picked Eva up and carried her over to the back seat of the car. She glanced at the cut knee as she did so. She was sure it was only a minor wound that could be sorted out quickly without any need for a doctor or hospital. But, she chastised herself, I really need to be more careful and keep a close eye on her in future.

Chapter Eighteen

Sicily, Wednesday 25th December, 2013

As soon as she stepped into the car, Hanna realised her mistake. Her head was swimming and her stomach was doing its own curious brand of gymnastics. She'd insisted that they should accept the invitation from Luciano's family: it was Christmas Day after all, and it was expected. Now in her second month of pregnancy, her appetite had waned and what little she did eat, she struggled to keep down.

Driving along the winding roads up to Luciano's family home only added to her misery. They had to stop several times en route so she could throw up. She felt light-headed and would have done anything to lie down.

"Are you sure about this? We can always turn back. I'll explain things to the family – they'll understand," said Luciano, looking concerned.

"No, I'll be fine later. It's usually just a morning thing. Besides, we want to tell them our news."

She took a swig of water from a small bottle and her stomach seemed to settle momentarily. But by the time they pulled up outside the house, she felt weak and rooted to the seat, unable to move.

Luciano rushed round to the passenger door to help her out. Hearing the car arrive, his mother, Arazia, opened the front door and let out a squeal of alarm when she saw them.

"What's happened, what's wrong with Hanna? Is she ill?"

"I'm fine, just a little…" Hanna wrestled to find a suitable response.

"You don't look at all fine," interrupted Arazia. "You're as white as a sheet and can hardly move. What's going on?"

"Don't fuss, *Mamma*. I'll explain later," said Luciano. "Help me get her into the house."

Hanna felt herself supported on both sides and was half carried into the house. The smell of cooking wafting in from the kitchen made her retch again. Luciano's sister Paola emerged, wiping her hands on a tea towel.

"Oh, Hanna, you look so pale. You shouldn't have let her come," she said, eyeing her brother crossly. "Here, let's get you to bed. You'll feel better after a lie down."

Hanna smiled weakly and let Paola take her to one of the guest bedrooms at the back of the house, far away from the aromas of the festive meal that was being prepared. The room was cool and quiet, the blinds closed to the winter sunlight. Paola helped her into bed, covered her with a warm duvet, and went into the adjoining bathroom for a glass of water. Hanna took a couple of sips before sinking back gratefully into the pillows. Paola pulled the door to as she left. Hanna closed her eyes and soon drifted off to sleep.

She was woken some time later by raised voices. Muzzy-headed from her short but fitful sleep, it took Hanna a few minutes to come to and remember where she was. The voices she could hear were not happy; it was more of a heated exchange, although she was too far away to make out the words.

Slowly, she pushed back the duvet and got up. The nausea seemed to have disappeared for the time being. She stumbled into the bathroom and splashed cold water on her face, grimacing at her dishevelled appearance in the mirror above the basin. Retrieving her handbag from the bedroom, she ran a brush through her hair and reapplied her lipstick. *Not great, but as good as it's going to get*, she thought. As she emerged from the room, the commotion calmed down as if its protagonists sensed her approach.

By the time she got to the lounge, the voices had subsided to a low chatter. The family were gathered there: Arazia and her husband Michele, Paola and Luciano's younger brother Giulio, but there was no sign of Luciano.

"Oh, there you are, *cara,*" said Arazia with a tight smile. "How are you feeling now? Any better?"

"Yes, thanks," replied Hanna. "I'm so sorry, I hope I haven't spoiled your arrangements on such a special day."

"Not at all," said Michele. "We're so happy you could join us. We're planning on eating in about an hour or so. Do you feel up to it?"

"I think I'll be able to eat something," said Hanna, conscious of the faint growls coming from her stomach. "Where's Luciano?"

"He's… err, had to go out to resolve some sort of problem in one of the wineries. He'll be back shortly," said Giulio. "Can I get you something to drink? Maybe a soft drink, a fruit juice, if you're not feeling too good?"

Hanna accepted a chilled pear juice and joined in the conversation which veered from the latest celebrity indiscretions to the island's political problems. Arazia and Paola kept popping out into the kitchen to make sure that the preparations were progressing to plan. Nothing more was said about Luciano's absence until he reappeared about half an hour later.

"So sorry," he said breathlessly, as if he'd been in a rush to return. "Just a problem we've been having with one of the machines. It was easier to go and resolve it on the spot rather than try and explain it to the duty manager. Hope I haven't missed anything? Glad to see you're up, Hanna – you look so much brighter." He went over to her and kissed her lightly on the cheek. "Are we ready for the Christmas toast then?"

Hanna sensed the mood lightening as Michele went to find the bottles of vintage champagne that he'd put aside for this purpose.

"Can I give you a hand?" she asked, feeling guilty that she'd contributed so little to the day. She followed him into the dining room where the table was already set and waiting for the festive feast.

"Yes, you can bring in the glasses if you don't mind. That

would be a real help," he said, pointing to a tray of tall elegant flutes standing ready on the traditional wooden dresser standing at the far side of the room.

"Fine, will do. Anything else?"

"Oh, and the canapés over there," he indicated another tray of small dishes filled with an array of *crostini,* along with salted almonds and pistachios.

"I'll take the glasses in first and come back for those," said Hanna, picking up the first tray.

By the time she returned to the lounge with the canapés, Michele was filling the flutes ready for the toast. Hanna set the little dishes down on a side table and joined Luciano, who handed her a glass.

"*Salute! Buon Natale a tutti!* Happy Christmas, everyone!" he declared, raising his glass and slipping his other arm round Hanna's shoulder.

"*Salute! Cin, cin!* Cheers, good health," echoed the family members, their glasses poised in mid-air.

"And before we drink a toast to another prosperous year, I have an announcement to make," declared Luciano ceremoniously, shooting Hanna a conspiratorial smile. "This is going to be a landmark year for our family, as Hanna has done me the honour of consenting to be my wife."

His words were met with a few seconds of stunned silence, followed by a ripple of applause. The news had obviously taken them all completely by surprise.

"That's wonderful news," said Arazia smiling, although her face seemed drawn and tight. "We're just a little taken aback, that's all. Everything has happened so quickly…"

"Don't mind my wife, Hanna," said Michele. "We're quite traditional in Sicily, set in our ways. The important thing is that this is what *you* want and are happy."

"I haven't finished yet, there's more news!" interrupted Luciano, eager to round off their bombshell. "You're going to become *nonni* – grandparents – and Paola and Giulio auntie and uncle. What do you think of that?!"

More applause and laughter, followed by the menfolk slapping each other on the back, the women exchanging hugs. Hanna smiled shyly, a little embarrassed at Luciano's flamboyant announcement but nevertheless delighted by the family's response. They all seemed genuinely pleased and each one in turn embraced her, kissing her on both cheeks.

"That explains the 'illness' then," said Paola, smiling. "I'd already guessed but didn't want to mention it until you did. I'm delighted for you both. When's it due?"

"Towards the end of July," confirmed Hanna. "I'm so excited but I want to get the first trimester over and done with, so I feel better. It's not been the best of starts."

"Never mind, you'll get there," said Arazia firmly. "But first things first. When are you planning the nuptials, before or after?"

"Just as soon as we can so that everything's in place before the baby's born," said Luciano beaming proudly, taking Hanna's hand. "We would have done it soon anyway. The baby just means that we're bringing it forward."

Arazia nodded as if this wasn't news to her. Had Luciano already told her? Maybe, but the important thing was that his family was happy and supportive. Otherwise, it would have been difficult or even impossible: they were such a close-knit family and Luciano wouldn't act against their wishes.

"We've had far too much excitement for one day, already!" declared Michele. "C'mon, tribe, don't know about you but I'm starving! If everything's ready, let's go and eat!"

Chapter Nineteen

North Wales, Monday 13ᵗʰ November, 2017

Today was the day. Hanna's first day at work and Eva's first day at nursery. Hanna had been dreading it, taking their first real step back into the world, starting to mix with strangers again. For the last few weeks, they'd been in their own little bubble, with only Rhys and Nerys and their furry friends Cosmo and Bryn for company.

Hanna had spent the last few days preparing. For her, it was straightforward enough and involved doing some research on the walking festival: what had been done in previous years, and what new ideas and opportunities she could think up for this year's event. But with Eva, it was quite a different matter and took no end of persuasion.

"It'll be fun, Eva, you'll see. There'll be lots of other children to play with and you'll be able to make new friends. Much better than being with boring grown-ups all the time. And it's only for a few hours…"

Eva's face set in a scowl and angry tears sprang from her eyes. "I don't want to go. I want to stay here. You can't make me," she wailed.

"It won't be so bad, and we can stop off on the way back and see the birds," said Hanna, referring to the RSPB nature reserve at Conwy – a sure-fire win with Eva who loved anything involving animals.

Eva's face brightened momentarily. "OK, but only if *Babbo* comes, too."

Hanna sighed. "Eva, you know that's not possible.

Daddy's busy working away and won't be back for a while. It's just you and me now, which is why it'll be nice for you to make some new friends."

The conversation continued in the same vein for several minutes. No matter how she cajoled, there was no pacifying her defiant little bundle of a daughter. Finally, in exasperation, Hanna said, "What about a visit to the bird place, a boat trip down the river, and an ice cream afterwards?"

A whisper of a smile appeared on Eva's petulant tear-stained face.

"I'll take that as a yes," Hanna said, relieved that her daughter was relenting at last.

"Only if Orsina can come," said the tot, as if determined to have the last word.

"Okay, but take good care of her and make sure you don't lose her."

"She's my best friend – she looks after me."

Hanna smiled. "In that case, I'd better have a word with her and make sure she does a good job!"

That was two days ago. Hanna felt it better not to broach the subject again until the actual day. Now it was here and she expected a tantrum, but Eva took it all in her stride and let herself be dressed in leggings and a flowery tunic without making a fuss, even singing one of her favourite songs in her usual jumble of Italian and English. *I'll have to warn the nursery about the Italian*, thought Hanna reluctantly.

Hanna dressed quickly, donning her burnt-orange sweater dress, opaque mocha tights, and matching boots. Smart enough to make an impression but not over the top, she hoped. A quick lick of make-up, a brush through her hair, and she was ready.

The slate clock on the kitchen wall showed it was nearly nine; time to go.

"Are we all ready?" she asked, having noticed Eva clasping Orsina to her chest. Eva gave a solemn nod without uttering a word. *She's still not happy about it*, thought Hanna. "C'mon, then, let's hit the road!"

Gathering up her bag and their coats, she bundled the lot into the car and fastened Eva securely into the car seat. The engine started with a splutter and seemed about to peter out before finally sparking into life. She pulled out slowly onto the track, which sparkled with a covering of light frost, and proceeded to negotiate the bends down to Conwy with care, although by now they were becoming quite familiar.

It was unusually quiet in the car; in the rear-view mirror, she saw why – Eva had already dozed off. That left Hanna free to ponder the day ahead and what it would bring. For her, this was to be a sort-of induction where she'd meet the Head of Tourism and the rest of the team and find out more about the job. She was looking forward to it now; it felt like ages since she'd had to apply herself to work and she relished the new challenge. For Eva, it would be a whole new world, one where children spoke a different language and played different games. Hanna wondered how she'd take to it. If it did work out, that might be difficult, too, as Hanna was hoping to do most of her work from home which would mean that Eva wouldn't be at nursery that often.

On reaching Conwy, the traffic thickened and Hanna concentrated on the road and the route ahead. Eva woke up just as they were approaching Bangor.

"Where are we? Where are we going?" she asked, clearly still muzzy from her nap.

"Remember, Mummy's starting work today and you're going to nursery to meet some new friends."

Hanna caught Eva's sour, grizzled expression in the mirror.

"Don't want to, want to stay at home," she began, kicking the car seat in protest.

"Look, we're nearly there now and the lady at the nursery said that there's a magician coming in today. You'll like that."

Eva's face brightened. "How long do I have to stay there?"

"Well, I'll drop you off on my way in, you'll have some lunch there, then there'll be the magic show in the afternoon, and I'll pick you up afterwards. If there's still time, we'll stop off at the nature reserve on the way back. If not, we'll go at the weekend. How about that for a plan?"

"Orsina likes it, so I have to, too."

Hanna laughed at the tot's logic. She'd finally managed to win her round.

By the time they drew up outside the nursery in Llangefni, Eva was back to her usual animated self, chattering away to Orsina in the back of the car. Hanna marvelled at Eva's mood swings, how she could go from being a little devil one minute to an angel the next, and her own ability to stay so patient with her.

Hanna released Eva from the car seat and took her hand as they approached the glossy red door of the Victorian terraced house where the Happy Tots nursery was located. The door was opened by a large woman in her forties with bright red hair and matching smudges of paint across her face and down the front of her smock.

"You must be Hanna! And is this little Eva?" the woman said in a strong Welsh lilt before Hanna got the chance to speak. She bent down to say hello, but Eva had taken refuge behind Hanna's legs. "Hi Eva, I'm Dilys. We've been expecting you. Come on in and meet the others."

"Nice to meet you, Dilys," said Hanna with a smile. "Thanks for taking her in, especially on such an ad hoc basis. I really appreciate it and hope she won't be too much trouble."

"Course, she won't. She'll be fine, won't you, pet?"

Eva smiled shyly as Dilys ushered them down the hallway into a large room that stretched the full length of the house. A group of excited toddlers milled around a handful of nursery assistants. A painting session was in full swing; huge expanses of white paper lay across the floor, half covered by multi-coloured handprints.

Eva squealed with glee. "Can I have a go, *Mammina?*" she asked. Without waiting for a reply, she let go of Hanna's hand and skipped over to join the others, her previous shyness now forgotten.

"Well, that certainly didn't take long!" said Hanna with a

smile. "And here's me thinking that she'd find it hard to settle in!"

"We don't usually find that newbies have too many problems," said Dilys, as she watched one of the assistants help Eva into a smock and start to show her what to do. "Would you mind stepping into the office for a couple of minutes while we finalise the details? Do you have time?"

Hanna glanced at her watch. Just under half an hour before she was expected at the Town Hall, which was only a couple of streets away. Plenty of time to complete the paperwork.

"Yes, no problem," she replied, hoping that the questions wouldn't be too searching.

"I hear Eva's mother tongue is Italian," said Dilys. "It shouldn't be a problem as we have a little boy, Ottavio, whose family is Italian. He speaks in a jumble of English, Welsh, and some Italian dialect. Sicilian, I think."

Hanna's blood ran cold.

Chapter Twenty

Sicily, Tuesday 17ᵗʰ February, 2014

Hanna couldn't believe how quickly the next few weeks flew by. At times she felt out of control, as if she were just a minor player caught up in the frenzy of arrangements the family was putting in place. The pregnancy was taking its toll, further adding to her feelings of helplessness. Arazia, her future mother-in-law, was determined that the wedding would go ahead before Hanna's bump became too noticeable, so the *bella figura* could be maintained.

But Hanna consoled herself with the thought that her relationship with Luciano was strong and this was what they both wanted for the future. He was quite happy to leave the wedding planning to his mother and her little band of helpers, who were all treating it like a military operation. Hanna would have preferred a small intimate affair, especially in the circumstances, but there was no chance of that. Not only was there the wedding and the baby to think of, but also somewhere more spacious for them to live. Luciano's apartment in Cefalu wasn't really suitable now there was a baby on the way.

She confided her thoughts to Ceri over coffee at the apartment they used to share in the old town. They'd just been to visit the sprawling new hospital development on the edge of town where she would give birth.

"Am I being selfish? I suppose I should consider myself lucky. Things with Luciano are going really well although he's still away a lot. I seem to be spending more and more time with his mother and sister, listening to their ideas and agreeing to all their elaborate plans. It's going to be such a high-profile affair, you'd think we were local celebrities."

"Well, it certainly saves you and Luciano the bother, especially as you've not been feeling too well," said Ceri. "Maybe you should let them get on with it and count your blessings. Don't stress, just relax and enjoy it."

"Maybe I should. Anyway, I couldn't back out of it now even if I wanted to. It's all a bit scary really, like being on a runaway train." Hanna giggled nervously.

"Yes, it's funny how things have changed so fast for both of us. Whatever happened to our carefree lives as tour guides? No responsibilities, no ties. Just look at us now – you about to get married into a prominent Sicilian family with a baby on the way, and me involved with a journo on a mission!"

They both laughed. At least they had each other to confide in. If it wasn't for Ceri, Hanna would feel pretty isolated. She could always rely on Ceri for her practical, no-nonsense take on life.

"And anyway, I'm facing my own dilemma," said Ceri, turning serious. "I'm not going to be able to afford the rent on this place when you've gone. I'll have to find somewhere else to live. Sergio wants me to move in with him, but his life is so chaotic. I don't know if that's what I want right now."

"I'm sure Luciano would help…" Hanna started hesitantly.

"Thanks, but I don't need his charity. I'll manage fine on my own," interrupted Ceri sharply.

"OK, I'd hate to think that you're being forced out of here because of me getting married."

Ceri's face softened. "Sorry, didn't mean to bite your head off. Just need to think about my options and where things are headed with Sergio before I rush into anything. It's been playing on my mind. So, are you going to fill me in on where the plans are up to?"

"You might want to make some more coffee – this could take a while!" Hanna joked as Ceri acted on her suggestion and disappeared momentarily into the kitchen to replenish the coffee pot.

Hanna's mobile rang. She checked the screen – it was Arazia, again.

"*Ciao, cara.* I've got some wonderful news. I've found the perfect place for you and Luciano. It's just outside Cefalu and has loads of room to bring up the little one. You just have to see it! We can all go up at the weekend and stop off for a spot of lunch. What do you think?" she enthused.

You couldn't doubt her enthusiasm and energy, thought Hanna. Exactly like a runaway train. She sighed inwardly. She should be grateful that Luciano's family was being so supportive. Half of the arrangements wouldn't have been done if they'd been left to Luciano. They agreed to meet up with the vendor that Sunday, followed by a late lunch at some restaurant that Arazia insisted was a 'must do'. Yet another of the family's plans that she was going along with.

Arazia was right. The house was set in an idyllic location, nestled in the foothills of the Madonian Mountains, above a lush green valley. Built of local honey-coloured stone, it sat bathed in wintry sunlight, warm and welcoming. Hanna and Luciano exchanged glances; the place was impressive.

Arazia and Michele were waiting for them outside with the owner, who was introduced as Salvatore. From the way the three of them were chatting, Salvatore seemed to be more than a passing acquaintance.

The house was enchanting, surrounded by a garden full of succulents and native plants that would be a blaze of colour in the spring and summer. And as Salvatore showed them around, the more Hanna saw, the more she liked. The only downside was that it might be a little rustic and isolated for someone used to the hustle and bustle of towns. But in every other respect, it seemed perfect.

"The property dates back to the seventeenth century but has been restored over time," explained Salvatore, opening the solid wood front door and ushering them inside. "You'll see that there are several buildings clustered around a cobbled inner courtyard which opens onto an extensive garden. The main house spreads over two floors. This is the living room."

Hanna cast an appreciative glance around the spacious room, lit by the rays of sun filtering through the windows. Furnished in a simple rustic style in warm shades of terracotta, it oozed character, from the wide open hearth, broad wooden beams, and exposed stone walls, to the heavy wooden shutters framing the windows and doors. Luciano caught her eye and smiled, evidently thinking along the same lines. The kitchen was equally as expansive and rustic but with the benefit of a modern, high-end range cooker and integrated appliances. Upstairs were four ample bedrooms, one of which had been converted into an office. There was plenty of space for their new family.

"So, *signori,* what do you think?" Salvatore asked at the end of the guided tour. "Is it what you're looking for and does it meet your expectations?"

Hanna couldn't contain her enthusiasm; she couldn't have picked anywhere better if she'd tried. "It's perfect. I love it," she replied, "and I'm pretty sure Luciano does, too, don't you?"

Luciano grinned and wrapped his arms around her protectively. "I'm sure we'll be very happy here. It's the ideal place to bring up a family. There's so much space – you can really breathe. We just need to agree a price and a date when we can move in."

Hanna smiled back in agreement. Luciano and Salvatore arranged to meet up the following week to discuss the finer details. It was only as they were driving away on the single-track road that Hanna realised how isolated it was. What would she do if she ran out of milk or the baby was ill? And what about company? *Don't be so silly*, she told herself, *trust your initial gut feelings.* Everything would work out just fine.

Chapter Twenty-One

North Wales, Tuesday 21st November, 2017

Hanna was sitting at her laptop, trying to concentrate on the screen. The deadline for submitting her proposal for the festival's opening event was fast approaching but she'd only managed to write a few paragraphs in the last couple of hours. It wasn't that she lacked ideas, just the best way to present them.

Everything seemed to be conspiring against her. The weather had turned bitterly cold and a fierce wind battered the cottage on all sides. Snow was forecast. The wood burner kept going out, making her realise how draughty a stone cottage in Wales could be at this time of year. Hanna shivered, took the throw off the back of the sofa, and wrapped it round her shoulders.

Eva was sitting on the rug, bored and restless, trying to thump out a tune on her toy piano. She hadn't been to nursery for several days and was already missing the company and constant activities.

"Has Cosmo come back yet?" she asked for the umpteenth time. Their adopted cat hadn't put in an appearance for the last few days, and Eva had asked about him so often that Hanna finally snapped.

"Can't you see I'm trying to do some work? How many times do I have to tell you? No!"

Startled by the outburst, Eva began to sob loudly, tears streaming down her cheeks. Hanna hurried over to console her, feeling guilty for losing her temper.

"Sorry I shouted, sweet pea. Mummy didn't mean it. I know you're worried about Cosmo, but he'll be back soon, you'll see. He's used to being out in the wilds. Cats often take themselves off hunting and come home when they've had enough. Come on, I'll read you a story if you like?"

Eva's sobs slowly subsided and she nodded, climbing onto the sofa and settling back into the cushions. Hanna put another log on the wood burner, hoping this would help raise the temperature, then sat next to her daughter and began to read. It was one of Eva's favourite stories about a fox that befriends a polecat, and together they set off on a series of adventures. Eva listened intently, butting in every now and again with her usual "why" question. Hanna answered by rote in a distracted way, but Eva seemed happy enough with the responses.

The wind continued to howl outside, and the log crackled as it caught fire, its flames helping to warm the draughty living room. Eva soon became drowsy, her eyes flickering until she eventually fell asleep.

Hanna covered her with the throw and returned to the laptop, but her heart wasn't in it. Truth was, her heart wasn't in anything right now. Waves of anxiety ebbed and flowed through her head, making it difficult to think clearly and concentrate on the matter in hand.

At times she felt they were safe, but she couldn't be sure for how long. But in more panicky moments, she feared they might be discovered at any moment. In many ways, Hanna hankered after her old life in the sun, the way Luciano had made her feel loved and protected, his touch on her skin. How had it all come to nothing almost overnight? But her life had been a lie; everything was just a façade, a grotesque cover-up. How could she have been so stupid, so naïve? Why didn't she realise sooner that it was all too good to be true?

And now she was torn, faced with the dilemma of deciding what to do with the information she had. She shuddered, realising that she couldn't put it off much longer. People would suffer if she chose to do nothing; but would she and Eva pay the price if she revealed the truth? Her mind flashed back to that last day in Sicily. What she couldn't quite work out was why Luciano had also been threatened.

Hanna blamed herself. It was all her fault, what had she let them get mixed up in? And why hadn't Ceri been in touch? She could do with catching up with her and getting some advice. Eva stirred in her sleep and shifted her position slightly, snoring softly. Hanna went into the kitchen to make a start on dinner, vowing to call Ceri later once Eva was in bed.

Above the sound of the wind and the rain lashing against the back door came a faint scratching noise. Hanna went over to investigate, cautiously opening the door. There, cowering on the doorstep, was a bedraggled Cosmo, his fur matted and bloody.

"Look at the state of you! Whatever's happened? Have you been in a fight or been trapped somewhere? C'mon, let's get you inside and have a look at you."

Cosmo meowed pitifully but allowed Hanna to pick him up for a closer inspection. Relieved to find nothing more serious than a few superficial cuts, she bathed the wounds with warm water, which met with an occasional whimper from the raggedy feline. When she'd finished, she set down a saucer of cat food which Cosmo devoured in one go before tottering off on unsteady legs into the lounge and settling down in front of the wood burner.

Eva started to stir. Opening her eyes, she shrieked with joy when she saw the cat lying in front of the fire. The noise startled Cosmo, who leapt to his feet and ran off to hide behind the sofa. Eva wobbled after him, calling his name. Cosmo eventually let himself be cajoled out of his hiding place and petted before curling up once again in the same place as before. Hanna watched in amusement as Eva plopped down beside him, carrying on her usual bilingual monologue, the cat doing his best to ignore this.

She went back into the kitchen, turning on the radio for the six o'clock news before starting to peel the potatoes for dinner. She listened to the various news stories: the latest terrorist attack; a Japanese car manufacturer closing factories in Western Europe; the pound dropping against the dollar. As the bulletin was coming to an end, the final breaking news item caught Hanna's attention:

"Earlier today, a number of arrests were made in Sicily connected with recent people-smuggling in the Mediterranean. Four men, believed to include a number of high-ranking officials, were taken into custody in Catania and in the capital Palermo to be questioned about their involvement and protection of the illegal trade. This is the result of a long-standing police operation into the trafficking, and further arrests are said to be imminent.

"The situation in the Mediterranean is reported to be worsening as large numbers of migrants from Africa continue to be picked up by coastguards off the Sicilian coast, many rescued from capsized boats. A large number of bodies continue to be found. The death toll is said to be at an all-time high, thought to have topped the 3,000 mark this year alone."

At last, some break in the investigation. Hanna was anxious to find out who'd been arrested. Strange that Ceri hadn't been in touch. Desperate for news, she picked up the phone, praying that she'd be able to get through. "Hi, Ceri, it's me. I've just heard the news. What's going on, who's been arrested? Why haven't you been in touch?"

"Oh, Hanna, thank God you've called. I've been trying to get through but the lines seem to be down. Luciano's father Michele's been arrested, along with Sergio's father, for some reason. God knows why when he's involved in the investigation. We're frantic with worry. It must be a mistake. We've been trying to find out what's going on…" Ceri's voice faltered.

"What the hell…? But isn't Sergio's father the deputy chief of police? And what have they got on Michele?"

"We just don't know at the moment. Sergio's still working on the story. He's trying to get to the bottom of it, but he'll be taken off it soon if they find out his father's implicated."

"Who else has been arrested?"

"Rino Milazzo, a local mover and shaker in the Democratic Party, and some mayor or other. They're both suspected of being implicated in some way or turning a blind eye. They could even have been protecting the ringleaders if they're not directly involved. We're waiting for more news."

"Any word about how Luciano's taking it?"

"Apparently, he's got one of the best criminal lawyers on the island on standby. Only problem is the guy's made a name for himself defending a couple of high-profile *pentiti* among his more legit clients. But Michele's not likely to turn state's evidence. He's bound to get off if they ever bring a case against him…"

"But what about Sergio's father? Wasn't he responsible for making a number of arrests in connection with the people trafficking investigation?"

"Yes, you're right. It might be that he was starting to get too close to the big bosses and they've set him up to get him out of the way, or to send him a warning to lay off. You know how things can work over here. But Sergio needs to get to grips with it before things get really serious."

"At least Luciano's got something else to occupy his head, rather than the two of us," said Hanna, realising as soon as she'd said it how selfish it sounded.

But Ceri continued to focus on Sergio. "He's like a bear with a sore head. There's no talking to him, he's hell bent on getting his father freed and finding out who's really behind the trafficking, rather than these token gestures. We'll have to see how it pans out. I'll keep you posted. Anyway, how are the two of you?"

"We're fine, some days better than others. It's not that easy getting to grips with being here. Eva's constantly asking when Daddy will be back. She's going to nursery and is really enjoying that. Quite the chatterbox in English now, with even the odd word of Welsh."

"No signs that you might have been traced?"

"Not really." The little boy at nursery from the Sicilian family came to her mind, and a cold shiver ran down Hanna's spine at the thought.

"Just be on your guard," Ceri warned. "You know what they say about '*la piovra*' – its tentacles reach the most obscure places."

"Thanks a bunch, that's all I need to hear," said Hanna, grimacing. "I'm here to get away from all that."

"And you need to make sure that it stays that way," said Ceri. "None of us can have that assurance, no matter where we are."

"We will, don't worry. And let me know if you hear any more about the arrests and Sergio's father. He's bound to be released soon, once they find out he's not involved."

"Let's hope so," said Ceri, sounding far from hopeful. "I'll be in touch as soon as I hear anything. Just be careful and take good care of yourselves."

"Will do. You, too. Speak to you soon. *Ciao.*"

Chapter Twenty-Two

Sicily, Thursday 23rd October, 2014

The sun came flooding through the kitchen window as Hanna folded another load of washing. Its rays played on the autumnal hues of the trees, making her think how much her life had changed in the last six months. A new house, a husband, and the birth of her daughter Eva. It had all happened relatively smoothly and without much effort on her part. At times, it felt surreal, as if this was someone else's life and not hers.

Even little Eva's birth had been straightforward. As if on cue, a gurgle rose from the Moses basket in the corner. Hanna went over to check on her. She was still asleep, her face crinkled into a frown, her tiny fingers curled around a corner of the blanket. Hanna smiled, a feeling of wonder and pride welling up inside her.

Throughout all of this was Luciano, handsome and attentive, always at her side whenever he could be. And her best friend Ceri, the only link to her old life and the one person who knew her better than anyone and who she could confide in.

Hanna had adapted easily enough to the new routine of frequent feeds, endless nappy changing and washing, snatching sleep whenever she could, as well as providing her baby with constant kisses and cuddles. Luciano adored Eva and was proving to be a doting and caring father, taking his turn with the chores and proudly showing off his little daughter to family and friends at every opportunity.

The buzzer sounded on the entry phone and Ceri's face appeared on the screen. Hanna pressed the release button for the gates and went to open the front door. A few minutes later, Ceri drove up the drive and parked her dusty old Fiat with a flourish, the wheels churning up the gravel and sending it spinning in all directions.

"*Eccomi,* I've arrived!" she shouted, getting out of the car, laden with bags.

"Yes, so I see! Still the same reckless driver as ever!"

"Well, I've had to adapt my driving habits to being here. At least I fit in now and can hold my own on the roads!"

"Where is he, by the way? Couldn't he come?" Hanna asked, as she helped Ceri into the house with the bags.

"Work, as usual. He's tied up with this story about all the migrants being picked up in the Med. Seems like it's a highly organised business and there's lots of money being made somewhere. I doubt if much will end up getting published."

Ceri dumped her bags on the terracotta floor in the kitchen. She noticed the Moses basket in the corner and rushed over, squealing with delight. "How's my little munchkin then? My, how she's growing! What are you feeding her on?"

Hanna smiled ruefully; Ceri was well aware that she was breastfeeding which, although going well for Eva, was taking its toll on her.

"You know full well! What's in all the bags?"

"Just a few presents for Eva, plus some goodies from Sergio's auntie's farm up in the hills – salamis, fresh cheeses, *sugo,* chutneys, that sort of thing."

"That's really good of you. You shouldn't spoil us so much!" said Hanna, hugging her friend. "Luciano really loves all that homemade stuff."

"So, how are things going? Not finding it a bit isolated out here? It's not really that far from town, but the roads are so windy and you can easily get lost."

"Actually, I really like the peace and quiet. And Arazia drops by whenever she can with childcare advice. That needs a bit of careful managing – I get the impression she'd like to be a more permanent fixture."

"I'll bet! You'd be better off with Netmums – at least there'd be no strings attached!"

A faint murmur came from the basket.

"Uh, oh – looks as if it's feeding time again. D'you want to be a love and put some coffee on? There's some ricotta cheesecake to go with it in the tin over there," said Hanna, indicating with her head as she gathered Eva in her arms. "She always wakes up hungry. You don't mind if I feed her, do you?"

"'Course not, carry on," said Ceri, already springing into action.

"It could take a while. Let me get her started, then you can tell me all about what Sergio's up to."

Hanna heard Luciano's Alfa Romeo screech to a halt outside, over the sound of the TV news. She glanced at the clock; he wasn't usually home so early. The key sounded in the lock and Luciano burst into the lounge, somewhat breathless.

"*Ciao, amore,*" he embraced Hanna warmly, before turning to Ceri. "*Ciao*, Ceri, *come va*?" He kissed her on both cheeks. "Nice to see you, it's been a while."

"That's 'cos you're always working!" said Ceri, playfully. "Someone has to keep Hanna company in your absence!"

"Well, today I finished early. Just wrapped up the negotiations on a lucrative new deal that'll keep us fed and watered for a good few years, and the rest of the family, too. How's Eva?"

"She's fine, taking a nap in the kitchen. Don't disturb her. Ceri, why don't you stay to dinner?"

"I can't, I'm afraid. It's Sergio's mum's birthday and we're going to that little restaurant in Mondello, the one she likes so much. It's a bit of a drive so I'll have to get going soon."

"I'll make us all an *aperitivo* then, a non-alcoholic one for Ceri seeing as she's driving," announced Luciano, disappearing into the kitchen.

Hanna and Ceri continued to watch the news, the sound of clinking glasses and ice cubes drifting through as Luciano busied himself in the kitchen, preparing the drinks. Graphic images of dead bodies washed up on the shore flashed across the TV screen as the newscaster explained:

"Earlier today dozens of migrants were reported missing after an overloaded fishing boat sank off the coast of Sicily. The Italian Coastguard received an alert that 350 people were in the water. 130 people have been saved so far and the Coastguard is still searching for others. About 30 bodies have been retrieved and the death toll is expected to rise. This is the latest tragedy to occur as a result of the profitable people-smuggling networks that arrange for the transportation of migrants from North Africa to Northern Europe via Sicily."

"There, that's what Sergio's investigating," said Ceri, pointing at the screen. "It's been going on for so long now that it's almost accepted. The cost of human suffering is enormous but it's big business for some, and getting bigger all the time."

"Yes, it's terrible," agreed Hanna. "Something needs to be done to stop it."

Luciano came in from the kitchen with a tray and handed round the drinks. "What's so terrible that needs to be stopped?"

"All the people-smuggling activities in the Med," Ceri replied. "It's Sergio's latest assignment – he's working with the authorities to uncover who's behind it."

"Really? He'll have a job on his hands then. Those involved will be intent on protecting their interests at all costs. He needs to watch out. It could be dangerous."

Ceri's face went pale. Hanna sprang to her defence, irritated by her husband's choice of words. "Luce, you're scaring Ceri. I'm sure Sergio can look after himself. It's not the first time he's been involved in investigating organised crime."

"Sorry, I didn't mean anything by it. I'm just concerned for him and his family, and Ceri too, of course."

"It's okay, I understand," said Ceri, the colour starting to return to her cheeks. "His line of work has always bothered me, but that's what he loves and I'm not going to stop him. You can't choose who you fall for."

Hanna shot Luciano a glance as if to warn him against pursuing the conversation. The news turned to the latest celeb scandal and they started to discuss that instead. But Luciano's earlier reaction continued to gnaw away at her long after her friend had left.

Chapter Twenty-Three

North Wales, Thursday 23rd November, 2017

A sudden crash at the lounge window made Hanna jump. But it was only the wind whipping up the bare branches of the trees and lashing them against the panes. Looking through the window, she could barely make out the blurry shapes of the bushes in the murky light. The sky was dark and brooding. It had never really got light all day, and seemed more like dusk rather than early afternoon. Hanna shivered and turned away, glad to be inside.

The constant barrage of wind and rain during the recent storms had turned the gentle Welsh hills into an almost hostile environment. Hanna was grateful for the welcome and much-needed sanctuary provided by the sturdy stone cottage, but its isolation was having an effect on her. Being confined indoors for so long was giving her cabin fever. But Hanna still managed to find solace within its walls, far away from the threats of the outside world, safe within its womb.

She glanced over at Eva on the rug in front of the roaring wood-burner. At least Cosmo was keeping her amused, the two of them best of friends despite the constant kiddie-babble that the poor old moggy had to put up with. Cosmo had settled in front of the fire ready for his afternoon nap, which Eva's bilingual monologue threatened to disrupt, when the phone rang. Picking it up, Hanna was relieved to hear Rhys's soft Welsh lilt.

"Hi, it's only me, *cariad*. Just thought I'd let you know that the road up to your place is blocked down in the valley.

A tree's come down in the storm and there's all manner of debris from the river that's burst its banks, as well as some local flooding. They're trying to clear it now, but I was worried about the two of you."

"We're fine, but we've not been out for days. I heard on the radio that the weather was causing problems, but I didn't know about the road up here being blocked. I've tried calling Nerys but the line's dead."

"Some of the phone lines are down. Just as well we manage to get a mobile signal most of the time. I was thinking of calling in later if you could use some company. The track over the hills should be passable in the Land Rover. Are you okay for food or do you want me to bring some over?"

Hanna's heart leapt at the prospect. "That'd be great! We'd both love to see you. I'm starting to go a bit stir-crazy from the remoteness up here. And we're running pretty low on food and logs for the fire. We could do with some bread, milk, and fresh veg, at the very least – some meat, too, or sausages if you can get them."

"OK, no problem. The Snowdonia Mountain Rescue's new home delivery service is on its way! I was rather hoping you might treat me to some of your wonderful cooking. Better than all the ready meals on my tod that I've had to put up with for the past week. I've been flat out at work and much too tired to be bothered cooking."

Hanna laughed. "I'm sure I can rustle something up. Better bring some wine as well."

"Will do. Should be with you about six-ish, all being well. Any problems, I'll let you know."

"Fine, see you then." Hanna put the phone down, feeling elated at the thought of company.

Eva looked up expectantly. "Was that *Babbo*? Is he coming home?" Her words brought Hanna back to reality with a start.

"No, sweetheart, it was Rhys, not Daddy. He's coming over later for dinner."

"Is he bringing Bryn?"

"Of course! He goes everywhere with Bryn."

A broad grin spread across Eva's face. "Oh, goody! Not seen Bryn for a-a-a-ages," she said, making Hanna smile.

"Well, you can help me to get ready and tidy up before they come." Hanna glanced around at the various toys scattered across the lounge floor.

"*Va bene, Mammina!* I'll help you!" Eva started to collect her things, piling them high in her arms. Cosmo lazily opened one eye before shutting it again quickly, no doubt glad to be left alone for once.

It took a while to put everything away as Eva dropped more than she collected, but finally it was done.

While Eva settled down on the sofa to watch her favourite cartoon on CBeebies, Hanna went to take a quick shower. The warmth of the water revived her spirits, but she couldn't afford to linger and leave Eva on her own. She dressed quickly in a pair of warm leggings and a deep pink and purple fleece tunic, adding a couple of layers of mascara, a touch of blusher, and lipstick, followed by a spritz of perfume to finish off. *Not bad for someone holed up in the Welsh hills*, she thought, checking her appearance in the mirror.

Back in the lounge, Eva was bouncing up and down on the sofa in time to the cartoon's signature tune, trying to imitate the words. The effect was so comical that it brought another smile to Hanna's face. At that moment, her mobile pinged an alert. She read the new message:

I just wanted to let you know that Luciano's and Sergio's fathers have both been released due to insufficient evidence. Hope you're both OK. Speak soon, Ceri xx

Hanna sighed, unsure whether this was good or bad news. *At least she and Eva were far away from that world and were safe,* she thought for the umpteenth time.

Hanna tiptoed out of Eva's room, softly pulling the door to behind her. She flopped onto the sofa next to Rhys.

"I thought she'd never nod off – too much excitement in

one day! After days of being cooped up with just me, having both you and Bryn here must have felt like a real treat. Well, I'm bushed even if she wasn't."

Rhys grinned. "It must be our Welsh charm, *cariad,* works every time! But I don't want to keep you from your beauty sleep. Besides, I'm up early in the morning. Maybe we can polish off the wine, then I'll make tracks." Without waiting for a reply, he padded out to the kitchen in his stockinged feet and came back with the bottle of South African Shiraz he'd brought earlier.

"It's pretty good, I must say. Not a bad choice of wine for a Welshman!" Hanna teased as he refilled her glass.

"You'd be surprised, some of us are almost cultured!" he said in an exaggerated Welsh accent. "There might be more sheep than people in Wales, but we make up in quality what we lack in quantity. Actually, we're quite proud of our history and heritage. You'll have to let me show you what we can offer. The National Eisteddfod is up in North Wales this summer and it's a great way to find out more about Welsh music and literature, as well as our mythical past. Would you fancy going? I'm sure you'd enjoy it, and there's always loads of fun stuff for kids, so it'd be good for Eva. What d'you think?"

"Sounds great, as long as we're still here by then," Hanna remarked ruefully, twisting her wine glass in her hands.

"Oh, I thought you were planning to be here for a while," said Rhys, a note of disappointment creeping into his voice.

"Well, it depends on how things work out."

"You know, you've never told me the whole story behind you being here. Ceri didn't tell me much more either. She just said you were in a precarious situation and were worried about Eva and needed to get away urgently to somewhere safe."

"It's complicated. I don't want to burden you with my problems…"

"I guess I'm sort of involved already. It's your call, though. I don't mean to pry," Rhys said in an apologetic tone.

Hanna took a gulp of her wine, feeling its warming effect

111

start to spread through her body. She relaxed, conscious of Rhys's presence close by, feeling a fleeting sense of security and wellbeing. Could she confide in him? What harm would there be? Maybe he *should* know – it was only fair, as he'd given her so much help when she needed it most. But how much should she reveal?

She tried to concentrate and think clearly, but this was hampered by her head, muzzy from the wine. *He has a right to know what brought us here*, she thought. *Maybe not the whole story, but the key parts at least.*

"Ok, you win. This is what happened…"

Chapter Twenty-Four

Sicily, Friday 31ˢᵗ October, 2014

"Are you sure you'll be okay looking after Eva?" Hanna asked for the umpteenth time, her face drawn into a frown. "And you know where everything is?" She'd been reluctant to enlist Arazia's help but it was really her only option. Ceri would have stepped in had she not already made plans to go away with Sergio that weekend

Her mother-in-law smiled, as if indulging a petulant child. "I've had two of my own, remember? I'm not exactly a novice."

"I know but it's the first time I've really left her for any length of time."

"Stop fretting, *cara.* We'll be just fine, won't we, *piccolina?*" Arazia glanced fondly at the granddaughter she was cradling in her arms. Eva gurgled in response and kicked her chubby legs in the air.

Hanna kissed the few dark hairs on the top of her daughter's head.

"Well, as long as you're sure. You *will* call if there's any problem, won't you?" she asked one last time, picking up her weekend bag and handbag, both made of soft fuschia-coloured leather.

Luciano came in the room and took them off her, impatient to get off. "We really need to get a move on, *amore*, otherwise we'll hit the traffic."

Arazia laughed softly, shooing them away with one hand as she accompanied them out to the car. "Go and have fun!

And let's hope you don't come back empty-handed!"

Luciano grinned. "I have every confidence that we won't! In fact, I'd put money on it if I were a betting man." He kissed his mother on both cheeks and steered Hanna to the car before she could raise any more concerns. "Don't worry, *Mamma* will be in her element looking after Eva, you'll see," he whispered in her ear.

Maybe, thought Hanna, *but I don't want to make a habit of it. She probably means well enough but would jump at the chance of being around more often.* Hanna smiled as she got into the car and waved to Arazia as Luciano started up the engine and drove slowly down the drive. Once the house had disappeared from view, she started to relax a little and contemplate the weekend ahead.

They were going to the island's annual wine awards ceremony at Catania's most opulent hotel. It promised to be a prestigious affair, with judges coming from across the globe along with the world's media. The family's wines were growing in reputation and starting to get a name for themselves outside Italy. So much so that they'd entered five of their best wines for this year's awards. Three had made the shortlist, much to the family's delight. As Michele was away on business the night of the award ceremony, it fell to Luciano to attend.

He had insisted that she buy a special outfit for the occasion. She had chosen a striking Alberta Ferretti full-length cocktail dress in black, an asymmetrical one-shouldered design with a slash across the figure-hugging bodice that revealed her cleavage and a triangular see-through panel at the waist. Luciano loved it so much that not even the price tag had put him off. Hanna was secretly looking forward to the event despite having to leave Eva behind. She couldn't remember the last time she'd had an opportunity to get dressed up

"Penny for them?" Luciano's words interrupted her thoughts.

"What? Oh, sorry, I was miles away. Where is it we're staying?" she asked.

"Capocastagne, just outside Catania. It's the perfect weekend hideaway – a little villa in the most exquisite location, perched on a headland overlooking the sea, with Mount Etna in the background. So-o-o romantic, you'll love it." He smiled and stroked her thigh affectionately.

His touch and the thought of a weekend alone together, apart from the awards ceremony, sent a tingle up her spine. She smiled. "Sounds amazing, can't wait!"

"Once we get to the *autostrada*, it'll take us a couple of hours, so sit back and enjoy the ride. I've booked a table for dinner at a nearby restaurant that serves some of the best seafood on the east coast. All that, and in the company of one of the island's most successful and handsome entrepreneurs! What more could a girl ask for?"

Hanna laughed at his tongue-in-cheek arrogance. He had a point, though; she couldn't quite believe her luck and the new life she'd almost fallen into as if by chance. With the sultry strains of a Sicilian blues singer playing softly in the background, Hanna watched the passing landscape change from lush cultivated valleys dotted with cattle and horses to one of rocky outcrops devoid of trees and populated only by the occasional flock of sheep. Luciano drove with one hand resting lightly on the steering wheel, the other gently caressing her hand.

When Hanna opened her eyes, it was dusk. She caught glimpses of citrus groves through the acacia and eucalyptus trees lining the road that was becoming ever narrower and rougher as Luciano drove on.

"Well timed, sleepyhead! We're nearly there, just a few minutes away now."

"Sorry, I must have dropped off."

The thick vegetation around them gave no suggestion of the coastline beyond. They could have been anywhere. But the road suddenly came to an end and they drew to a halt in front of intricate wrought iron gates flanked by high security fencing. Luciano rummaged through the glove box and pulled out a set of keys. He jumped out of the car to tackle the heavy padlock securing the gates.

They drove on, and when the villa came into view, Hanna had a sharp intake of breath. It was much larger than she'd been expecting. Built of local stone, it spread over a small headland, its lofty position commanding impressive views over the coast in both directions.

"Wow, this is fabulous! Who did you say it belongs to?"

"Domenico, an old friend of mine. He's quite prominent in the film industry and uses it for entertaining. It's quite something, isn't it? Come on, I'll show you round," he said, getting out of the car.

Hanna followed Luciano as he flicked a switch, bathing the outside in a soft glow of light. Among lush gardens filled with exotic plants and palm trees sat a kidney-shaped swimming pool, its waters shimmering. Overlooking the sea was an expansive dining area, served by a bar and a spacious food preparation area cleverly concealed from diners behind bamboo screening.

The interior was equally stunning. The lounge was split-level, no doubt designed for separate business discussions to take place simultaneously, with cream leather sofas and an array of striking abstract prints on the walls. Modern and minimalist. Each of the four generous bedrooms had been decorated in a different colour palette. The one Hanna chose was grey, white, and pistachio, with an oversized bed and yet more striking abstracts on the walls.

"Well, it's not exactly the cosy little romantic hideaway I'd imagined! It's well impressive!"

Luciano's face fell. "What, you don't like it?"

"Don't be silly, it's wonderful! But, more importantly, what time's dinner booked for? I'm ravenous!"

Luciano laughed. "That's more like it! There's just time for a quick shower and a change of clothes. We need to leave in about 45 minutes."

Hanna pecked him on the cheek. "Fine, I'll call Arazia first to check everything's okay with Eva."

Strolling along the beach hand in hand with Luciano on their way back to the car, Hanna almost glowed with happiness. It could have had something to do with the amount of wine she'd drunk over dinner – a sumptuous affair of local *antipasti*, *pasta alle vongole (*pasta with clams), and a huge platter of freshly-caught fish and seafood. The two of them had chattered incessantly throughout, glad of the opportunity to catch up. Quality time together had been in short supply since Eva came along.

Now they walked in companionable silence, relaxed and sated by the food and wine, the sea lapping the shore. There was a gentle breeze and just enough moonlight to cut through the darkness. Hanna could make out something lying on the beach a few metres away by the water's edge.

"That's weird. Do you remember passing that on the way to the restaurant?" she asked, pointing at the shape.

"No, but I probably wouldn't have noticed it. I'm not as observant as you," Luciano replied. "It's probably an animal that fell into the sea, or even a dolphin or porpoise that's washed ashore. It happens from time to time."

It struck Hanna as strange they'd not spotted it before, given its size. Wondering what it could be, she approached for a closer look. A strangled cry escaped from her throat as she realised to her horror what it was.

Not animal but human: the body of a dead child.

Chapter Twenty-Five

North Wales, Thursday 23rd – Friday 24th November, 2017

Hanna was coming to the final part of her tale. Rhys had listened without interruption. The only other sounds were the occasional crackling and spitting of the wood on the fire and the odd snore from Bryn stretched out on the rug. She'd managed to keep her voice steady and unemotional up to now, as if recounting a situation that had happened to someone else. It felt almost like a confession, although she was not the perpetrator but the victim. But now she was approaching the end, her emotions resurfaced and her voice started to quiver.

"Over time, I got the impression that something else was going on. I overheard strange whispered conversations between Luciano and his father and brother that made no sense, and furtive meetings and phone calls were still taking place at all hours. Then one day Luciano left his laptop on at home and I sneaked a look at his files. I was shocked; they made reference to goods being 'imported' and exorbitant amounts of money changing hands. Nothing explicit, but the dealings clearly had nothing to do with the wine business."

"Did you ever discuss it with Luciano? There might have been a reasonable explanation."

"I was too scared. There was so much in the media by that time about the refugee situation and the ruthlessness of the people behind the trafficking. So, I copied all the files with the intention of going through them to find out the truth.

Before I got the chance, I came home one day to find an envelope on the doormat with three silver bullets inside – one, I imagine, intended for each of us. There was no clue as to who'd sent it and where the threat was coming from. It was the final straw: I just freaked out and knew I had to get Eva out of there straight away to keep her safe. Nothing else mattered."

Rhys flinched and shook his head in disbelief. "My God, I'd no idea that things were this bad."

"Ceri was the only person I felt I could trust, and she was the one who helped me escape. The rest you know."

"So, what will you do now?" he asked softly

Hanna shrugged and sighed deeply, feeling relieved to have confided in Rhys, almost as if she'd shaken off an invisible burden. He seemed stunned by what he'd heard, the shock clearly etched on his face.

"It's impossible to know what to do for the best. I feel a moral responsibility to report the whole business to the authorities, but that would only jeopardise our safety. But even if I do nothing, there's still a real danger that we'll be tracked down anyway sooner or later, wherever we are. I blame myself for being so naïve and not seeing the signs, but I could never have imagined a situation like this." A single tear trickled down her cheek, and she brushed it away quickly.

Rhys moved closer and slipped a comforting arm across her shoulders. "I really don't know what to say or how to advise you. Something like this is completely out of my league."

Hanna wondered fleetingly whether she'd done the right thing in telling Rhys what had happened. *A bit late for second thoughts*, she reflected.

"I shouldn't have told you. It'll be a burden to you as well now."

"No, you did the right thing. It's better for me to know what I've let myself in for."

Hanna looked at him quizzically.

"Sorry, just trying to lighten the situation a bit in my own clumsy way," said Rhys with a wry smile. Maybe we should sleep on it and talk some more in the morning."

"Maybe."

"It's late and I really should be going, but I don't want to leave you both on your own. Maybe I could stay on the sofa bed tonight?"

Hanna felt relieved at his suggestion. "I'd really appreciate that. Telling you has brought it all back and made it more vivid, if that's possible. I'd feel better knowing that there's someone else around tonight, if you don't mind."

"Long as I get a decent breakfast before I get off to work in the morning, I'm all yours!"

"No problem, that'd be a small price to pay," said Hanna, with a faint smile. "Let me find you a spare duvet. I'm sure I've seen one somewhere."

"Allow me. I know exactly where it is," said Rhys, going straight to the cupboard under the stairs. "By the way, there's a friend of the family, a lawyer, who's had some experience of human rights cases. He might be able to help."

"Okay, let me think about it. Thanks for listening and for all your support. I guess I need it right now," said Hanna. She kissed him lightly on the cheek. "Sleep well, see you in the morning."

"You, too," Rhys said.

She could feel his eyes follow her as she turned and disappeared into the bedroom, with almost a pang of regret.

Hanna woke to a clattering of crockery coming from the kitchen. She realised with a start that it was late and she must have overslept. She heard Eva giggle at something Rhys had said, although she couldn't make out the words. Her head was thumping; sleep had eluded her long into the night, her mind churning after sharing the events of the past few months with Rhys. When sleep eventually came, it had been deep and dreamless but still left her feeling drained.

It was Friday, the day she'd agreed to go into the office and take Eva to nursery, if the stormy conditions had abated. She peered through the curtains; the sky was murky and a thin drizzle was falling. No excuse for not going in, and it would do Eva the world of good to be with other kids again after being cooped up in the cottage for so long.

Wrapping herself in a warm dressing gown, Hanna went into the kitchen to find Eva sitting cross-legged on the floor, still in her pyjamas, playing with Cosmo. "Morning, munchkin," she said, ruffling Eva's hair. Rhys grinned and thrust a mug of steaming coffee into her hands.

"Thanks. Sorry I overslept. Took me ages to get off, then when I did…"

"Don't worry, I've only just got up myself. It was Eva who woke me, chatting to the cat in Italian."

"I thought you had to be at work early?"

"I did, but I've called in to let them know I'll be late. I've got some errands to run on the way in, anyway.

Hanna took a sip of her coffee. "Come on, Eva, it's nursery today. Let's get you washed and dressed."

"Think about what I said about the lawyer last night. It might be useful to get some professional advice. Put you in a better position."

"I will, and thanks again for all your help. I've been trying to push things to the back of my mind, but I need to make a decision sooner or later. There's no easy solution. I just feel so torn."

"Well, I need to be off," said Rhys, giving Hanna a peck on the cheek and swinging Eva in the air, much to her delight. Grabbing a piece of buttered toast in one hand and his car keys in the other, he made for the door. "I'll give you a ring later. Have a good day, both of you, and mind how you go."

Alerted by the jingle of the car keys, Bryn rose sleepily from his place in front of the dying embers of the fire and followed Rhys out to the car. Hanna waved them off from the window before starting to get ready for work.

The roads were quiet, which was just as well as they were still treacherous, slick with rain and scattered with debris brought down by the recent storms. Visibility was poor in the sparse daylight. Hanna drove slowly as she did her best to negotiate her way through, trying to concentrate through the torrent of kiddie-chatter from the back seat. She felt like a novice driver, after several days of not being behind the wheel.

Not long after they'd left the cottage, she noticed a pair of piercing headlights some way behind them, high off the ground as if coming from an off-road vehicle of some sort. They were distinctive, more like fog-lights. As she steered the Peugeot down the last stretch towards the main coastal road, the headlights disappeared for a while, but Hanna could have sworn that they were back a few minutes later. As the traffic got busier, it became difficult to differentiate between one vehicle and the next. *My God*, she thought, *I'm being paranoid. Maybe I should speak to the lawyer as Rhys suggested. Better than trying to deal with it on my own.*

It was getting lighter, the clouds thinning to reveal a pallid sunlight. A silly song from CBeebies came on the radio and Hanna started to sing along with Eva. Eva didn't know all the words and used whatever came to mind, a curious mix of English, Italian, with the odd word of Welsh. The result sent both of them into a fit of giggles. Hanna started to relax.

It was only when she pulled up at the main traffic lights in Llangefni that Hanna thought she recognised the headlights of the 4x4 several cars back. *Don't be ridiculous*, she admonished herself, *it can't be the same one.*

But somehow she couldn't shake off the feeling, and when she drew up to drop Eva off at nursery, she got a fleeting glimpse of two dark-haired men as the high-sided vehicle passed by. One looked vaguely familiar, but it could just have been her imagination in overdrive. She spent the rest of the day on tenterhooks, worrying about Eva, even phoning the nursery three times to check everything was okay.

When Hanna finally arrived to pick Eva up, she found her sitting on the floor daubed in paint, giggling and chattering away in Italian with a dark-skinned, curly-headed little boy who she assumed was Ottavio.

"C'mon, Eva, time to go home now," she said, grabbing

the toddler by the hand.

Eva's face fell. "But I was playing with Ottavio…"

"Not any more, you're not," said Hanna, whisking her away and popping her head round Dilys's office to let her know they were going. In the hall on the way out, a dark man with an aquiline nose hurriedly brushed past her. At first, she thought it was Luciano and her heart leapt into her throat, her body trembling. But when she looked again, she realised that this man was shorter and stockier. He made straight for Eva's playmate, calling him by name. *Ottavio's father*, Hanna thought, hurrying Eva out of the nursery and back towards the car.

As soon as she got home, she called Rhys to tell him what had happened earlier. He sounded concerned, which made her all the more worried as if it hadn't just been her imagination.

"Listen, I hope you don't mind but I've spoken to Dafydd Williams, the lawyer friend, and he's happy to come over in the next day or so and give you some advice if you want. It'll give you a better idea of where you stand and what the options are. What do you reckon?"

Hanna was unsure, but she had to face up to the situation and make a decision one way or another. Nevertheless, she was loath to share the information with a total stranger, even one who'd be able to give her professional advice.

"Okay," she said reluctantly. "It makes sense. Go ahead and arrange it."

"Until then, stay at the cottage and keep off the roads. Anything suspicious, call me right away."

Hanna felt an icy chill creep through her body at the thought that the cottage might no longer be the safe haven she'd hoped for.

Chapter Twenty-Six

Sicily, Friday 31st October – Saturday 1st November, 2014

An exasperated voice trickled through the loudspeaker of the mobile phone: "*Eh, signore, pazienza!* Just stay where you are, we'll be with you shortly. It's a busy night, I'm afraid."

Luciano continued to pace up and down the beach; it was the fourth time he'd called the *carabinieri*, each time getting a similar response, as if he'd called about something trivial. It was approaching 1am now, almost two hours since they'd made their gruesome discovery. And they were expected to stay there until the police put in an appearance.

They'd moved a little distance away so they couldn't readily see the shape of the body in the moonlight, but it was no less distressing for Hanna. She couldn't stop shivering, partly from the night air which had turned chilly under a clear sky, but mostly from shock. Luciano slipped off his jacket and wrapped it round her shoulders.

"Sorry, *amore*. We're just going to have to hang on here. You heard what the police said on the phone. It shouldn't be much longer now."

"You'd think they'd take the death of a child seriously and make it a priority," she muttered.

"I guess for them it's just one more body out of all the migrants who are found dead on our shores and out to sea." Luciano shrugged dismissively.

"How do you know it's a migrant?"

"Well, it's more than likely, given the current situation."

Hanna felt her chest tighten and the bile begin to rise in her throat. She'd seen the constant stream of news reports about people fleeing from the shores of North Africa in makeshift boats to escape war and atrocities in their own countries. She couldn't begin to imagine how the refugees might feel. Many of them never even managed to reach Sicily, dying or drowning en route. But experiencing it first-hand and in such shocking circumstances was horrifying. Did human life really have so little value? The gulf between these refugees desperate to escape their homelands and the comfortable lives of the islanders seemed enormous. She felt guilty that she hadn't made more of an effort to help out in some way.

"I guess we should all be doing our bit to help them. After all, it's not their fault. Any family would resort to desperate measures faced with a similar situation, anything to get away to safety."

Luciano pulled a face, seemingly unmoved. "That might be the case for the minority, but if you watch the news reports, you'll see that most of them are young single men who've heard they can make a better life for themselves in Europe without too much effort. They want to come here for economic reasons, not political ones. Many of them are criminals, and probably more than a handful are terrorists who come here to commit atrocities in Europe."

"That seems a bit harsh. You don't know that for sure." Hanna was horrified; she couldn't remember Luciano ever expressing such sentiments before. "What about the men who've been persecuted and tortured in their native countries, and the women and children caught up in conflict?"

"And just how do you differentiate between those in need and those with an excuse? Either way, they're coming to Europe to sponge off our people. It needs tackling, if you ask me. Charity begins at home."

Luciano's apparent lack of concern left Hanna dumbfounded. It wasn't an issue that they'd discussed in the past. In fact, they rarely disagreed on anything. Before she could respond, the distant wail of a police siren floated towards them on the night air, quickly intensifying in volume as the police car drew nearer.

"About time, too," said Luciano. "A few questions and we should be out of here."

Hanna couldn't bring herself to say anything; she was too taken aback by his reaction to the plight of the refugees.

The siren built to a deafening crescendo as a police car screeched to a halt on the gravel road that ran parallel to the beach. Two uniformed *carabinieri* got out and made their way towards them, moving slowly across the sand.

"*Buona sera, signori.* Sorry for the delay. I take it that you are the people who've found the body of a child on this beach? Can you show us where it is?" It was the older officer who spoke while the younger stayed several steps behind him, a bored expression on his face.

"Yes, I'll take you there," said Luciano. "Hanna, do you want to stay here with the officer?" She nodded. The young policeman forced a smile and Luciano led the older officer over to the body. Hanna could hear them talking but couldn't make out the words. It wasn't long before they were back.

"You'll both need to come down to the station, I'm afraid, and answer some questions so we can file a report. We'll try not to keep you too long," the older officer said, ushering them to the waiting police car.

The next few hours passed in a blur, most of it spent waiting for someone to take their statement. At that hour, the police station was quiet; a sole officer manned the front desk, and the duo who'd brought them in had been called out again straight away. Eventually, the desk sergeant called for assistance but only after a heated exchange with Luciano in dialect that Hanna could barely decipher. A stern uniformed official appeared within minutes and steered them into a back office.

Hanna shuffled uncomfortably in her seat as the police officer confronted them with a string of questions. He recorded their words on a computer, typing laboriously with two fingers and showing little interest in the answers. For him, it seemed to be just a routine matter, but for Hanna it was a major tragedy. She was shocked at the way the people around her were dealing with this. After all, it was a dead child they'd discovered on the beach, not some washed-up animal which would have been bad enough. She began to wonder if she was overreacting, judging by the behaviour of others. Luciano continued to be dismissive and seemed more interested in not missing the award ceremony later that day.

By the time they'd completed the formalities and got a taxi back to the villa, it was starting to get light. Through the picture windows, Hanna was taken aback by the spectacular views of sunrise over the bay, in stark contrast to the horrors of the night before. Luciano made straight for the drinks cabinet and poured out a generous measure of brandy.

"Here, drink this," he said, handing the glass to Hanna. "It'll help calm your nerves. Then I think we should try and get some sleep if we're going to be in any fit state for tonight."

"Thanks, I certainly need something. It's been a hell of a night." Hanna flopped onto the sofa and took a gulp of the amber liquid, appreciating its warming effect. She felt exhausted and in no mood for the awards ceremony but didn't want to let Luciano down. The awards were important, not just for him but for the family business.

"D'you think the police will be back in touch to let us know if there's any news?"

"I doubt it," said Luciano, taking a seat next to her. "They'll only contact us if they need any more details. They won't update us on any investigation. Not that there'll be much of one."

"Why not? Surely a dead child is a matter of concern?" Hanna could feel her cheeks flushing with anger.

"One more dead child is just collateral damage in their eyes, given the situation as a whole. The police won't waste much time in investigating one death when they've got so many on their hands."

Hanna's cheeks were smouldering now. "So, we might

have just as well not have bothered reporting it?"

Luciano shrugged. "Well, somebody had to, I guess. Anyway, let's try and get some shut-eye before tonight. Don't know about you, but I'm whacked."

"Me, too. Though I think I'm too wound up to sleep. Maybe the brandy will help."

She finished off her drink before following Luciano into the bedroom where she undressed and slipped between the sheets. Her mind was in turmoil. She couldn't believe that people could passively accept this horrific situation without wanting to do something about it. Thoughts continued to churn through her head.

Luciano had already fallen asleep, breathing in slow and rhythmic waves as if untroubled by the night's events. *Maybe I don't know him as well as I think,* she mused, turning over. Nagging doubts gnawed away inside her head, keeping sleep at bay.

Chapter Twenty-Seven

North Wales, Sunday 26th November, 2017

"Oh, Rhys, thank God I've reached you at last! Eva's disappeared! She was playing in the garden one minute, the next she'd gone. I've been all over looking for her but there's no sign of her anywhere. It's as if she's been swallowed up. And the weather's getting worse…"

Sobs smothered Hanna's words. Her hand clenched around the mobile phone, the skin drawn tight and white across the knuckles. She wanted to scream, beat her fists against the wall. She'd been in the kitchen and had only taken her eyes off her daughter for a few minutes, just as she'd done so many times before. *How could I have been so careless?* she thought. Something must have happened. Eva couldn't have got far on her own; she'd have found her by now.

Someone must have taken her. There was no other explanation. But how could that be when she'd heard nothing, not a sound, and certainly hadn't seen anyone lurking in the vicinity. A cold knot of fear snaked through her body.

Rhys's calm voice broke in. "Hanna, try not to panic. Anything could have happened. We'll find her, don't worry. She might have fallen and hurt herself. I'm on my way, stay where you are until I get to you."

An image of Eva lying in a ditch, battered and bruised, flashed in front of Hanna. She shuddered. "Hurry, Rhys. Something bad's happened, I just know it. I'll never forgive myself if it has. I should have kept my eye on her. It's all my fault…" Her voice was rising to a crescendo again. She was on the verge of hysteria now, sobbing and trying to speak at the same time, the words coming out in a jumble.

"Try and calm down. Everything will be fine. She won't be far away and there'll be a perfectly good explanation, you'll see." Rhys's soothing tone had little effect.

"I just hope you're right…"

"Sit tight, I'll be with you in no time at all. I'm only at the bottom of the valley. Maybe she wandered off and got lost. Stay in the cottage. You need to be there if she does make her way back. Try not to worry. We'll get her back safely, you'll see."

His attempts to reassure her rang hollow. She felt a vast aching void in the pit of her stomach. There was more to this, she felt sure. She ended the call and slipped the phone into the pocket of her waterproof. Tearing herself away from the window where she'd been keeping a lookout for any sign of Eva, she hurried outside again. The wind had increased, whipping through the trees as if in a hurry to get to its destination. Hailstones started to fall, striking and stinging her face with their force.

Stifling her sobs, she began to call out, "Eva, Eva – where are you? Can you hear me? Eva, come on home now. *Vieni qui.* Eva, Eva, Eva-aa…" She paced up and down, calling her daughter's name repeatedly. Each time the wind whipped the sound away, reducing it to a pathetic whisper.

It was only early afternoon but already the light was fading, dark storm clouds scudding menacingly across the sky. With the temperature dropping, more snow could be on the way. What hope could there be of finding Eva in these conditions? She trembled at the thought of what could have happened.

Going around to the back of the cottage, she called again, louder this time, still competing with the wind. Still no answer. She scanned the surrounding countryside with a pair of old binoculars she'd grabbed earlier from a kitchen drawer. It was increasingly difficult to focus in the bad light and she struggled to see through blurry eyes. There was no option; she'd just have to stay put and wait for Rhys.

"Still no sign?" Rhys shouted through the open window of the Land Rover as he brought it to an abrupt halt in front of the cottage. Bryn squeezed his muzzle through the gap and started to bark as if sensing something was wrong.

"No, nothing, not a peep, and the light's starting to go. We'll never find her…"

"Don't talk daft, Hanna. Jump in and we'll find her before long, you'll see."

Hanna wasted no time clambering up into the passenger seat. Rhys switched on the vehicle's powerful main beam and accelerated away from the cottage, heading for the track leading up to Nerys and Lars' place. Trees swaying in the breeze cast ominous shadows on either side.

"Keep a lookout for her as we drive," he shouted over the roar of the engine. "Could she have gone as far as Nerys's?"

"On her own? I very much doubt it." Hanna grabbed the side handle of the Land Rover as it lurched and bounced over the rough track. "I tried calling them before but there was no answer. If she'd shown up there on her own, they'd have called straight away. But it's quite a long way from the cottage. She's unlikely to be there."

"But she might have been on her way up there when something happened, or else she's wandered off en route," said Rhys. "It's worth a try, anyway, don't you think?"

Hanna sighed, unconvinced but at a loss to suggest anything better. They continued on their way in silence for a few minutes when Hanna suddenly spotted a dark shape at the side of the track. "Stop the car! What's that over there?"

"Stay here, I'll go and take a look." Rhys pulled up and disappeared from view, returning with a shake of his head. "It's not her. Just a dead badger." Hanna felt both relieved and dismayed.

They started off again. Their neighbours' cottage loomed up ahead, dark and foreboding, not a light to be seen. Clearly, there was no one home.

Rhys must have sensed Hanna's thoughts. "I'll just check

quickly that she's not in any of the outbuildings before we go," he said, hastily rummaging through the glovebox for a torch. "Won't be long."

He left Bryn whining in the back as he slid out of the driver's seat and shone the torch across the flagged yard, creating arcs of light as it flickered from place to place. The only sound was from the wind whistling through the trees. No sign of life. He returned, grim-faced. "She's not here. Let's head down the track and check around the cottage again before we go any further. We need to make sure she's missing before we report it to the police."

So, Rhys is starting to believe she's missing, too, thought Hanna with a heavy heart, as he steered his way across the tracks behind the cottage. They stopped at regular intervals to call her name, straining to hear any response. But there was nothing. Driving down the valley, they repeated the process. Still nothing.

They continued to scour the countryside for an hour or so, their efforts hampered by the darkness and occasional flurries of snow, but there was still no sign of Eva. Their feelings of frustration and anxiety were now running at a peak.

"This is hopeless. We're just not getting anywhere on our own. We'll have to call in the police and the mountain rescue team," said Rhys with an exasperated sigh, as he climbed in the Land Rover again and turned the key in the ignition. "They're more used to getting results with this sort of thing."

"We can't, Rhys, not in the circumstances…" Hanna started to say but her words were interrupted by the sound of a text alert from her mobile phone. She pulled it out of her pocket and stared at the screen, her blood turning cold as she read the message, written in Italian:

EVA STA CON NOI – We have Eva. You have information that we need. Wait for further instructions. Don't alert the authorities if you want to see her again.

Chapter Twenty-Eight

North Wales, Sunday 26th November, 2017

Hanna's heart continued to hammer as Rhys drove back to the cottage through the darkness. The message confirmed her worst fears. Her head throbbed, threatening any attempt to think clearly, the knot of fear in her stomach swelling by the minute. But one thought prevailed: she had to get Eva back, whatever it took

"It's all my fault," she wailed, pounding her thighs with her fists. "Why didn't I confront things sooner? I was kidding myself. It all seemed so safe here, far away from everything that happened in Sicily. I've been an idiot."

"You shouldn't blame yourself, Hanna. You were only doing what you thought was right for the two of you." Rhys paused before adding, "I don't know what you're thinking of but whatever it is, you can't do it on your own, Hanna. It's far too dangerous and you can't risk Eva getting hurt. You have to report it, despite what the message says." He glanced at her, his concern almost palpable.

"You don't understand. I don't have any choice," Hanna responded in a despondent but exasperated tone. "We're not dealing with some petty low-life criminals here. This is big business, with millions of euros at stake. They must have found out somehow that I've got evidence on a memory stick. Without proof, it would just be my word against theirs. Ruthless bastards, they'll obviously stop at nothing to get the information back."

"But if you start negotiating with them, whoever they are,

you're putting yourself in danger, too. Can't you see that? There's no guarantee that the two of you will come out of this safely even if you turn over the information they want. Remember the silver bullets?"

She did, vividly; her main reason for escaping in the first place. But who was behind Eva's disappearance? Luciano had the most to lose from the incriminating information she held. But was he so callous as to snatch his own daughter away from under her mother's nose? And how had he tracked them down? If it wasn't him, who else could it be? His family, his associates? So many unanswered questions plagued her mind.

She was vaguely aware of the noise of the engine, the bumpy track back to the cottage, and Rhys's voice, pleading and cajoling her to see sense and call in the authorities. That was out of the question. What if she never saw Eva again? It was too painful to contemplate. She wouldn't be able to live with herself if anything happened to Eva. She felt sick at the thought. All that mattered now was getting her daughter back. She didn't care about bringing the people trafficking operation down. Even with her evidence, that might never happen anyway. Too many people, often in high places, were embroiled for that to occur.

Rhys eventually pulled up outside the cottage, a dark silhouette barely visible under the overcast night sky. Hanna shivered as she went inside and turned on the lamps; it was nearly as cold inside as it was outside.

He busied himself making up the fire, hampered by Bryn's efforts to turn it into a game. Hanna sank onto the sofa, still deep in thought but at a loss to know what to do next. The place seemed eerily quiet without Eva. She checked her phone in the vain hope that she might find out who'd sent the text. Chillingly, her daughter's name appeared but with no clue as to the sender's number.

Rhys went into the kitchen and returned with two large brandies. He handed one to Hanna and sat down next to her, his face pale and drawn. Hanna absentmindedly ran her finger round the rim of the glass as she stared at the flames licking the glass window of the wood burner, lulled by their hypnotic spell. Thoughts raced furiously through her head in no coherent order. She felt faint, so desperate was her concern for Eva.

"So, what's the plan?" Rhys ventured, interrupting her thoughts. He seemed to realise that his efforts to talk her into notifying the authorities had been in vain.

Before Hanna could reply, her mobile beeped again with another text alert. She snatched the phone and stared at the brightly-lit screen:

We have unfinished business to resolve. Get the next flight back to Sicily if you want to see Eva again.

A wave of anguish ripped through Hanna; she felt dizzy and light-headed as panic threatened to engulf her.

"What is it? Is it the kidnappers again? What do they want?" he asked.

"Oh, my God, it's Luciano, it's got to be him. He must have found out somehow about the information I've got on him and he's blackmailing me to hand it over so I'll get Eva back. What a bastard! How could he stoop so low?"

She started to sob, her hands trembling as she fumbled for a tissue. Rhys attempted to put his arm round her shoulders in a comforting gesture, but she shrugged it off, her sobbing becoming more intense.

"I keep trying to tell you that we need to—" Rhys started to say hesitantly, a helpless look on his face.

Hanna's sobs subsided in an instant and she rounded on him, almost angrily. "You really have no idea what we're dealing with, do you? I've got no option. I'll have to go back to Sicily straight away and settle this once and for all. I knew it had to come to a head but just not quite like this. I need to call Ceri and let her know what's happened."

Rhys must have realised from her determined look that there was no point arguing. He sighed deeply and picked up Hanna's laptop lying on the coffee table. "Okay, you do that, and I'll try and get you on the next flight back to Sicily."

Hanna slipped her jacket on and took her mobile outside on the pretext of getting a better signal. She didn't want to run the risk of involving Rhys any more than he already was and of giving him more information that might persuade him to go to the police.

With trembling hands, first she checked the messages again for any details as to their source. Nothing. The information must have been blocked by the sender. Then she called Ceri, who picked up after a couple of rings although it was now in the early hours of the morning in Sicily.

"Hanna, what is it? What's happened?" Ceri asked in a concerned voice.

"It's Eva. She's… she's been kidnapped. I've been told to come back to Sicily otherwise I'll never see her again," Hanna whispered into the handset between sobs.

"What the…!"

"It must be Luciano. He must have found out where we'd gone and that I've got information on him. I just hope he won't harm Eva. He wouldn't harm his own daughter, would he?"

Hanna could sense a slight hesitation on the other end of the phone.

"I'm sure he wouldn't. I'm surprised he's gone to such lengths, but it's not unheard of. Not in the circumstances. What are you going to do? D'you know for sure it's Luciano? Have you reported it to the police over there?"

"Course not. Rhys was trying to persuade me to. I've got to get back as soon as possible. I can't risk them harming her. I have to get her back whatever it takes, even if I have to hand over all the information I've got. Rhys is trying to get me on a flight tomorrow."

"Let me know what time you're arriving and we'll pick you up at the airport."

"Have you heard anything at your end about a possible kidnapping?"

Again, a slight hesitation before Ceri responded. "Well, things are hotting up even more now. There's talk of a turf war, with African gangs moving in on traditional mafia territory. Nothing specific about a kidnapping, though, or anything about Eva. But the most important thing is we'll help you to get her back safe and sound. Both Sergio and his father are well connected. We'll have Eva back before you know it."

Hanna started to cry again, tears of relief on hearing Ceri's reassuring words. She made it sound so straightforward; Hanna feared it wouldn't be. Right now, she felt terrified and exhausted, her head and emotions all over the place, wondering where Eva was and praying she hadn't been harmed in any way.

"Okay, I'll let you know about the flight. See you tomorrow hopefully. And thanks, Ceri. Let's just hope we'll be able to get Eva back OK…"

"We will, you'll see. Try not to worry too much and get some rest."

"Speak to you soon." Hanna ended the call, her hands still trembling, and went back inside.

Rhys sprang up from the sofa, closing the laptop. "I've managed to get you on the early afternoon flight to Catania tomorrow. I'll stay over and drive you to the airport in the morning. How did Ceri react to the news?"

"She didn't seem overly surprised, as if she was expecting something would happen. She'll pick me up from the airport tomorrow. I need to pack a few things and let her know what time I'll arrive."

"I wish I could do more. Maybe come over to Sicily with you?" Rhys suggested in a subdued tone.

"Thanks for the offer, Rhys, but you've done more than enough already. Ceri and Sergio will be more than enough support. They know how things work out there and Sergio's got lots of contacts and his father's in the police. At worst, I'll just have to hand over the information to Luciano if it's going to save Eva. I just hope that'll do it…" Hanna realised how brittle and rattled she sounded.

A shiver slid down her spine at the prospect of having to confront this situation head-on. But there was no choice. She had to stay strong for Eva's sake. This was no time to feel weak and helpless. She had to get her daughter back, no matter what.

From the corner of her eye, Hanna caught Rhys looking at her.

"Sorry, I don't mean to be rude or ungrateful, Rhys. You've been a real rock these past few weeks. We couldn't have survived without you."

"Try and get some sleep. You must be exhausted," he continued gently, a wounded expression on his face. "I'll see you in the morning."

Hanna kissed him lightly on the cheek and turned away quickly, bidding him goodnight as she retreated to the haven of her bedroom. She threw some clothes into a cabin bag. *I'll need to take some clothes for Eva, too*, she thought, vowing to do it in the morning, not wanting to confront Rhys again that night.

And her passport. She wondered how Eva could have been taken back to Sicily without it. Probably using fake documents or bypassing the authorities somehow.

Not forgetting Orsina; wherever she was, Eva would be missing her battered old teddy by now. Hanna's eyes filled with tears again. She could only hope and pray that her precious little daughter wouldn't be harmed in any way.

Chapter Twenty-Nine

Sicily, Monday 27th November, 2017

Hanna looked out of the window as the plane started its descent through the wispy clouds towards Catania airport. She'd dozed off during the flight following a restless night with little sleep. But images of Eva had plagued her: Eva tied up, crying, hungry, hurt. A nightmare that didn't disappear on waking. As if part of her had been cruelly torn away and her mind and body were mourning its loss.

Her thoughts drifted back to Rhys, the journey to Manchester airport, the stilted conversation, and their awkward goodbye. She had grown fond of him during her time in Wales, and the feeling seemed to be reciprocal. But the important thing now was getting Eva back without anyone getting hurt, whatever that entailed. Hanna shuddered at the thought.

Before long the sprawl of the city came into view, locked between the shimmering waters of the Mediterranean and the majestic snow-capped peak of Mount Etna, its white plume sharply etched against a perfect blue sky. She couldn't help feeling impressed by the stunning sight despite the grim circumstances of her return to the island.

The pilot made a smooth landing and the plane taxied along the runway for a while before juddering to a halt. Passengers tussled with each other as they retrieved their hand luggage and scrambled to the exit. Hanna left them to it; she'd be off the plane soon enough and had the advantage of not having to retrieve any additional baggage.

But there was a queue at Passport Control. The checks seemed to be unusually methodical and the line edged forward slowly. When it came to her turn, the uniformed police officer glanced at the photo in her British passport before looking her up and down suspiciously. She was glad she'd left her passport in her maiden name so it couldn't be connected to Luciano in any way.

"Reason for your visit, *signora*?" he asked gruffly.

"I'm visiting friends," she answered nervously.

"Here in Catania?"

She wondered whether he'd ask for an address and replied, "No, in Cefalu."

"How long do you intend to stay?"

"A couple of weeks."

He stared at her again before handing her passport back and waving her through. "*Va bene, signora. Buon soggiorno.* Enjoy your stay." He turned his attention to the elderly man waiting behind her.

"*Grazie, buongiorno.*" Hanna put her passport back in her handbag, grateful she didn't have to face any in-depth questions, and made her way towards the exit. The arrivals hall thronged with people. She searched the crowd for Ceri and was about to give up when she heard a familiar voice calling her name.

"Hanna, I'm over here!" Ceri was stuck behind a group of noisy schoolchildren being reunited with their families. Hanna fought her way through the mayhem and flung her arms round her friend.

"Oh, Ceri, I'm so pleased to see you…" Being back in Sicily in such a situation and seeing her best friend again was just too much for Hanna, and the tears streamed down her cheeks as the two women hugged each other. "I'm so worried. I can't let them harm Eva, I just can't…

"Come on, let's get away from here," said Ceri, steering her towards the exit. "Sergio's waiting outside in the car. We can talk on the way home, unless you're hungry or want to get a coffee first?"

Hanna shook her head. "I had a bite to eat on the plane,

thanks. I just need to work out how to get Eva back. Can't think of anything else right now."

"That's understandable," Ceri said, leading the way towards the exit. Sergio was waiting nearby at the wheel of his Fiat 500 in a space reserved for emergency vehicles. He got out of the car as he saw them approach and hugged Hanna warmly.

"*Come stai, cara?* I can't believe that Luciano would stoop so low as to snatch Eva from you."

"Me neither, but I guess he's got a lot to lose…" Hanna said, slipping effortlessly back into Italian.

Sergio opened the car boot and put Hanna's cabin bag inside.

"I have to get Eva back if it's the last thing I do…"

"Obviously, and we'll do everything we can to help you," said Sergio as he got in the driver's seat with Ceri next to him, and Hanna settling in the back. "It's a bit of a drive to Cefalu so there's plenty of time to discuss our options. I've put out feelers among my contacts but nothing's come back as yet. However, it's only early days."

A chill spread over Hanna. "Surely you'd have heard something by now?" she asked, trying to mask the desperation in her voice.

Sergio revved the car up and accelerated into the busy airport traffic. "These things can take time. It's not unusual in such cases. And people are often reluctant to talk…"

"You make it sound as if it happens often," Ceri said, flashing Sergio an angry glance.

"Sorry, I didn't mean to sound unsympathetic, but you'd be amazed. All sorts of stuff happens here that never sees the light of day."

Is he trying to tell me that our efforts will prove useless? Hanna thought in alarm.

"That's not making Hanna feel any better," Ceri responded crossly. She must have sensed Hanna's reaction.

Hanna fought back the urge to burst into tears again and asked quietly, "So what are the chances of getting Eva back?"

"I guess it depends what happens," Sergio answered. They

were crawling through the traffic on the ring road now. "And whether you're prepared to give up the information you have and not do anything about it."

"I'd do anything to get Eva back," Hanna said softly, her eyes brimming with tears again. "I just want her to be safe and for us to have a normal life again, if that's possible, away from danger and threats."

Sergio shot her a look in the rear view mirror as if if to say *You must be kidding, given what Luciano's up to.*

They fell silent as Sergio joined the slip road heading for the A19 motorway. The outskirts flashed past, fleeting images that Hanna hardly noticed.

"So, what do we do? Just sit tight until they contact us again?" she asked, shifting nervously in the back seat.

Sergio turned his head slightly towards her. "I don't think it'll be long before they do. They'll want to resolve this as soon as possible. There'll no doubt be a rendezvous where you can hand over the information and get Eva back. We just have to wait. We may get some leads in the meantime. I guess the main decision is whether you're prepared to hand over the information in exchange for Eva, or whether you still want to bring Luciano and his family to justice and put an end to their people-trafficking."

He paused, waiting for Hanna's response.

"Realistically, what are the odds of doing both? How dangerous would it be? I don't want anyone getting hurt in the process."

Sergio exhaled loudly in frustration. "Hanna, *cara,* this isn't a game – these are hard-nosed criminals we're dealing with, who stand to lose their business interests and their status in the local community. It's bad enough that you disappeared with Eva in the first place, but to threaten the business—"

Ceri jumped to Hanna's defence. "That may be, but it's not really helping Hanna's state of mind, is it? She was just protecting both of them after the… the… threat. What else was she supposed to do?"

Sergio shrugged. "Go to the authorities, maybe?"

Ceri laughed bitterly. "Yeah, right. Here in Sicily where the authorities are often more corrupt than ordinary people. Great idea."

"But we have to fight back," Sergio insisted. "And attitudes are changing. People are challenging the old traditions. Some businesses have stopped paying protection money to the mafia. We have to start somewhere."

"Not necessarily with me when my daughter's life is being threatened," Hanna said, flashing an angry look at Sergio.

"Sorry, Hanna, you know we'll do everything we can to support you and get Eva back safe and sound." Sergio shrugged his shoulders again, this time by way of apology.

"It's a difficult time for everyone," Ceri intervened. "But Hanna has a point. Just what are the chances of being able to turn Luciano and his family in once we get Eva back?"

If *we get Eva back,* thought Hanna, noting that the conversation was steering clear of the possibility that this might not happen. The thought made her feel ever more despondent. Hunched in the back seat, she let her mind wander, thinking about what might happen.

Ceri and Sergio fell silent, as if they'd run out of ways to pacify her. The truth was that they were all in the hands of whoever had snatched Eva. A feeling of helplessness surged through Hanna. The situation was totally out of their control.

After a while she began to feel drowsy from the warmth of the car and her lack of sleep the previous night. Her eyelids drooped as she struggled to stay awake. She must have dozed off ,for when she opened her eyes again it was dark and they were approaching the outskirts of Cefalu. As Sergio turned into the road where he now shared the apartment with Ceri, Hanna's mobile phone buzzed.

She snatched it from her bag. The kidnappers. Her hands trembled as she read the text:

Welcome back, Hanna. Eva is missing you. Don't alert the authorities if you want to see her again. We will send further instructions tomorrow. Buonanotte.

Hanna stared at the brightly lit screen of her phone, feeling increasingly nauseous. They must be watching her movements closely, maybe even right now. She glanced around instinctively, aware of her growing paranoia. They wouldn't dare get that close, or would they? But one thing was certain: whatever this was, it seemed personal.

Chapter Thirty

Back at the apartment in Cefalu, Hanna continued to dwell on the situation over dinner later that evening. She was feeling drained as the full force of the last twenty hours started to hit her. Her head ached and she shifted uncomfortably in her chair. All the talking was getting them nowhere. It seemed pointless even to talk about the situation, in a way. There was little more they could do for the moment. Eva's fate lay in the kidnappers' hands. They would just have to wait for their next move, however distressing this proved to be

A brief lull in the conversation gave Hanna the chance tomake her excuses and retreat to the guest room. She undressed quickly and slipped between the cool sheets. Tired though she was, sleep proved elusive, her mind churning, images flashing through her head like sequences in a film: Eva tied up, crying, calling out to her. Eventually fatigue overcame Hanna and she managed to drift off into a troubled sleep.

It was no real surprise when she woke with a start in the middle of the night. She sat bolt upright in bed, covered in a cold sweat, struggling to get her breath in the stuffy little bedroom. *It must be hell here in the stifling Sicilian summers without air-con*, she thought.

She padded across to the window, the stone floor cold on her bare feet. Opening it a fraction, she gasped as the sharp night air rushed in. There was a faint sound, an agitated voice talking in hushed tones. Through the window, Hanna could see Sergio out on the balcony adjoining his bedroom next door-but-one to hers. He was silhouetted against the streetlights, his mobile pressed to his ear. She strained to hear the words but they came fast, in a thick, gutteral dialect that would have been impossible to decipher even if she'd been able to hear properly. As it was, she only caught the odd word, not enough for her to guess the nature of the conversation.

Probably to do with work, she thought. Nevertheless, she felt uneasy. After a few minutes, Sergio disappeared from view and the apartment fell silent again. Hanna glanced at the luminous figures on the bedside clock: 3.22am. Surely, it couldn't be work, or could it? *Journalists probably get tip-offs at all hours,* she tried to reassure herself. But the doubt continued to gnaw away long after she returned to bed.

By the time Hanna rose shortly after 7am the following morning, there was no sign of Sergio. Ceri was already busying herself in the kitchen, clattering pans and dishes as she put them away. She must have sensed Hanna's presence and turned around, with a forced smile.

"Hi, there. Did you manage to get any sleep?"

Hanna shrugged. "Not much."

"Coffee?"

"Please. Is everything okay? You seem a bit upset."

"I'm a bit annoyed that Sergio's had to go off on some urgent job, today of all days. Talk about timing!"

"Well, we can't do much anyway until the kidnappers make contact again. He may as well be doing something useful rather than hanging around here."

Ceri came over and wrapped her arms around Hanna. "You're right, of course. Just wish it was all over, with Eva back safely. You're being so brave…"

Tears pricked at Hanna's eyes as she rested her head against Ceri's shoulder. "Not really," she said. "I just want Eva back. It sounds selfish but I don't care about anything else at the minute, not the memory stick or the people trafficking…"

Ceri stroked Hanna's hair soothingly. "I'm sure it'll all be over in next to no time once they get what they need. You'll see."

"Just hope you're right," said Hanna, sighing deeply, and freeing herself from Ceri's embrace before her emotions got the better of her.

The espresso pot on the stove gurgled as the water bubbled up through the coffee. Ceri poured the contents into two cups and handed one to Hanna. She waited while it cooled a little, then downed it in one go. The shot of caffeine was just what she needed to help her face the day ahead. God knows what it would bring.

Her thoughts started to wander again, interrupted by a cheery Italian pop song: the ring tone on Ceri's mobile phone. Ceri answered, saying little but listening intently.

"*Sei sicuro?*" she asked finally. Hanna couldn't hear the conversation but imagined that it was Sergio calling. She was right.

"That was Sergio," Ceri explained when she ended the call. "He's on his way home. He needs to see what's on the memory stick. Apparently, this story's much wider than the transport arrangements for the people trafficking, as if that wasn't bad enough. Even the immigrant centres are part of the racket, it turns out. It seems to have become a real industry, with stacks of money being made by those involved."

Hanna recalled how her suspicions about Luciano had deepened. He'd left his laptop open to take a call in the next room. Glancing casually at the screen, Hanna had noticed a list of payments for "imports", some from humanitarian organisations. She was curious about the large amounts involved and why they should relate to imports. *What could that possibly have to do with the wine business?* she'd wondered, but was loath to broach the subject with Luciano in case he thought she was prying.

She shuddered now. "Does that make it better or worse for Eva?"

"That's what Sergio's trying to get to grips with. If it's as big as he thinks, it's not only Luciano and his family who've got a lot to lose."

"I sense there's something you're not telling me."

"It's just that…" Ceri hesitated. "Well, it might not even be Luciano behind the kidnapping."

Hanna went cold as the implications of this struck her.

"Christ, I'd not even thought of that. If it's someone else, they won't care about harming Eva or keeping her alive. It doesn't bear thinking about…"

"We just don't know, which is why we need to see exactly what's on the memory stick. Didn't you say that you'd not looked at the files since copying them from Luciano's computer?"

"Well, I opened the first few and it seemed to be all about the trafficking arrangements and how they worked. That was bad enough. Then shortly afterwards the silver bullets were delivered. I didn't want to see or hear any more at the time, I just wanted to get out of there."

"That's understandable, but we need to look at the contents now if we're to get Eva back safely. Sergio's coming straight over to go through them and—"

Her words faded as the shrill ring of Hanna's mobile cut through the air.

Chapter Thirty-One

Sicily, Tuesday 28th November, 2017

Before Hanna could answer, the phone went dead. She gazed at the blank screen in dismay, thinking that she'd missed contact with the kidnappers. But a text alert followed straight after. She opened the message with trembling hands. It was them, with instructions for the memory stick drop-off.

On Thursday morning, take the SS285 turn-off for Caccamo from the E90. Shortly before Caccamo, take a sharp right towards Lake Scalzano and follow the road until it becomes a dirt track. Leave the car and continue on foot. Come alone. After about 500m, you'll find the hollow stump of an old chestnut tree. Leave the memory stick inside the stump and text back when it's in place. Don't contact the police. Don't try and trace this phone. We'll send instructions of where to find Eva later once we've verified the content.

Reading the message, Hanna's eyes filled with tears and a sob caught in her throat. Thursday, the day after tomorrow. They had until then to work out some sort of plan. But even then it wouldn't be over; they'd still have to wait to get Eva back. And even then, there were no guarantees. She wondered how the kidnappers knew about the memory stick

"What is it? What does it say?" asked Ceri, straining to see the screen over Hanna's shoulder.

"There, see for yourself." Hanna handed the phone over as if it were red hot, her voice shaky. "We've got until Thursday to deliver the information."

Ceri quickly scanned the screen. "Okay, at least we've got something to work with now. Go and get the memory stick and let's have a look at what's on it. It's got to be pretty important for them to go to such lengths to get it back. We'll get a head start before Sergio gets home."

Hanna moved towards her room as if in a trance, her head a jumble of mixed emotions. To her relief, the memory stick was still there, sitting in a little embroidered bag tucked into the zipped pocket of her handbag. No reason why it shouldn't have been; she'd checked it a thousand times since leaving the cottage in Wales.

If only I'd looked at it before now, I could have gone to go to the authorities and Eva would still be with me, she thought, her eyes welling with tears as she returned to the kitchen. *It's all my fault. I shouldn't have been so damn complacent.*

Ceri almost snatched the memory stick in her eagerness to see its contents. She inserted it into her laptop which immediately sprang to life, exposing a myriad of folders on its brightly-lit screen.

"At least there's no password protection, that's something," Ceri said, "but even that's strange if the content is so sensitive..."

Hanna watched as her friend started to click into the individual files. But every time the result was the same; each time the content appeared as a mixure of indecipherable symbols and numbers.

"But, but...I just don't understand. What the hell is this?" Hanna stammered in surprise. "I was able to access the files easily enough and copy them. How come they're suddenly unreadable? Have they been corrupted or encrypted in some way?"

"I don't know that much about computers, but maybe you could view them as you were logged onto Luciano's computer. In saving them, maybe they've either corrupted or reverted back to the encrypted originals."

"Does that mean that the information's lost?" Hanna could feel a wave of panic rippling through her body. She flopped onto a kitchen chair as if the stuffing had been knocked out of her.

"I wouldn't have thought so, but I'm no expert. Sergio'll have a better idea of what to do when he gets here."

The information won't be any good to the kidnappers encrypted, or will they have the means to decrypt it? Hanna thought. *If we can't give the kidnappers what they want, there's no hope of getting Eva back in one piece.* It was too painful to contemplate.

As if reading her mind, Ceri said, "It'll be okay, we'll be able to retrieve the information, you'll see."

But Hanna couldn't see. Her vision was blurred with tears. She tried unsuccessfuly to blink them away. "But how?" she cried, giving vent to her emotions. "We've only got until Thursday. That's no time at all…" Images of Eva bound and bleeding flickered before her eyes. Was she still alive? Had they hurt her in any way? Hanna shuddered as she recalled instances in the past where children had been found dead and mutilated, with no real explanation or the perpetrators ever being brought to justice. She couldn't let Eva become yet another victim.

Swallowing the bile rising in her throat, Hanna resolved to stay strong and do everything in her power to get her daughter back safely. "We're never going to get Eva back on our own. We'll have to go to the police."

"I'll call Sergio. He'll know what to do," said Ceri, reaching for her phone. A hurried one-sided conversation ensued, at the end of which she declared, "He'll be back any minute – he's only about 10 minutes away. Apparently he's got a colleague at work who does this type of thing all the time and can sort it out. He needs to collect the memory stick and take it back to the office for the guy to work on."

"But can this guy be trusted? Will he tell someone? I can't risk—"

"Hanna, we really don't have any choice or time to do

anything else," Ceri interrupted firmly. "It's our only course of action in the circumstances."

Hanna stared at her friend, a flurry of questions gathering in her head. "What about going to the police? I know they said not to but it's got to be an option, or would it be too risky? I don't want to put Eva in even more danger than she already is."

"Let's see what Sergio says when he gets here. He knows how the police works better than most people with his dad being in the force."

Ceri went over to the stove and picked up the espresso pot, emptied the grounds into the sink, and refilled it with water. "I think we need another coffee while we wait."

Hanna nodded in a resigned manner, more to appease Ceri than with any real conviction. She had a sinking feeling in her stomach that things weren't going to work out in their favour.

"*Minchia!*" Sergio exhaled loudly as he examined the laptop's desktop, trying to access the files with growing frustration. Each file displayed a jumble of symbols and numbers just as before, and just as Ceri had described over the phone. "How long have we got?"

"We're due to deliver it on Thursday morning, the day after tomorrow. Will your colleague be able to decipher it by then?" Hanna asked, her face etched into a deep frown, willing the answer to be in the affirmative.

"I'll take it over there now and get him to start work on it straight away. He's a whizz at this sort of thing, but God knows how difficult it will be," Sergio responded, grim-faced. "But it's the only option we've got." He closed all the open files and removed the memory stick from the laptop.

Hanna was sick of hearing that they had no choice. She noticed how Sergio had managed to dodge answering her question. The situation seemed hopeless. They'd be forced into handing over the information without ever seeing it for themselves. Or maybe it was better that way, never knowing the truth.

"If he does manage to decipher the files, can we be sure

he'll keep the information to himself?" she asked, trying not to panic and give in to her heightened sense of alarm.

"Pietro and I go back a long way. We've been friends since we were kids. We grew up together, went to school together. He's like a brother to me; he wouldn't risk doing anything that would jeopardise either our personal frienship or our professional relationship. Believe me, he can be trusted." Sergio gave a faint smile. Hanna realised that he'd quickly copied all the encrypted files onto the laptop as he was talking. "But you can never be too careful; at least this way we'll have our own copy just in case," he added with a shrug by way of explanation.

In case of what? Hanna was tempted to ask but decided against it. The thought that Sergio might be involved in some way still lingered in her head.

Chapter Thirty-Two

Sicily, Tuesday 28th November, 2017

Back in the kitchen later that evening, Ceri served up a simple dinner of chicken breasts in lemon and white wine with pan fried greens. The food looked and smelt delicious. Hanna tried to eat, but after the first few mouthfuls she felt nauseous and took a gulp of chilled Grillo wine to compensate.

"Sorry, I'm just not feeling hungry," she said, noticing that Ceri was also pushing her food around the plate with little enthusiasm.

"Neither am I, but we have to eat something to help get us through this."

"Yes, you're right." Hanna forced herself to eat a little more.

Sergio continued to tuck in, apparently unaffected. There'd been no word from Pietro. She glanced at Sergio. As if sensing the unspoken question, he met her gaze and shrugged. "Well, he did say it might prove difficult and could take some time…"

"But we don't have time. He's not going to manage it, is he?" Hanna said, her voice starting to crack. "We're never going to find out the truth about what's been going on. And if Luciano's not behind this and the kidnappers can't access the information, then Eva…" She began to sob and Ceri jumped up and went over to give her a hug.

"If this isn't going to work, maybe we should just go to the police and let them deal with it?" Ceri suggested.

"*Ma, dai!*" Sergio said, quickly swallowing his last mouthful. " You've both been in Sicily long enough to know that the police can't always be trusted either. I think we'll get a better idea of what we should do if we can just get to see what's on the stick."

"And if that doesn't happen, then what?" Hanna asked in an anguished voice, the sobs relenting a little.

Sergio sighed. "Then we'll have to decide whether we go along with the instructions or involve the police or some other authority. If it *is* people trafficking, we could always approach one of the charity organisations involved. I could do an exposé for the newspaper but that would take time and need hard evidence to back it up. That wouldn't help get Eva back any time soon."

"It's hopeless, we're never going to get her back," Hanna groaned, shaking her head despondently.

"C'mon, Hanna, stay positive. We're doing all we can," said Sergio. "I'll call Pietro now and check if he's made any progress." He reached for his phone and started to dial, leaving the kitchen to make the call. Hanna looked at Ceri quizzically.

"The reception in here is pretty awful; it's much better in the living room, and even better on the balcony," her friend explained, sitting down again beside her.

That would explain the call the night before. Maybe Sergio wasn't being so secretive, after all. But it had still been the middle of the night.

Fragments drifted through to the kitchen, odd words and phrases animated and tense, but not enough for her to get the gist of the conversation. Sergio returned to the kitchen a few minutes later, a faint smile on his face.

"*Allora,* Pietro's been able to access some of the files, not all. At least that should be enough to give us an idea of what Luciano's been up to. He's on his way over here now to show us what he's managed to uncover – it'll take him half an hour or so."

Hanna glanced anxiously at the clock on the kitchen wall. It was already just after nine.

"That's great news," said Ceri, smiling broadly, getting up and starting to clear the table.

"Let's just hope it'll be enough for the kidnappers," said Hanna, feeling the tension in her shoulders relax a little. "Here, let me give you a hand." She was grateful to have something to do to distract her and work off some of her nervous energy.

Sergio took three delicate shot glasses out of the cupboard and lined them up on the table, filling each with a dark viscous liquid from an unmarked bottle. Handing them out, he said, "Drink this, Hanna. It's a local *amaro* that'll do wonders to settle your nerves. *Cin, cin*. Here's to getting Eva back *sana e salva*, safe and sound." He raised his glass in a toast.

Hanna murmured in agreement although she knew it would take much more than a local brew to make her feel better. She took a tentative sip. It tasted herby, almost medicinal, but left a welcome afterglow. Conscious that she needed to keep a clear head, she took another mouthful and left the rest. She looked at the clock again.

"As I said on the phone to Sergio, I've not been able to access all the files," Pietro explained, as he waited in the kitchen for the laptop to boot up. "And even those I've been able to get into won't always let me back in. There's no guarantee that what we see now will still be accessible an hour from now. Unless you're the original owner of the material, of course."

Huddled over the screen, the three friends watched over his shoulder as the desktop sprang into life and he clicked to access the memory stick.

"The easiest files to get into were the videos, and there are quite a few of those. I've not been able to view them all in the time. The audio files were the hardest, and the documents fell somewhere in the middle. I've kept the original memory stick in its encrypted form and then transferred the files that decrypted successfully onto this one," Pietro nodded towards the laptop, indicating that they were looking at the latter, and retrieved what must have been the original memory stick from his wallet.

"Sergio didn't explain much about what this is all about, just that you needed the information urgently. I can leave it with you or I can hang around a while in case you get any problems," he added.

"Pietro, you're a star!" said Sergio, clapping him on the back. "If you could stay while we have a quick look through, that would be great." He slipped into the chair that Pietro had just vacated.

"You're welcome to wait in the lounge," said Ceri. "Can I get you a coffee or a glass of wine?"

"A glass of wine wouldn't go amiss, thanks." Pietro smiled gratefully as Ceri filled a glass with the last of the Grillo and ushered him into the room next door.

"I'll keep you company and leave Sergio and Hanna to it," she told him. "Three of us around a laptop is a bit much."

Hanna drew up a chair next to Sergio and focused on the screen as the numerous decrypted files started to appear. There was a lot of material – a mixture of documents, audio files, and videos. Most seemed to be opening without any major problem. Sergio clicked into a number of documents which all seemed to be about shipping cases of wine. Was this really wine or was it a euphemism for something else?

"Nothing of much use here," he said grumpily. "Makes you wonder why they bothered encrypting them if the content was so innocuous."

Hanna continued to look intently at the screen. "But if you look, there's a lot about importing shipments. If it was really about wine production, surely it would be mainly about exporting."

"You're absolutely right but there's nothing specific about the nature of the shipments, which is unusual in itself. There may be something somewhere but we'd need to check all the files to be sure, and that would take time. Let's try the audio files instead for now."

He started clicking into them but the sound quality was poor. "These seem like the recordings of meetings but it's difficult to make out what's being said. Maybe the encryption or the decryption has managed to corrupt the original recording."

"Let's try the videos," said Hanna with growing impatience, feeling disheartened.

Sergio clicked into the first video file. It started to play but quickly froze. He restarted it but the same thing happened. The second file did the same. The third was going the same way but Sergio eventually managed to get it to play.

The footage was grainy and dark, and the audio came in waves. It showed a group of about seven or eight men discussing payment for a "shipmen", with ludicrously high sums being mentioned. It couldn't possibly be to do with wine. The camera panned each man in turn but none were familiar to Hanna. As the camera focused on the last man, the colour drained from Sergio's face.

"What's the matter? Do you recognise someone?" she asked.

"*Porca miseria!* He's in disguise but I'd know that face anywhere. It's my father."

Chapter Thirty-Three

Sergio continued to stare at the computer screen. "I just can't believe my father's involved in some way," he said, running both hands through his thick, dark hair, his voice distraught. "There must be an explanation, maybe some sort of undercover operation."

"Your father's only come up once so far. Let's see if he appears anywhere else," said Hanna. "Strange there's been no sign of Luciano as yet."

Sergio glanced at her briefly with an odd expression before he turned back to continue working through the files. "Maybe this is all about him monitoring other people and keeping a record of his business transactions, rather than his own involvement."

It was shortly after one in the morning. Pietro had left a couple of hours earlier, having been thanked for his efforts. Hanna and Sergio had carried on going through the files to see what they could find, but some wouldn't even open while others were full of gobbledygook, signs, and symbols that made no sense. The quality of the audio and video files was often poor, the sound muffled, and the images grainy and pixellated as if they'd been taken hurriedly and in secret.

Hanna's eyes ached with tiredness and she stifled a yawn as she tried to focus on the screen again. She had to stay awake.

Ceri brought over two steaming mugs of *caffè latte* and set them down beside the laptop. "Here, this should help keep the two of you going."

"Thanks, Ceri, just what we need," Hanna smiled gratefully.

Images continued to flick across the screen as she took a sip without thinking; the coffee was still much too hot and scalded her tongue. She hurriedly put the mug down and turned back to the screen.

"Hold on, what's that?" she said, pointing at the image on display. "It looks like Luciano…"

Ceri came over again and stood behind them, watching as Sergio rewound and enlarged the picture so they could get a better look. The picture quality here was better. Luciano and Michele could clearly be seen talking to two men – one in his sixties who looked like an elder statesman; the other, a handsome man in his fifties with greying hair and dressed in an expensive suit. A number of younger men hung around in the background.

"It's him alright and that's his father Michele next to him. Who are the others?" Hanna asked.

"*Minchia,* that looks suspiciously like the Mayor of Postigliano," Sergio said, indicating the younger of the two men. "But hold on a minute. One of the men in the background bears a striking resemblance to my brother Pino. It could well be him. My family's not seen or heard from him in years, but he was always involved with the wrong sort of people, even from an early age. It wouldn't surprise me if he was involved in this."

Hanna looked at him in horror. Two members of Sergio's own family implicated in some way? Could Sergio be trusted, or was he too caught up in this dirty business? If so, what were the chances of getting Eva back safely?

"Can you make out what they're saying? You can barely hear anything and what you can hear is all in thick dialect," said Hanna quickly, trying to mask her suspicions.

Sergio plugged in the headphones and turned the volume up to maximum.

"More talk about *spedizioni* – shipments, I think you'd say – without specifying what's being shipped. Hang on, now there's mention of charitable aid and the 'shipments' being bound for a number of refugee centres along the west coast and on the offshore islands. They're saying that on the island of Lampedusa, there are more 'shipped goods' than locals."

"The content of the few files I saw when he left his laptop on was pretty damning, that's why I copied the lot. It's proof that Luciano *is* involved after all, just as we thought," Hanna said in a low voice, her chest heaving with the effort to mask the bitter disappointment that burned inside. "Let's just hope that he's behind the kidnapping and will release Eva once he gets the information back. It still seems incredible that he'd kidnap his own daughter."

"There's a lot at stake, and the evidence speaks for itself. He wouldn't want this to fall into the wrong hands, that's for sure," said Sergio.

Hanna noticed that he seemed pleased, almost triumphant, to have uncovered proof of Luciano's illicit business dealings. Just what did this mean? Was Sergio on her side, or was there more going on? Could he be mixed up in this in some way? After all, both his father and his long-lost brother had turned up in the video evidence now. She wondered yet again whether he could be trusted.

"Let's see what else is on there," she said, stifling another yawn.

"You should really get some sleep…" Ceri suggested. "We should all get some sleep. We can pick this up tomorrow and make our decision then about what to do next."

Hanna looked at her with pleading eyes. "C'mon, Ceri. I need to see just how mixed up Luciano is in all this. Another half hour?"

"OK, you win," Ceri replied wearily. "Then we *all* go to bed, right?"

Hanna squeezed her friend's hand gratefully, tears springing to her eyes again. "You're a good friend, Ceri. I don't know what I'd do without you."

Ceri wrapped her arms round Hanna's shoulders and lightly kissed the top of her head, saying dismissively, "You'd do the same for me."

"Enough of that, *ragazze*," said Sergio. "Come on, let's try and finish viewing these video files before Ceri's curfew."

More evidence came to light the following morning as Sergio scanned through the remaining files. Hanna noticed the dark shadows under his eyes and coarse stubble on his cheeks and chin. He'd evidently not had much sleep, but then neither had she. Troubled images of Eva lying hurt and wounded had played through her head on a constant spool, keeping sleep at bay. Eventually, she gave up trying and resorted to scouring the local news channels on her phone for any mention of a kidnap, but there was nothing.

Piecing together the fragments of information from the memory stick was difficult, and trying to making sense of it all was even tougher. It was a complex, tangled web of human shipments that seemed to involve not only Luciano and his father but also several upstanding figures of the community, according to Sergio. His own father had only appeared once more, in the background of a short dimly-lit video clip which appeared to have been shot in a cave. He claimed his brother hadn't shown up again.

Turning to Hanna, he said, "Well, *cara*, it looks as if Luciano and his cronies are well implicated in people trafficking. If he knows you've got this information, he's quite capable of doing anything, even kidnapping his own daughter, to get it back. Once he does so, he's bound to release her unharmed."

"How can we be sure?"

Sergio shrugged. "We can't be, but the chances are…"

"D'you reckon that Luciano and his father are the ringleaders in all this?" Hanna asked.

"It's not clear from what we've seen. But it's certainly a lucrative business, judging by the sums being quoted. There's also talk about charitable funds being siphoned off. That's worth a packet alone."

Hanna could sense that Sergio was loath to follow this up, possibly because of his father's and brother's potential involvement. "Let's just focus on getting Eva back safely.

The rest can wait for now. So, given all this, do you think we should make the drop-off as instructed?" she asked tentatively.

"*Francamente,* I don't see why not. After all, we'll still have the back-up stick, should you want to take any further action. But you probably won't, not after what's happened. You wouldn't want to risk it happening again, or something even worse. They'll be aware that we could have copied the contents, but this kidnapping is to scare you off from going to the police."

He seems very sure, thought Hanna, *as if he knows more than he's letting on.* Could he be yet another of the *compari,* one of Luciano's cronies? But surely Ceri would have suspected something by now? But it had taken Hanna ages to doubt Luciano, so maybe not.

"What d'you think, Ceri?" Hanna asked.

"I'd go with Sergio. He's got much more knowledge about this sort of thing and the likelihood of getting a positive result."

"I just want to get Eva back safely and then get the hell away from here. It may sound selfish, but I don't care about taking any further action. If there's already a police investigation underway, then Luciano's bound to be caught at some point anyway," said Hanna, her voice quivering between anguish and pain.

"Ok, that's settled then," Sergio replied. "I'll drive you there and you can do the drop-off bit on your own, but I'll have your back should anything go wrong."

Hanna cast her mind back to the reason she and Eva had fled from Sicily in the first place. The three silver bullets. One for each of them. That implied that someone else was involved, unless it had all been part of some devious scheme of Luciano's. She couldn't shake off the idea that it might not be Luciano behind the kidnapping after all. Her imagination conjured up scenarios of how this could all end very differently.

Paralysed by fear, she realised she might not come back at all. Nor might Eva.

Chapter Thirty-Four

Sicily, Wednesday 29th – Thursday 30th November, 2017

Sergio left the apartment later that morning, saying he had an urgent assignment to finish at work. No sooner had he left than Hanna's mobile started to vibrate. She snatched it off the kitchen table, alarmed that it might be the kidnappers to say that things had changed and the drop-off had been cancelled. But it was only a message from Rhys, asking if she'd made any progress with getting Eva back.

She hadn't really given Rhys another thought since she'd returned to Sicily; she'd been totally focused on rescuing Eva. A feeling of guilt welled up inside her. Rhys deserved better, after all he'd done for them both.

"Everything okay?" asked Ceri, looking worried,

"It's just Rhys, asking how things are going." Hanna started to text him back. "I'll let him know about the drop-off tomorrow and I'll call him when it's over. I don't feel like talking right now."

"Talking of my brother, how were things working out in Wales?" Ceri asked.

"Rhys was a great help and it was all going so well. It really seemed like a new start for me and Eva. I'd even begun to forget about the past. Until this happened."

"Well, hopefully it'll all be over soon. We'll get Eva back and you can start again where you left off," said Ceri, squeezing Hanna's hand.

"Let's hope so." Hanna doubted that life would ever be the

same, even if Eva was returned safely. She didn't want to think about what she'd do if not. Life wouldn't be worth living.

"I don't know if Luciano will ever forgive me taking his daughter away. But if he's responsible for kidnapping Eva, he's certainly getting his revenge and making sure that I suffer and won't ever reveal the details of his business affairs."

"And what if it's not him? Once you get Eva back, you might be able to patch things up with him and reach some sort of arrangement so he won't cut too much of a *brutta figura* and look bad in front of his family and associates."

"Seriously? Ceri, he's a people-trafficker, for God's sake. Nothing can condone that," Hanna said, exasperated that her friend could even contemplate such an idea. "There's no way I can live with that, and no way I can allow Eva to be brought up in that world."

Her eyes filled with tears again at the mention of her missing daughter. She thought back to the three silver bullets. Why had there been three? It still suggested that a third party was involved, someone who wanted to threaten the whole family. But surely this was all about Luciano trying to retrieve the damning evidence she had of his business dealings? And in the only way he knew how, by kidnapping Eva. Or was it? She felt sick at the thought that someone else might be behind it all.

"You okay?" Ceri interrupted Hanna's thoughts.

"Just thinking about everything's that happened. Nothing we haven't talked about already."

"Why don't we go and get some fresh air?" her friend suggested. "It'll be ages until Sergio gets back, and we don't want to stay cooped up here until then. We can take a stroll along the beach."

"Good idea, it might help to take my mind off things. I'll get my jacket."

After dinner that evening Hanna and Sergio spent more time browsing the files on the memory stick. They didn't uncover anything of particular interest, just more videos showing similar small groups of men huddled together, discussing "shipments" in thick dialect, according to Sergio. No more appearances from Luciano or Sergio's father or brother. Fortunately, they'd had the foresight to copy the files the day before, as not all of them would open and some had reverted back to their encrypted form. Tiredness finally defeated both of them and they gave up and went to bed.

But as soon as Hanna's head touched the pillow, her fatigue vanished. Thoughts streamed through her head of what might or might not happen the following day at the drop-off. Images of being reunited with Eva, of seeing her hurt, of never seeing her again… or even worse. The frenzied thoughts eventually subsided enough for her to fall into a fitful sleep. She continued to toss and turn, finally waking shortly before 7am, her head pounding and her skin clammy from sweat. It was as if she hadn't slept at all.

Reluctantly, she forced herself into the shower. The pulsating jets of warm water revived her and left her feeling ready to face the day ahead. After towelling herself dry, she pulled on a warm sweater and jeans and headed for the kitchen, where Ceri and Sergio were talking in low voices. They both looked up as she came in, as if she were interrupting something

"Morning," Hanna tried to sound cheery. "Did either of you manage to get much sleep? I know I didn't."

"Not really," said Ceri, "but it's not really surprising in the circumstances, is it? Sit down, I'll make more coffee and get you some breakfast. What time are we planning to leave?"

Sergio shot her a glance. "We talked about this last night and I thought we'd agreed that it'd be just Hanna and me going? Just in case of any trouble."

Hanna felt a twinge of alarm. "We're not expecting any, are we? After all, I'm supposed to be doing this on my own. I'm scared enough as it is." She flopped wearily onto the nearest chair.

Sergio looked annoyed. "Whoever is behind this wants the information on the memory stick at all costs, so they won't want to do anything to stop you delivering it. So no, I'm not really expecting any trouble, but there's no reason for Ceri to come."

"Not even to give Hanna a bit of moral support? You could do with it, couldn't you?" Ceri directed the question at Hanna.

Hanna shrugged. "Honestly, whatever you think best. I want to get it over and done with so I can get Eva back as quickly as possible."

"Ok, it's decided then. Just you and me, Hanna. Ceri, you stay here just in case," said Sergio, without specifying in case of what.

"What time do we need to leave?" Hanna asked.

"It'll take us a good 40 minutes to get there, and then we need to find the exact location of the drop-off point," explained Sergio. "Why don't we leave as soon as the rush hour's over? That will give us plenty of time to get there by mid-morning. *Va bene?*"

"Fine with me," said Hanna. Her mouth was dry and her stomach was doing somersaults. It was an effort to drink the fresh *caffè latte* that Ceri had made, but she managed to force down a couple of mouthfuls of croissant. Afterwards, she helped clear away and wash the breakfast dishes.

The three friends fell into an uneasy silence. Shortly after 9.30am, Sergio picked up his car keys from the kitchen worktop. "OK, Hanna, time to make a move," he said. "Are you ready to go? Got the memory stick?"

Hanna nodded nervously, patting the pocket of her jeans in response. "Let's get this over with," she said, slipping on her jacket and transferring the memory stick to one of its zipped pockets for safety.

"Sure you don't want me to come, too?" asked Ceri, directing the question to her partner.

"Quite sure," replied Sergio firmly. "Stay here close to your phone in case we need anything."

"Okay, will do. Good luck and take care, both of you. Let me know how it goes." Ceri gave Hanna a quick hug and Sergio a peck on the cheek.

"Course we will," said Sergio. "We'll call as soon as it's done."

Chapter Thirty-Five

Sicily, Thursday 30th November, 2017

Hanna and Sergio left the apartment and walked over to the car which was parked in one of the nearby narrow streets. Hanna climbed into the passenger seat and Sergio took his place behind the wheel then deftly manoeuvred the Fiat 500 out of the tight parking space and into the heavy morning traffic.

They'd just reached one of the town's main streets when he was forced to brake sharply to avoid an elderly lady who had stepped into the road in front of them. They were both flung forwards towards the windscreen before their seatbelts jerked them back.

"*Oh, signora, stai attenta!* Lady, watch where you're going!" Sergio shouted through the open window. "Are you okay?" he asked, turning to Hanna before driving off again.

"I'm fine," said Hanna, although she felt a little shaky. "Just a bit nervous about today. I just want it over and done with. D'you think the kidnappers will be there at the drop-off, watching us?"

"Maybe, maybe not. But they won't be far away; they'll be eager to get their hands on the memory stick as soon as they can." He glanced at her anxiously. "It'll all go well, you'll see. Eva'll be back safe and sound before you know it."

"God, I hope so," said Hanna, with a deep sigh. "How soon do you think it'll be before I get her back?

Sergio shrugged. "Who knows? We'll just have to wait,

I'm afraid." He turned towards her briefly with a smile, patting her hand.

Hanna mused over his vague answer and wondered how dangerous the situation really was. Maybe they should have reported it to the police, after all. She could feel her heart hammering in her chest, her head thumping in tandem. How she wished that none of this had happened and she could have her old life back. But no point on dwelling on that now.

People and shops flashed by without her really registering anything. In contrast, Sergio seemed surprisingly relaxed as he navigated the streets out of the town, one hand on the steering wheel, the other resting on the gear stick.

Soon they reached the main road which would take them west towards Palermo and the turn-off to Caccamo. On a normal day, Hanna would have appreciated the beauty of the coastal road, flanked by the majestic Madonian Mountains on the one side and the Tyrrhenian Sea shimmering in the sunlight on the other. But not today.

"So, this is how I suggest we play it," said Sergio. "I'll drive as far as the turn-off for the lake. Then you take over driving and I'll hide in the back seat out of sight." He indicated a rug he'd brought along to cover himself with. "As long as you can find the right spot for the drop-off – the chestnut tree stump they mentioned – I don't think you'll have any problems. They won't want to show their faces but they'll be watching. Any problems, just call me and I'll come running."

Hanna nodded, taking this in, and checked her phone for the umpteenth time to make sure Sergio was on speed dial. "Seems to make sense. How long do you think it'll be before they get in touch afterwards?"

"Well, once they've checked that all the information is there, they've got no reason to keep Eva any longer. They'll just need to make arrangements to get her back to you."

This sounded much too straightforward. Hanna fell silent and Sergio switched on the radio to fill the void. A local news bulletin came on reporting the discovery of two mutilated bodies in a burnt-out shack out in the country somewhere in the province of Palermo. The place name meant nothing to Hanna, but Sergio seemed to be listening intently to the report.

"Is that near here?" she asked, alarmed, wondering if the incident could in some way be related to her own dilemma.

"Don't worry, it's the other side of Palermo," Sergio replied. "Probably family feuds or immigrant gangs. You'd be surprised just how often this sort of thing happens around here. Yet another story for us to follow up at *La Gazzetta della Sicilia*."

Hanna shuddered, realising how protected she'd been from the dark side of Sicilian life. Or maybe she'd chosen not to see it. Now it all felt very real and threatening. She said a silent prayer begging for Eva to be returned safely so they could both leave the island for ever.

They continued their journey in silence, each lost in their own thoughts, until they reached the turn-off for Caccamo where they headed inland. Sergio negotiated a number of hairpin bends as the road started to climb towards the hillside town, dominated by a colossal medieval castle built on a steep rocky outcrop.

"Wow, that's quite spectacular. It's like something out of a film set," said Hanna in spite of herself, peering out of the windscreen at the town ahead.

"Yes, it's a picturesque little town," agreed Sergio. "The castle is one of the largest on the island, and one of the oldest – it's Norman, dating back to the 12th century. We can't be far from the rendezvous now."

The road continued to wind round the contours of the countryside, the car just managing to cope with the steeper inclines. After about ten minutes, a battered roadside sign for Scalzano Lake came into view, quickly followed by a sharp right-hand turn into a narrow road. Sergio made the turn, then pulled up on a grass verge.

"Let's swap places here. It shouldn't be much further now. Just drive on until it becomes a dirt track…"

"…and continue on foot from there," Hanna finished his sentence. "You don't have to remind me. I remember the

171

instructions well enough."

"Sorry, I didn't mean to…" Sergio got out of the car. Hanna shuffled over and took his place behind the wheel while he crouched down in the back of the car, covering himself with the rug.

"No problem," said Hanna, starting up the car. "No more talking. Just in case…"

Sergio obliged and fell silent as Hanna drove off. The condition of the road quickly started to deteriorate, and she struggled to manoeuvre around potholes and boulders strewn along the way. She could hear Sergio shifting uncomfortably in the back. After just a few minutes, the tarmac ended abruptly, the route continuing onwards as little more than a mule track. Hanna stopped the car and looked around nervously. All she could see were a few clumps of trees nearby and the odd sheep in the distance. She opened the car door and got out. A light breeze rustled through the remaining leaves on the trees. Otherwise, nothing. She slammed the car door shut to let Sergio know that she was leaving.

Trembling, she started to make her way down the track, glancing nervously from side to side. All around her was eerily quiet. There was really nowhere for anyone to hide. Even so, she quickened her pace, eager to get the drop-off over with. She spotted a large tree stump in the track ahead. But when she reached it, it was solid, not the hollow stump that had been mentioned in the instructions. She wondered if this was all just a trick to get her out here on her own and maybe kidnap her, too.

The track was now starting to dip towards the lake, and Hanna could just make out a low dark shape in the grass verge ahead. Maybe this was it? She hurried towards it. Sure enough, it turned out to be a hollow stump, similar in shape to other trees growing nearby. Wary that it could be a trap, she approached cautiously, glancing around for any sign of the kidnappers. But there was nothing, just the wind soughing in the branches.

Hanna slipped the memory stick out of her zipped jacket

172

pocket. She'd put it in a plastic bag to prevent it from getting wet. With trembling hands, she placed it in the middle of the stump, checking that she was alone. Still no sign of any company.

Retracing her steps, she started to hurry back towards the car. Just then, a deafening crack shattered the silence, quickly followed by another, the sounds reverberating across the countryside. Gunshots. Hanna froze, then broke into a sprint. As she approached the car, she could hear the engine running.

"Get in!" yelled Sergio from behind the wheel, flinging the passenger door open. She hardly had time to shut it before he accelerated away at speed up the narrow road.

Sergio dropped Hanna off at the apartment and apologised for having to go back to work. Over lunch, she told Ceri what had happened.

"Oh, my God!" said Ceri when she related the final part. "D'you think the gunshots were meant for you, or was it just a warning?"

Hanna shrugged. "Who knows? But it scared me shitless. I've never experienced anything like this before. I feel so desperate, so helpless. And guilty that I didn't do enough to protect Eva. It's my fault this has happened. I don't know what I'd do if they hurt her in any way."

"Let's just focus on getting her back now," said Ceri. She seemed to be struggling to find the right words so as not to upset Hanna even more.

"It's hell all this waiting for news. I'm still not sure that we should be handling this on our own," said Hanna.

"Well, we've got no choice but to wait now. We can still involve the police if things don't go as well as we hope. But that should be the last resort. We discussed this with Sergio, remember, and decided that it'd be too risky."

"That's true but I'm really struggling to deal with this whole situation. I can't bear the thought of what Eva's going through and how she'll be feeling…"

Ceri squeezed her arm. "It'll all turn out okay, you'll see."

"I just hope you're right," said Hanna, feeling uneasy and unconvinced.

By the time Sergio returned to the apartment that evening, Hanna still hadn't heard any news from the kidnappers. She was mad with worry, thinking the worst. What had happened? What could have gone wrong? A constant stream of fears flooded through her head. The thought occurred to her that she might not hear anything ever again and that Eva might just disappear. Surely they wouldn't harm a child? But Hanna knew from previous media stories that it had happened before.

The strain of keeping her emotions and imagination in check was proving unbearable and she could feel her composure slipping again.

"I feel so helpless, just sitting around waiting for news," she said. "Is there really nothing we can do to get Eva back quickly?"

"I'm afraid not, *cara*. We have no option but to wait. I know that's not what you want to hear," Sergio replied. He looked weary, with dark circles under his eyes

"I need some space. I feel like I'm going mad cooped up in here. I'm going out to get some fresh air," said Hanna, pulling on her jacket and making for the door.

Ceri and Sergio exchanged worried glances. "Will you be okay on your own? Sure you don't want any company?" asked Ceri.

Hanna shook her head. "No, I'll be fine. Don't worry, I won't be long. Sorry, but it's all getting too much. I'm just not coping."

She pecked Ceri on the cheek, hoping her friend would understand. Ceri smiled briefly in response.

Hanna opened the front door and stepped out, her vision blurred by the tears welling in her eyes. By the time she'd reached the street, they were in full flow, falling in silent torrents down her face.

Hanna's mobile vibrated, accompanied by its usual shrill alert. She didn't feel as if she'd been asleep for long as she groped around on the bedside table to find it. 6.13am. An incoming message. But there was no message, only a short video clip.

It shows Eva, looking dirty and dishevelled, tied up and gagged. A dark figure approaches and rips the gag off. (Hannah flinched.) A plaintive cry – "*Mamma, aiutami, vieni presto!* – Mummy, help me, come and get me!" Then the gag is roughly taped back over her precious little daughter's mouth and the screen goes black.

Chapter Thirty-Seven

Sicily, Friday 1st December, 2017

Hanna opened her eyes. She was lying in a crumpled heap on the bedroom floor, a nest of mice doing a clog dance in her head. Slowly she tried to focus. Her mobile was lying on the floor next to her. Of course, the video clip of Eva. She must have blacked out for a minute. She sat up and grabbed the phone, playing the clip over and over, looking for any clues as to where it might have been filmed. The only thing she noticed was the camera panning briefly to show a copy of the previous day's edition of *La Gazzetta della Sicilia.*

Eventually, she gave up and knocked on Ceri and Sergio's bedroom door. "The kidnappers have made contact," she shouted through the door. "They've sent through a video of Eva. Come and see."

She could hear footsteps and Ceri opened the door, Sergio close behind her. They followed Hanna into the kitchen.

"Is she OK?" asked Ceri, her face drawn and tense.

Hanna nodded, tears in her eyes. "She seems to be. Here, watch it. See what you think."

"Well, it's good news in a way," said Sergio, after watching the clip several times. "At least we know they've not harmed her. Strange there's no message, though."

"But what I don't understand is why they've sent this now," said Hanna, pacing up and down, her head fuzzy and confused. "We've done as they asked and returned the memory stick, so they've got what they want. What the hell's going on?"

"These people, whoever they are, aren't stupid," said Sergio. "They'll be only too well aware that we could have copied the information so we still pose a threat. Maybe this is just a reminder that they're in control and to warn us off from going to the authorities. There are no clues in the video as to where she's being held, so I'm afraid we're back to square one, waiting for news."

"Poor Eva, God knows what she's going through. She must be terrified," said Hanna, wringing her hands. "But it doesn't add up. I just feel that there's something else going on here. Not that I'm familiar with these situations…"

"We need to play it carefully by their rules, however painful that may be," said Sergio gently. "We can't take any risks."

"You think that they might still hurt her?" asked Hanna, her heart beating faster.

Sergio shrugged. "We just need to wait it out."

"I don't think I can take any more of this." Hanna's voice cracked. "My head feels as if it's going to explode."

Ceri, who had been listening intently to the exchange, opened a cupboard door and retrieved a box of pills.

"Here," she said, taking two out of a blister pack and putting them on the table with a glass of water. "Take these – they should help ease your head and calm your nerves. You might want to try and get some rest. We can monitor your phone and let you know as soon as there's any news."

"Maybe," Hanna said reluctantly, "but you'll let me know as soon as they make contact?"

"Of course we will. We all want this to be over as quickly as possible." Ceri smiled briefly to reassure her.

"Okay, then," said Hanna, washing the pills down with several mouthfuls of water. "I could do with some sleep. I didn't get much last night. Can you wake me in an hour or so?"

"Will do. Try not to worry too much." Ceri gave Hanna a hug.

"See you in a bit, then. And thanks, both of you, for all your support."

Hanna went off to her room and laid on top of the bed. She could feel her eyelids getting heavy, drowsiness seeping in, and wondered briefly what was in the tablets she'd just taken. The last thing she remembered before she fell asleep was the murmur of voices from the kitchen.

Hanna awoke to find Ceri standing over her, tugging at her arm

"What the… what's going on?" she asked, still groggy from sleep and stirring herself to sit up.

"It's them, the kidnappers, they've got back to us with a rendezvous to collect Eva," said Ceri, her voice animated. She held out Hanna's phone with the new message displayed on the screen. It was short and clipped, giving a location and a time for the day after next.

Hanna read the message several times before the contents registered. This was it, the end. She was going to get Eva back. Everything she'd hoped and prayed for. She felt elated, giddy with joy.

"Oh, my God. At last! That's wonderful, I just can't believe it!" Tears trickled down her cheeks.

"I'm so happy for you," said Ceri, hugging her yet again. "It's nearly over. Eva will be back soon."

"See, it'll all work out okay now," said Sergio, who was hovering in the doorway. He seemed hesitant to come closer. "I think this calls for a celebratory lunch, if you're up to it, Hanna?"

Hanna smiled. "It's probably a bit premature, but I have to admit that even my appetite is coming back now. I'll ring Rhys and tell him the good news."

"And I'll ring Ciccio's and see if he can find us a table."

Ceri laughed. "Typical Sicilian. Everything in life is celebrated with food."

Lunch turned out to be a welcome distraction for Hanna. The busy little family-run restaurant was a favourite of Ceri and Sergio's for its fresh ingredients and reasonable prices. Hanna realised how little she'd eaten over the last few days;

her stomach was rumbling and she felt hungry for the first time in what seemed like ages.

The waiter ushered them through the bustling restaurant to a corner table. On his recommendation, they opted for pasta with swordfish and aubergines, followed by a large platter of grilled seafood and green salad, washed down by a chilled Grillo. They talked little as they tucked into the delicious food. Eva's impending return had restored their appetites. Over coffee, the conversation turned to Sergio's line of work.

"So, why did you choose journalism?" Hanna asked. "Particularly investigative journalism. It can't be an easy career to pursue in Sicily."

"You're right, in fact it can be downright dangerous. I've been threatened and shot at several times. One of my colleagues died in a shoot-out. The newspaper's offfices have been broken into and trashed several times. So why did I choose journalism? I have memories of my father being involved in the police investigation into the killing of the two anti-mafia judges Falcone and Borsellino in Palermo in the early 1990s when I was a young boy. I guess I grew up wanting to make a difference. You know how it is, you become an idealistic student, get into politics, and think you can change the world single-handedly. The arrogance of youth."

"You weren't tempted to follow your father into the police?" asked Ceri, to Hanna's amazement. Surely they must have discussed this before now?

"To me, the police only ever managed to scrape the surface. If they were lucky, they might end up arresting those immediately responsible but rarely those who were pulling the strings, the ones with real power and influence. I thought that being a journalist would give me the freedom to dig deeper."

"And has it?" Hanna asked.

Sergio lowered his voice, although the chances of being overheard in the lively restaurant were slim. "Up to a point, yes. We've had some successes but they usually come at a price. As I said, one of my colleagues died and another lives on the mainland under an assumed identity with round-the-clock protection."

Hanna's eyes widened. "But I thought the mafia years were largely over?"

He shrugged. "Many of the old brigade are either dead or in prison. The rest have had to regroup and find new outlets and activities, particularly as more people are prepared to take a stand against them now, lawyers and politicians, even local business owners. There are fewer murders, but the feuds between rival clans and families still exist. And now we have the immigrant gangs as well."

His voice tailed off. The conversation had brought them back to the present, destroying their earlier optimism and good spirits. Hanna's thoughts returned to what she'd discovered about Luciano's activities. She shuddered. If she couldn't take any action, maybe Sergio could reveal the truth in a story for his newspaper?

But what then would become of Luciano? And did she still care?

Chapter Thirty-Eight

Sicily, Saturday 2nd December, 2017

All Hanna could think of when she woke the next morning was the rendezvous with the kidnappers and the prospect of seeing Eva again. It was arranged for 3pm the following day at a farmhouse up in the Madonian Mountains. She didn't know how she was going to get through the empty hours of waiting that loomed ahead.

Her mind was a whirl of mixed emotions: on the one hand, she was overjoyed at the thought of getting Eva back; on the other, the nagging doubt that all might not go smoothly bothered her. Lying in bed turning things over in her head wasn't going to help. She got up and wandered into the kitchen where Ceri was busy making coffee and putting croissants in the oven.

"Hi, Hanna. How are you feeling? Did you manage to get any sleep?"

"Actually, I did. It must have been the relief at hearing from the kidnappers. Plus all the wine we drank over lunch."

Ceri smiled. "Yes, that might explain it. Thinking about today, d'you remember when we were tour guides the one thing we always meant to do in Cefalu and never got round to?"

"Course I do. How could I forget? Go up to La Rocca."

"Well, today's the day, if you're up to it. It's a bit of a climb but it's a fabulous day, crisp and clear. The views from up there will be breathtaking. What d'you think?"

Hanna hesitated. "I'm not sure. I've not done anything like

that for a while."

"Oh, come on. We've got all day and it'll take your mind off tomorrow."

"Yes, you're probably right," said Hanna, warming to the idea.

"Sergio's already gone into work, but he's promised to research the route and the location of the rendezvous ready for tomorrow, so there's nothing much else that we need to do. We can talk it over tonight when he gets back."

"How long will it take us to get up there?"

"Probably a couple of hours, there and back. You're the same shoe size as me so I'll lend you some walking boots – you'll need them, as the paths are quite stony. We'll take the walking poles, too, and a packed lunch, so we can take our time. You okay with that?"

"I just hope I'm up to it."

"You will be. It's not that challenging, from what I hear. Looks worse than it actually is. And it should be quiet out of season without the tourists."

Hanna had to admit that it was a good idea, probably just what she needed. Diversional therapy. "Okay, you're on. Just let me pull some clothes on and we can make a start."

As she got dressed, Hanna contemplated the trip ahead. It was a good idea, and she was grateful to Ceri for suggesting it and for providing her with a focus. The alternative was being left to brood for hours on end. She knew which she'd rather have.

As the two friends approached the imposing rocky crag that dominated the town, Hanna started to have second thoughts. It looked challenging and slightly menacing despite the almost perfect conditions: a cool breeze and bright sunlight. But perhaps it was just her imagination.

Ceri paid the entrance fees to the park and they passed through the turnstile, stopping briefly at an information board. Originally an Arab citadel, the remaining castle ruins dated back to Norman times. The site had been favoured by local people taking refuge from waves of marauding pirates.

Interesting stuff, thought Hanna, reminded of her days as a tour guide.

Adjusting the straps of her backpack, Hanna followed Ceri as they started to climb the stony path, a series of steps that ascended gradually towards the summit. Walking in single file hampered their conversation although Ceri stopped every now and again to make sure she was keeping pace. Hanna was starting to get into a rhythm. She could feel her calf muscles stretch as her legs propelled her up the path. The exercise, she told herself, would do her good and the fresh air would help clear her head.

Few people were around; it was a popular spot with holidaymakers in the summer but not at this time of year. As they gained height, the views over the town, the harbour, and the sweeping bay beyond were hard to ignore. Hanna was tempted to stop every few minutes to take them in but Ceri was ploughing on relentlessly, so she followed suit.

After about twenty minutes, they reached a stretch of well-preserved battlements set among olive and pine trees.

"Breather?" asked Ceri, herself a little breathless.

"Yes, please," replied Hanna, who'd been struggling to keep up with her..

Ceri peeled off her backpack and flopped down on a grassy verge, her back propped up against the battlements, facing the town. Hanna collapsed next to her.

"Struggling?"

"Just a bit. I'll be fine." Hanna took a swig from her water bottle and gazed out over the town. "But it's worth it for the views alone."

"They'll be even better from the top. Sure you'll be able to make it okay?"

"Should do, as long as we take it easy. You know me, I'm not at my best with hills."

Ceri laughed. "We're not in any hurry. We can have a break in another twenty minutes or so, but if you want to stop before then, just yell."

"Okay, walk leader. You always were the bossy one."

"Look who's talking!" Ceri punched Hanna playfully.

The going got harder as they continued to climb. As they left the steps behind, the path became stonier and they had to pick their way carefully around the boulders strewn along its length. Hanna's mind focused on maintaining her balance and keeping up with her friend, grateful for the support from the walking pole.

"Hey, wait for me, will you?" she panted. "How come you're so fit?"

"I've started going to the gym. It gets a bit addictive and you start to get agitated if you don't keep it up. Sorry, I'll slow down." Ceri grinned, hands on her hips, waiting for Hanna to catch up.

"Sure you're not in training for the army?" grumbled Hanna.

"That's me – Sergeant Major Thomas at your service!" Ceri did a mock military salute.

Hanna smiled. "C'mon, it's not going to beat me."

"We can reward ourselves with lunch when we get to the top."

"Sounds like a plan. *Andiamo!*"

By the time they reached the summit, the wind had picked up and they decided to delay lunch until they found a more sheltered spot.

"You cheated me!" growled Hanna good-naturedly. "No lunch!"

"But totally stunning views, you have to admit!" said Ceri, throwing her arms wide to demonstrate the 360 degree views. "We couldn't have picked a better day. You can even see the Aeolian Islands!"

Hanna stood still for a few minutes to admire the breathtaking view – it had certainly been worth the strenuous climb. The Madonian Mountains rising majestically behind them, the wide curving bay below, fringed by the Tyrrhenian Sea shimmering in the sunlight, boats bobbing along the coast, the dark mass of the Aeolian Islands in the distance. Truly spectacular. But thoughts of her little daughter being held captive somewhere out there, no doubt miserable and afraid, came flooding back and Hanna started to cry.

"C'mon, it's not that bad," said Ceri, putting her arm around her. "Lunch is ten minutes away at the most!"

Hanna smiled through her tears. Ceri always knew how to make her feel better.

Chapter Thirty-Nine

Lunch was a quick affair. Mozzarella, *prosciutto*, and tomato *panini* eaten behind a clump of low bushes, sheltering from the wind. Soon they were ready to start the descent. In many ways the downward path proved more challenging than the ascent, as it was strewn with loose boulders, almost scree in places. *Thank God for the walking pole*, thought Hanna, who stumbled several times despite gripping it firmly.

The wind dropped as they went downhill. Hanna could hear a faint noise, a clatter of rocks falling on rock. She looked over in the direction of the sound and saw that they had company.

"Ceri, look over there!" she shouted, pointing. "Wild goats!"

Three goats with shaggy white and tan coats were making their way, one after the other, across a narrow ledge on a steep and rugged cliff face that ran parallel to the path.

"We're lucky to see them. They're usually quite shy. Trust them to take the most difficult route!" said Ceri.

"I guess it's in your DNA if you're a mountain goat. I wish I had some of those genes."

"Stop your grumbling. You're enjoying it really!"

"I am, actually. It was a really good idea. I just don't want to break my neck."

The sight of the goats made Hanna think about Eva again and her love of animals. The tot would have been chortling with delight if she'd been here. Hanna's thoughts turned to their reunion the following day and her heart filled with joy at the prospect of holding Eva in her arms again. She had to remain positive and strong until this situation was resolved once and for all.

The goats soon disappeared from view and Hanna and Ceri carried on making their way downhill. Although they'd encountered only a handful of people en route, Hanna had an uneasy feeling that they were being watched. Probably her imagination again.

They'd barely reached the halfway mark when she stepped on a loose boulder, the walking pole knocked out of her grip, and was sent sprawling to the ground. She yelped in surprise as she fell. Ceri turned round and came running up the path. Hanna was lying on the path in a heap, one leg twisted awkwardly under her body. She felt light-headed, waves of nausea washing over her intermittently.

"Whatever happened? Are you okay? Have you hurt yourself?" Ceri asked.

"I'm… I'm…" The words wouldn't come.

"Can you move?" asked Ceri, trying to help her up.

Hanna remained lying on the path, still in shock, unable to move.

"My leg…" she stammered, pointing to her torn trousers which revealed a nasty gash below the knee that was oozing blood.

"Can you manage to sit up?"

"Give me…a minute…"

Ceri took the water bottle out of her backpack and held it to Hanna's lips.

"Here, take a sip. Get your breath back."

Hanna did as she was told. The water revived her slightly and she shifted her position, moving her twisted leg into view.

"Are you in pain?" asked Ceri, reaching for her backpack again.

"Just my leg."

Ceri manoeuvred her into a sitting position and frowned as she inspected the wound. Retrieving a microfibre towel from her backpack, she applied it to the gash, holding it firm to stop the bleeding. Hanna's dizziness was passing now.

"What the hell happened?" asked Ceri.

"I just lost my footing, that's all. On a loose boulder."

Ceri turned her attention back to Hanna's leg which had stopped bleeding. "Keep this on your leg a minute." Hanna obliged while Ceri rummaged in her backpack again, bringing out a rudimentary first aid kit.

"I knew this would come in handy one day." She grinned, making a makeshift dressing from a piece of gauze and surgical tape. "If you can make it back down, we'll get it looked at properly and cleaned up so it doesn't get infected. Okay?"

Hanna nodded and let Ceri help her to her feet.

"I should be fine, just a bit shaky. At least the bleeding's stopped."

"Try putting your weight on it gently. We can take it easy and we'll be back to the steps in a few minutes, so the going'll get a lot easier."

Hanna lent on Ceri and took a few tentative steps. "It's a bit painful but I should be able to manage. I just need to be right for tomorrow."

"Here, take a couple of painkillers. They should help for now."

Hanna took the tablets and swallowed a couple, washed down with a swig of water.

Gingerly, they set off again, Hanna limping with Ceri by her side. As her friend had predicted, they soon reached the stone steps where a guard rail provided useful support for the rest of the way down. But they made slow progress, and it was gone 3pm by the time they reached the park exit.

Hanna collapsed in a heap on a nearby bench, her leg throbbing with pain.

"Come on, my girl," said Ceri, getting out her phone and starting to dial. "I'll call a taxi to take us over to the *Pronto Soccorso* at the hospital to get that leg looked at."

Chinks of sunlight filtered through the shutters in Hanna's room, settling across the bed and gently shaking her from her slumber. She rubbed her eyes, conscious of the dull throbbing from the wound on her leg. At *Pronto Soccorso,* they had cleaned it up, removed several shards of rock, put on a fresh dressing, and given her a tetanus injection. Nothing serious and no stitches needed; it would heal on its own, they said. She'd been lucky, it could have been a fracture that would have put her out of action.

Today of all days. The day that she was going to be reunited with Eva. The thought filled her with elation and spurred her out of bed. She showered quickly, covering the dressing with a plastic bag to keep it dry, and threw on some clothes. Ceri and Sergio were waiting for her in the kitchen.

"*Salve.* How's the wounded soldier this morning?" asked Ceri jovially.

"A bit sore but that's only to be expected. I probably got away lightly."

"Maybe my idea wasn't so great after all. Sorry," said Ceri.

"I'd been enjoying the walk up till then."

"Well, as long as you're okay, that's the main thing," said Sergio, bringing the coffee pot over to the table. "Let's have breakfast and we can talk things through for today. Hopefully, it should be straightforward enough if it's simply a matter of collecting Eva, but…" His voice trailed off.

"But what?" asked Hanna, frowning.

"We need to make contingency plans just in case. We don't want to run any unecessary risks."

"Why, what d'you think might happen?"

"You never know with these things. I can always alert my father to have some of his team on standby," said Sergio.

"Absolutely not," said Hanna emphatically. "We've been told not to involve the police in any way. If they get wind of any police involvement, they could stay away altogether and I might never get Eva back."

"And we still don't know for sure who's behind this," said Ceri. "We're assuming it's Luciano but…"

191

Sergio glared at her. "That's less than helpful, Ceri, at this moment. Who else would be after the information on the memory stick?"

They fell silent, each lost in their own thoughts. Hanna wondered why, if it was Luciano, Eva would have been left so dirty and dishevelled. Maybe it was his henchmen acting on his orders and he wasn't directly involved. But surely he wouldn't let his daughter be neglected or mistreated in any way?

If all went to plan, she would be seeing Eva soon enough, she tried to reassure herself.

Sergio was the first to break the silence. "Okay, let's just talk through the arrangements."

Chapter Forty

Sicily, Sunday 3rd December, 2017

It was almost 2pm when they left the apartment. This time, they'd decided that all three of them would go. The kidnappers had stipulated no police involvement and that Hanna was to come alone to the rendezvous. Ceri would stay in the car, parked some distance away, while Sergio would track Hanna on foot but stay hidden from view. Hanna suspected that he may have been armed but this hadn't been mentioned in their discussions, nor had she asked.

The rendezvous was at a farmhouse high up in the Madonian Mountains. Sergio had plotted the route using the GPS co-ordinates the kidnappers had given, but it wasn't clear how accessible the farmhouse was by car. The maps of that area were notoriously inaccurate, he said, due to the constantly evolving nature of the landscape. A road or track that was there one minute could have been washed away or blocked by a landslide the next. With that in mind, they'd allowed themselves plenty of time for what should have been a forty-minute drive.

The first part of the journey reminded Hanna of happier times when Eva had been a baby and she and Luciano had lived in this area. How long ago it all seemed, a world away from now. The winding roads linked houses and the occasional church. There were few villages, and even fewer shops. Many of the houses had smallholdings growing an array of crops. The soil here was fertile, and the landscape thick with trees – cork oaks, carobs, and olives – and the ubiquitous vines. As they climbed, the trees thinned out, the road narrowing until it was little more than a stony mule track, just wide enough for the car to pass through.

Few words were exchanged, except for Sergio cursing and muttering about the shortcomings of his Fiat 500, wishing it was a four-wheel drive instead. Hanna kept glancing nervously at her watch, anxious that they might not arrive in time. Ceri sat in the back, tense and silent. Hanna had left the navigation to Sergio, but even he didn't know this area well and had to focus on following the sat-nav instructions.

As they were nearing their destination, they were forced to an abrupt halt by an enormous fallen tree blocking the way ahead.

"Okay, folks. That's as far as we can get with the car," he said, unfolding a large-scale map. "Sorry, Hanna, you're going to have to go the rest of the way on foot. I'll show you on the map. It can't be more than a 10-15 minute walk. Will you be able to manage it?"

Hanna wondered briefly how her leg would hold up, but she nodded, determined to see this through. She checked her phone. It was shortly after 2.30pm, enough time as long as she didn't get lost. "At least the mobile reception is good. I'll call if there are any problems."

Sergio marked the route on the map and took a photo of it on both his own phone and Hanna's.

"Should be quicker and easier this way," he explained. "Focus on finding the farmhouse. Forget about me following you. Don't look back. If you get into any difficulty, call me. I won't be far behind. Ceri, turn the car round so we can make a quick getaway."

It was Ceri's turn to nod.

"Hanna, you go on ahead. I'll follow in a few minutes. Will you be okay?"

Hanna swallowed nervously. Her leg had started to twinge in protest. "Hope so."

"See you back at the car with Eva. Any delays or problems, let us know."

Hanna took the bottle of water from her backpack and had

a swift swig. She took a deep breath in an attempt to calm her nerves and her racing heart. "Fine, wish me luck," she said, getting out of the car.

"*In bocca al lupo*," said Sergio, getting out the other side.

An unfortunate choice of words, thought Hanna. Although the expression translated as "good luck", it literally meant "into the wolf's mouth". She hoped that wasn't where she was heading.

Hanna circumvented the tree trunk blocking the road, and continued up the stony track. She was trembling and unsteady on her feet, unsure of what lay ahead. Soon she left the car behind, the track veering off sharply to the right. There was no sign of any buildings, just clumps of trees dotted across the hillside, but according to the map she still had some way to go. The track continued to rise and Hanna struggled to watch her step, follow the map, and keep a lookout for the farmhouse at the same time.

Dark clouds gathered above, masking the sun, and the wind brought a chill to the air. Hanna shivered and speeded up. She checked her watch. 2.42pm. She'd been walking for ten minutes already. The farmhouse shouldn't be far away now. She checked the map on her phone which confirmed this, showing its location to be just over the brow of the hill. With a renewed spurt of energy, she set off again. Sure enough, an old stone farmhouse came into view. Not what she was expecting. It was a ruin; the exterior walls were still standing but the doors and windows had long gone, the roof caved in. Was this the right place?

She looked around wildly, then back at the map. There was nothing else for miles around, and they had followed the GPS co-ordinates to the letter. It must be here.

Hanna approached the ruined farmhouse cautiously. It was quiet, no sign of the kidnappers or of Eva. Maybe they were waiting for her to arrive and then bring Eva to her. Maybe they'd approach from a different direction. She glanced round. There was no sign of Sergio either. Something seemed wrong.

She stepped gingerly through the gap in the wall where the front door had once stood. Inside, it was dark and gloomy, filled with an acrid stench of animal droppings. Collapsed beams leant across the stone walls at various angles. A couple of rickety chairs were placed at a scarred table, as if for a meeting. This struck Hanna as being odd and out of place with the rest. She had a horrible sinking feeling in her stomach. The screen on her mobile told her it was 2.55pm. All she could do was wait.

Hanna's nerves were in shreds. She perched on one of the rickety chairs, the light fading rapidly in the gloomy, ruined farmhouse. It was eerily quiet. No-one had appeared – not the kidnappers, not Eva. She wondered how long she should wait. Had something gone wrong? Had they found Sergio? She didn't know whether to call him or not. It was 3.20pm. Maybe they'd been delayed. There was still time. She'd wait another ten minutes, then text him.

The gaping hole in the roof revealed a leaden sky, a brisk wind howling around the old stone walls of the ruin. Hanna drummed her fingers on the table. A palpable sense of fear hung over her, her mouth dry and sour-tasting. Any hope of being reunited with Eva was dwindling fast. 3.35pm. It wasn't going to happen.

She sent Sergio a text asking how much longer she should stay. He responded immediately, saying that she should give it until 4pm before leaving, adding that he hadn't seen anyone in the vicinity from where he was watching the farmhouse a short distance away. At least she wasn't totally alone. Another twenty-five minutes to kill.

The minutes ticked by. Still nothing from the kidnappers. No appearance, no text. The sky had turned inky black, a faint rumble of thunder in the distance signalling an approaching storm. Soon the first raindrops started falling. Still no sign.

Hanna heaved a deep sigh, all her hopes dashed. What had gone wrong? She waited until shortly after 4pm before she alerted Sergio that she was leaving. He confirmed yet again that there was no sign of life outside.

She used the torch on her phone to pick her way across the rubble to reach the doorway. She was just about to leave the farmhouse when from the corner of her eye she noticed something glinting. There, by the side of the doorway, hanging from a rusty nail was a length of coarse string.

Attached to the string were three silver bullets.

Chapter Forty-One

Sicily, Sunday 3rd December, 2017

Hanna stumbled out through the doorway of the farmhouse, her eyes thick with tears. Sergio emerged from his hiding place in the ruins of a nearby outbuilding and ran over to her. She was so overcome with sobs that she could hardly move.

"What the hell's happened, Hanna? Are you okay?"

Hanna opened her mouth to speak, but the words wouldn't come. Her whole world had become a blur, seen through a veil of tears. Why the bullets again? Had they harmed Eva, or was it just another sick threat?

"C'mon, let's get back to the car. We can talk about it later once we're away from here." Sergio put his arm around her and guided her away from the farmhouse, back towards the car.

As Hanna gradually calmed down, they were able to move more quickly despite the driving rain. Sergio remained vigilant, constantly checking their surroundings for any sign of the kidnappers. He sent a quick alert to let Ceri know they were on their way back, and she was waiting for them with the engine running. They piled gratefully into the car, water dripping from their clothes and hair. Ceri looked at them questioningly but said nothing as she put the car into gear, scattering stones as she accelerated away.

The rain was relentless now, the downpour dislodging boulders and depositing broken branches along the track ahead. Potholes sprang up in places that hadn't been there on the way up. Ceri struggled to manoeuvre the car around all the obstacles and seemed relieved when Sergio offered to take over the driving. They swapped places and started off again. Hanna sat in the back seat, chilled and trembling, her mind awash with thoughts of Eva and what might have happened to her.

The storm raged around them, now in full force, with flashes of forked lightning and claps of thunder at regular intervals. The track was fast turning into a torrent, and Sergio was struggling to control the car in the extreme conditions. No-one spoke. The storm only started to ease once they arrived back at the coast, although the driving rain persisted.

Hanna could tell that they were all relieved; the atmosphere lifted in the car as they exhanged nervous smiles, glad to have made it back safely. She felt sick, partly from the journey through the ferocious storm, but mostly because of her experience at the farmhouse. *What had gone wrong?* she wondered. *Why were they toying with her like a mouse at the mercy of a cat?* These thoughts continued to torment her back at the apartment as she peeled off her wet clothes and took a hot shower.

After about twenty minutes and a change of clothes, all three gathered around the kitchen table. Ceri had made hot chocolate and toasted smoked provolone cheese and mortadella sandwiches. For Hanna, the food provided some comfort despite everything she'd just been through. She took a sip of her hot chocolate and winced as it scalded her tongue.

"So, what the hell happened, Hanna?" Sergio asked, through a mouthful of sandwich.

"Well, I got there in good time time but the farmhouse was deserted. As you know, I waited a full hour in case they'd been delayed, but nothing. No Eva, no message, nothing," Hanna's eyes started to brim with tears again. "Then, just as I was leaving, I noticed something glinting on the inside of the doorway. Three silver bullets. Just like before. They must have been left hanging there deliberately, in a place where I couldn't fail to see them on my way out."

Ceri's hand flew to her mouth in dismay. "Oh my God! And still you didn't see anyone?"

Hanna shook her head. "It can't be Luciano behind this, can it? It must be someone else. But who? And why haven't they returned Eva? We've given them what they asked for."

"Beats me," said Sergio. "But whatever it is, I think we need help to resolve it, and quickly. It's too big to be tackling it on our own now. You've had two death threats, for God's sake."

Hanna studied Sergio's face. "You mean it's too dangerous?"

"It just seems too…" he struggled to find the right word, "…involved. We need to secure Eva's release and make sure no-one gets hurt in the process."

"But what can we do?" Ceri asked.

"Well… I've been thinking. What I could do is discuss this with my father and see what he advises. It would be on a personal level and confidential, not as part of a formal police investigation at this stage." He looked nervously at Hanna, as if unsure of how she would respond to his suggestion.

"You might be right. Let me think about it," she said, feeling more open to police involvement given what had just happened. Desperate measures were needed now.

"Don't take long about it – we need to act quickly. The kidnappers could be back in touch at any time with further demands."

"But we've got nothing else to offer them," said Hanna, frowning. "What more could they possibly want?"

"That, we don't know. I just think we need to be fully prepared, that's all," he replied resolutely.

"Sergio's right," said Ceri. "Especially with the recent increase in feuding that's in the news. We really don't know what we're up against, or what's going on behind the scenes."

Hanna felt a hot stab of anger rush through her. Why was this happening? She'd never done anything to harm anyone. But she had to admit that both Sergio and Ceri had a point and they were taking risks, too. What if—

A text alert. Hanna grabbed her phone. A message from the kidnappers:

Don't fuck with us. Not all the information was on the memory stick. Some files encrypted. Try again if you want Eva back. Wait for further instructions.

"OK," she said quietly, putting the phone on the table so Sergio and Ceri could read the message. "Let's do it. Let's talk to your father."

Chapter Forty-Two

Sicily, Sunday 3rd – Monday 4th December, 2017

Sergio called his father straight away and arranged to go over to his parents' house that evening. At first, Hanna had insisted on going, too, but Sergio managed to persuade her that they'd be able to talk more frankly without her. He pointed out that she was in no fit state for the journey, let alone the discussion. She felt completely drained, physically as well as emotionally, and accepted that she'd be better staying behind with Ceri.

Once left on their own, all conversation soon dried up. There was nothing new, not until Sergio had spoken to his father. Ceri switched on the television news – the usual reports of global disasters before turning to those closer to home. More arrests in Sicily in the run-up to the local elections amid allegations of corruption linked to the migrant centres across the island. Aid had not been reaching the needy and was being siphoned off. They watched in silence until Ceri switched it off.

"D'you think Sergio'll be much longer?" asked Hanna.

"It'll probably be late before he's back, I would think. No point you waiting up. You must be exhausted. You need some sleep," said Ceri. "If there's anything urgent, I can always wake you but it's unlikely there'll be anything that won't wait until tomorrow. We can talk in the morning."

"You're probably right," said Hanna reluctantly, trying to stifle a yawn. "You will wake me if anything happens?"

"Of course I will. Try and get some rest."

"Okay. See you in the morning then."

When Hanna woke the next morning, the first thing she did was reach for her phone yet again. She'd barely slept and had been constantly checking the mobile throughout the night. The only message that had come through was from Rhys, asking how things had gone.

She got up and went into the empty kitchen. As she started to make coffee, Ceri appeared in a dressing gown, her hair dishevelled, looking as if she'd just woken up and was struggling to cope with the new day. There was no sign of Sergio.

"Morning," Ceri mumbled. "You okay? Any news from the kidnappers?"

"Nothing as yet. Rhys has been in touch, asking about yesterday. I'll call him in a minute and let him know what's happened. How did Sergio get on last night with his father?"

"I don't really know. It got late at his parents' place and he decided to stay over. He should be back anytime now, so we'll soon find out. Let's have some coffee before we do anything else."

"I was just making some," said Hanna. She finished filling the coffee pot with water and put it on the stove.

Just as the pot started to gurgle, Ceri's phone rang and a message alert sounded on Hanna's at exactly the same time. Vaguely aware of Ceri's voice in the background, Hanna grabbed her phone and opened the message. It was the kidnappers again:

Make sure all the information is on the memory stick this time. Same drop-off as before – the old tree stump near Lake Scalzano outside Caccamo. Tomorrow morning. No tricks. Don't fuck up or you'll never see Eva again.

She collapsed onto a chair, feeling as if the blood was draining from all her vital organs.

Ceri was just finishing her call. "That was Sergio," she explained. "He's dropped the memory stick off with Pietro so he can have another stab at decrypting the remaining files. He should be back here in about 15-20 minutes or so…" Her voice trailed off. "Hanna, what's happened?"

"The kidnappers. They want the information by tomorrow morning. Christ, Pietro better be able to do it in time. What if he can't? We can't afford any problems, otherwise we're in big trouble. Did Sergio say anything about the discussion with this father?"

"Only that they've got a plan which he'll talk to us about when he gets back," said Ceri, pouring milk into two cups of coffee and handing one to Hanna. "I'm going to get dressed quickly."

"Yes, I'll do the same," muttered Hanna, taking her coffee back to the bedroom.

When will this nightmare end? she wondered, her heart racing and her head starting to throb again.

True to his word, Sergio arrived back at the apartment shortly after nine. Sitting around the kitchen table, Hanna told him about the latest message from the kidnappers.

"That seems straightforward enough, as long as they don't pull any tricks," he commented.

"So, what did your father have to say?" asked Hanna impatiently.

"Well, predictably enough, his view is that we were mad to contemplate tackling this on our own, especially with a child involved," said Sergio, "even if we thought it was just a family issue. There's too much at stake – this is organised crime we're talking about, not some petty street thugs. You've heard about the surge in criminal activity and the recent arrests. Apparently even figures of authority are involved. You'll remember that my father was arrested at one stage, although it turned out to be a case of mistaken identity. There's a lot of police undercover work going on and further arrests are likely.

"His advice is not to take any more chances and get police back-up for any future drop-offs or meetings. He can keep the whole thing low-key and confined to a few trusty colleagues rather than turning it into a formal investigation. Seems like a reasonable plan to me. What d'you reckon?"

"It makes sense," said Hanna slowly, as she turned it over in her mind, trying to put her emotions aside for a moment. "At least we'll have back-up which should help. Did he say anything about our chances of getting Eva back safely?"

"Not really. He didn't want to speculate and give us false hope."

"So we're agreed that we shouldn't try to tackle this on our own from now on?" Ceri asked.

A murmur of assent rippled around the table. Hanna was still unsure about the idea of police involvement but she kept this to herself. At least the police could offer a safety net. The thought gave her a greater sense of hope, but it wasn't without its risks.

"Good, that's settled then," said Sergio, reaching for his phone. "My father and his colleagues are on standby for the next drop. I'll let them know it's tomorrow morning. Pietro, too. I've left him working on the files. He'll be in touch later to let me know how it's going. All we can do now is wait."

Hanna's heart plummeted. She was so weary of waiting, especially when the outcome never amounted to anything positive. She clung desperately to the belief that this time they would have more success.

Chapter Forty-Three

Sicily, Monday 4th December, 2017

Patience had never been one of Hanna's virtues, and the waiting around, along with the feeling of helplessness and fear that Eva might be harmed in some way, were almost too much for her to bear. She tried to while away the time by flicking through a number of magazines, blind to their contents, her mind churning. What if Pietro had no joy with the memory stick and couldn't retrieve all the files? What would happen to Eva then? It was too awful to contemplate. Would the police be able to intervene?

Sergio was working on a feature story for that week's edition of the paper, while Ceri attempted to tidy up. Few words were spoken between them. The tense silence hung in the air like a noxious gas. The kitchen clock provided the only audible reminder of time passing.

Just before noon, the shrill ring of Sergio's phone shattered the quietness. He listened to the caller, only adding the occasional word to the conversation, before hanging up.

"That was Pietro. He's not quite there yet, but he's gone through each file and made some adjustments so they won't revert to their encrypted form. Just one or two that he's having problems with, but he's confident he'll be able to crack it and have it all finished by tonight."

"Thank God for that," said Hanna, feeling the tension in her shoulders ease slightly. "Maybe, this time, we really will get Eva back."

The rest of the day passed quickly in contrast. Hanna felt more optimistic and jumped at Ceri's suggestion that they go for a walk along the harbour if her leg was up to it. Being out and among other people would take her mind momentarily away from her ordeal. Sergio stayed behind to finish his feature, but promised to call the minute he had any news.

Just as they reached the far end of the harbour, Hanna's phone rang. She fished it out of her jacket pocket with trembling fingers, relieved to see from the screen that the caller was Rhys.

"Hi Hanna, it's Rhys. How are you? How are things going? Have you managed to get Eva back yet?"

"Hi, Rhys. Good to hear from you. Eva's still missing, I'm afraid."

She moved onto the beach to avoid being overheard speaking English by people passing by, and gave Rhys a brief summary of where they were up to. He listened without interrupting until she'd finished.

"Probably for the best that you've got police back-up. Is there anything I can do? Would it help if I came over?" he asked.

"Thanks for the offer, but I think we're doing everything we can."

Out of the corner of her eye, Hanna caught sight of a lone, burly man approaching along the beach. He looked out of place somehow and she hastened to finish her conversation with Rhys. "Just hope it goes well this time and we can get Eva back. Sorry, but I've got to go now."

"Okay. Well, good luck with everything. Keep in touch and let me know how it goes. I'll be thinking of you."

Hanna watched the man as he changed direction and headed away from her. She was struggling to focus on the conversation and keep her emotions in check.

"Thanks, Rhys, much appreciated. Talk soon."

"Give my love to Ceri."

"Will do. Bye."

Ceri was looking at her with raised eyebrows as she ended the call.

"What is it? What are you thinking? Don't let your imagination run away with you."

"You forget that I know Rhys inside out. He's my brother, after all. Beneath that tough, rugged exterior, he's just a sentimental soul at heart."

Hannah shook her head. "He's only being supportive, Ceri. No more than that. Anyway, in the circumstances—"

Their conversation was cut short by Ceri's phone ringing. Hanna could hear Sergio's voice but couldn't make out the words. As Ceri listened, saying little, she gave Hanna the thumbs up. "That's great news. Fingers crossed this time that it'll be enough," she said into the phone. "See you later."

Ceri put her phone back in her jacket pocket. "All set," she announced. "Pietro's finished with the memory stick and all the files are there, so Sergio's gone to pick it up. He's meeting him in a bar on the outskirts of town. Should take him about an hour or so. Enough time for us to get back and start getting dinner ready. You hungry?"

"A little," Hannah admitted. "I suppose I should keep my strength up. I'll be needing it."

Everything was in hand for the drop-off the following day. Sergio had collected the memory stick, and a copy, from Pietro, having first checked that all the information was there as it should be. He'd then alerted his father, who'd arranged for the police to stake out the drop-off point.

After dinner, feeling more hopeful but still anxious, they settled down to watch a light-hearted film that Ceri had chosen to try and take their minds off the following day. The film turned out to be a perfect choice and was serving its purpose well until just before the end, Hanna's phone rang and broke the spell.

Another short video of Eva. This time, she was sobbing and wailing, "*Mamma, ho paura* – I'm so frightened. Where are you? Come and get me! I miss you, *Mamma...*" Then it cut off and a curt message flashed up:

Remember what's at stake. No tricks. Come alone.

208

Chapter Forty-Four

Sicily, Tuesday 5th – Wednesday 6th December, 2017

The rendezvous the next day went smoothly. For Hanna, it felt strange, like reliving a habitual dream or replaying a familiar scene from a film, but somehow less threatening than before. Maybe it was knowing that the police were on hand should something go amiss.

They repeated the same steps as before, with Sergio driving, then hiding in the back of the car while she made the drop-off on foot. The same eerie silence, except for the birds chattering in the trees. No gunshots this time. She made her way back to the car at a steady pace, and they drove away calmly as if it was just a normal outing into the countryside.

Once back at the wheel, Sergio shot her a sideways glance.

"So?" he asked. "How did it go?"

"Straightforward. I made the drop, didn't hear anything or see anyone. No gunshots, no threats of any kind."

"Good," Sergio replied, although from the incredulous expression on his face it was clear that he thought it almost too good to be true. "Let's get back and wait for them to contact us again."

This time, the kidnappers wasted no time in getting back to Hanna. Early the same evening, back at the apartment, a short cryptic message pinged through on her phone:

All files received. Handover will take place tomorrow afternoon. Location will be confirmed in the morning. Don't do anything stupid.

Hanna's eyes filled with tears. It seemed like an eternity since she'd last seen her precious daughter. Although it had only been just over a week, they'd never been apart for more than a few days before. She'd do anything just to hug her again. The thought of Eva filled her with anguish and her body ached as if a part of her had been torn out. She agonised over how the tot was coping with her ordeal. She must be terrified. Hopefully it would soon be over and they'd be reunited at last.

Ceri put her arm round her. "That's great news! At last!"

Hanna smiled through her tears, overcome with emotion, but she could see that something was troubling Ceri.

"Did you talk to your father about tracing these messages?" asked Ceri, turning to Sergio.

"I did, and I've even tried myself, but they're obviously using some form of blocking device to hide both the number and the location of the calls," said Sergio. "Even if we manage to track their location, it'll change every time they contact us, so the information would be pretty useless. Anyway, it looks as if it'll all be over soon."

"Kidnapping children is pretty low, even for organised criminals," Ceri continued.

Sergio sighed. "You're forgetting that this is Sicily, *cara*. There's a different code here, a different set of rules, and even that keeps changing. I think we're going to have to be satisfied with getting Eva back, and forget about retribution."

Hanna nodded in assent. "I just want Eva back safe and sound, that's all. That'll be more than enough." She tried not to think of all the misery and danger the migrants were facing.

"You're right, of course, but it seems so wrong that these people can get off scot-free," said Ceri.

"Well, that might not be the case," said Sergio. "Dad didn't give any details but I got the impression that the police investigation into the people trafficking is close to making a breakthrough. There could well be further arrests. Plus, I know from our own sources that the rivalries between clans are gaining momentum. It may only be a matter of time."

"Can we change the subject?" asked Hanna wearily, the last of her emotional and physical energy ebbing away.

"Sorry, you must be exhausted," said Ceri. "I think we all deserve a little *aperitivo,* then I'll make a start on dinner."

"Good idea!" said Sergio. "I'm famished!"

The two girls smiled at each other. It would take a lot to put Sergio off his food.

The ruined farmhouse comes into view, this time in brilliant, blinding sunshine. She has to shield her eyes as she thrashes through the undergrowth, approaching the building from a different route. Shouts come from within. Gunshots ring out. A child's shrill cry pierces the air. She breaks into a sprint. Shadowy figures flee from the building. Inside, Eva lying on the ground, a pool of blood forming underneath her. She flings herself on Eva's body, desperately looking for any sign of life. But there is none. A bloodcurdling scream escapes from her throat. Her little girl has gone…

Hannah's phone buzzed and she awoke with a start, trembling and sweating, terrified by the vivid images. Then a gradual flood of relief as she realised that it was only a nightmare, quickly followed by a sudden feeling of dread that it could be a premonition.

She reached for her phone. One new message. The kidnappers, this time with a different location for the handover. At least that part of the nightmare couldn't come to fruition. But the ending still could.

The nightmare had left Hanna feeling groggy. Bleary-eyed, she stumbled into the bathroom, turned on the shower, and let its soothing jets revive her. After dressing quickly, she went into the kitchen where Ceri and Sergio were deep in conversation.

"I've got the location for the handover," she blurted out, skipping the usual morning pleasantries. "A message came through this morning. Seems like they're keen to get Eva off their hands now that they've got what they want."

Ceri raised an eyebrow. "Well, they probably are. She's

served her purpose, I guess."

Hanna felt a sudden flash of anger. "It's my daughter we're talking about, not some some sort of unwanted present."

"Sorry, I didn't mean to upset you. I only meant…" Ceri looked mortified.

"I know, I'm sorry, too. It just touched a nerve, that's all. I'm a bit overwrought, I guess."

"That's perfectly understandable in the circumstances. Sit down and let me get you some breakfast."

Hanna flopped onto a chair, remembering the final images from her nightmare. Should she tell them about her fears that it could be a premonition? Even relating it might somehow give it credence and prove too painful. She decided to keep it to herself.

"Let me see the message," said Sergio.

Hanna handed over the phone. Without another word, he took a note of the GPS co-ordinates and started to scour his laptop to pinpoint the location of the handover.

Minutes later, he said triumphantly, "Got it! It's up in the mountains again, about an hour's drive from here. The maps of these areas aren't always very up-to-date or detailed. Just as well we've got the GPS co-ordinates. We'll need to leave about 2pm to get there in time. I'll let my dad know so he can arrange to get his team up there in advance."

Sergio moved out onto the balcony to make the call as Ceri brought a pot of fresh coffee to the table and a plate of warm croissants.

"Sorry for earlier," she said. "I only meant—"

"I know," Hanna assured her quickly. "I'm a bit agitated, wondering how it's all going to work out."

"I can imagine. Sergio and I both feel for you, you know that. I shouldn't have been so insensitive."

"Don't worry, no damage done." Hanna forced a smile, helping herself to coffee and a croissant. After a couple of mouthfuls, she felt too nauseous to continue. That final image of Eva from the nightmare continued to plague her. She was deep in thought when Sergio came back into the kitchen.

"It's all arranged," he said. "I just need to pop out and pick something up before we go. Won't be long." He disappeared before the girls could question him further.

Chapter Forty-Five

Sicily, Wednesday 6th December, 2017

The front door of the apartment slammed shut, announcing Sergio's return. He came into the kitchen, his arms laden with plastic-covered garments which he dumped on the table. He launched into an explanation for his rapid exit and the reason for the garments.

"You want us to wear what?" Hanna asked incredulously.

Sergio shrugged apologetically. "It's on my father's advice. Personally, I think he's right to be cautious. These are the latest models – lightweight, and specially designed with the female form in mind."

"Small consolation," said Ceri, examining the bulletproof vests more closely. "But your father must think there's a need, otherwise he wouldn't have mentioned them."

"Well, there's a heightened risk with the recent surge in gangland activity. To be honest, he'd rather we didn't remain involved at all and just let the police handle it directly."

"Is that what you think, too?" asked Hanna, worried by this latest turn of events. The police were obviously expecting trouble. Or was this just a normal precaution?

"He's probably being a little overprotective in the circumstances, but it pays to be vigilant. I sometimes wear a vest for work. Not in the office but when I'm out on a story," said Sergio.

Ceri looked horrified; this was obviously news to her.

"It's fine by me, as long as I can breathe and move in it," said Hanna, looking at the cumbersome vests with resignation.

"Okay. It's a deal," Ceri said with a sigh, "as long as we can all fit in the car wearing them."

Sergio laughed at her attempt at humour. "That shouldn't be a problem. Let's go through the logistics so we're all prepared." He moved the bulletproof vests to a chair and spread a large-scale map out on the table.

"This is where the handover will be, according to the GPS co-ordinates," he said, pointing to a large X marked on the map. "It seems to be an industrial location of some kind, but what I don't know. I can't find any images online. There appear to be several buildings in the same location, which might pose a problem as we can't be sure which one they'll use unless they send further instructions. I'd say they'll probably pick the largest, but I could be wrong."

Both girls nodded.

"We can only get so far by road, then there seems to be a track, but I can't manage to trace it online so we're going to have to play it by ear. The police team are going up in advance and will position themselves out of sight. They'll keep in contact with me by phone.

"Once Eva has been handed over and we make a safe getaway, they'll try and apprehend the kidnappers, if they can. But only once we're well out of the way. Ceri, you stay in the car as before. I'll follow Hanna on foot and keep out of sight. It's hard to anticipate whether the kidnappers will put in an appearance or whether they'll leave Eva in one of the buildings for us to collect her. Hanna, once you have Eva, the police will cover your journey back to the car. If anything else happens or something goes wrong, the police will intervene. I'll give you their number if you need to call them directly. *Chiaro*?"

"Clear enough, thanks," said Hanna, with a shiver of trepidation. She was overjoyed at the prospect of seeing Eva again but so scared that something would go wrong and prevent this from happening. The final image from the nightmare rose before her eyes like a spectre.

Hanna helped Ceri prepare a quick tuna salad for lunch, although no-one was really hungry. After several strong coffees, they went through the arrangements again, then checked and double checked they had all the relevant numbers stored in their phones.

Finally, they donned their bulletproof vests. Sergio slipped his on in no time at all, then helped each of the girls in turn with theirs, as they were struggling. For Hanna, it felt like a straitjacket, bulky and restricting, but she'd just have to get used to it. But what about Eva? They all had protection but she'd be exposed and vulnerable. A worrying thought.

In the hallway as they were about to leave, she caught sight of her reflection in the mirror and almost didn't recognise herself; she looked at least two sizes bigger. In another situation, they would have made a joke and laughed about it. But not today.

Sergio went to retrieve the car from a nearby street and picked up the two girls outside the apartment shortly before 2pm. They soon left the town behind and headed inland under an overcast sky. Sergio explained the route as he drove, and went over the arrangements again. The girls said little, their concentration totally focused on Sergio. The atmosphere was strained, the tension palpable.

As they turned away from the coast towards the mountains, the winding road passed first through groves of walnut and hazelnut trees, then climbed up through pine forests. Hanna shifted in the front passenger seat, uncomfortable and sweaty in the bulletproof vest, feeling nauseous from the constant bends. She opened the car window to get some air. Sergio negotiated the bends with ease, slowing down a little at the girls' request.

About halfway through the journey, Ceri asked, "Can we stop a minute? I'm feeling really queasy in the back."

"No problem," Sergio replied, pulling off the road.

Hanna got out of the car and stood up slowly, her legs stiff and unsteady. She leaned on the car to get her balance while Sergio disappeared into the woods for a pee. Ceri was standing by the roadside, bent over, her chest heaving.

"Are you okay?" Hanna asked, going over and putting a hand on her back.

Ceri took a couple of deep breaths and straightened up, her face pale and slightly green. "It's the bendy roads. I've always suffered with car sickness. I even used to get it on the coach sometimes in our tour guide days. I'll be fine once I've got some fresh air and stretched my legs. Be back shortly."

Hanna watched her go into the woods, realising that she'd been left alone. *No reason to be alarmed,* she told herself. She followed their lead, taking a pee under the cover of the woods before returning to the car where Sergio was waiting. She breathed deeply; the mountain air was fresh and smelt sweet and slightly fragranced. Ceri appeared, still looking grim.

"Feeling any better?" Hanna asked.

"Think so. I just need some water before we set off again."

"Do you want to swap places and sit in the front?"

"No, you need to be at your best. We can't have you going sick." Ceri returned to the car ahead of Hanna and had a quick conversation in low tones with Sergio before taking her place in the back again. She retrieved a bottle of water from her bag and took a long swig.

The break had helped Hanna shake off her own nausea, and she felt refreshed as they set off again. Soon after they reached a little market town, Sergio's phone rang. He listened for a few minutes on his headset, then rang off.

"That was the police. They've just reached the handover point and are taking up position now. There's no sign of the kidnappers as yet. There are several buildings, just as we thought. We need to focus on the main one while they'll hide in the outbuildings. But you'll have to be careful, Hanna, as there won't be much cover on the way in and out. Apparently, the location is quite exposed: it's a deserted quarry."

Chapter Forty-Six

Sicily, Wednesday 6th December, 2017

After passing through a small town, the road became narrower as it continued to climb through scrub and patches of forest, passing only a handful of houses and farm buildings and a deserted water mill. Sergio glanced at the sat-nav.

"We should be nearly there by now but I can't see where this turn-off is. I need to pull up and look at the map."

He braked sharply and brought the car to a sudden halt. "Sorry," he said, seeing the girls' reaction. "Old habits." He spread the map across the steering wheel and peered at it closely.

"I need to spend a penny," said Hanna, opening the car door. "Must be nerves. I won't be long."

She took cover behind a clump of bushes while the other two stayed in the car. It was only on her way back that she noticed a roadside shrine with a plaque underneath and a bunch of fresh flowers. Curious, she drew closer. The plaque marked the death of a 21-year-old man killed just fourteen months before in a family vendetta. She shuddered and hurried back to the car.

"Found it!" announced Sergio, pointing to the map. "It's a couple of hundred metres further on to the right. It's not showing up on the sat-nav, maybe because it's not very navigable. See, this is the rendezvous and this is where we are now. Even allowing for the last part being on foot, you should get there by about 2.45pm. Can you keep hold of the map in case we need it again?"

"I've got it on my phone, remember? I need it to get to the rendezvous. And back again," Hanna replied, beginning to feel really nervous now. "You've got it on yours as well. We checked before we left."

"Of course, but it probably only covers the route from the end of the track to the rendezvous. Humour me and keep the map open."

"Okay, okay," said Hanna impatiently, keen to get the ordeal over with.

The turn-off was no more than a little-used track, overgrown with brambles that scratched the paintwork as they drove slowly past.

"This is no route for a Fiat 500," said Sergio ruefully as they bumped along the rocky trail. "We could have done with a 4x4."

The track continued for some way before dipping steeply and bringing them into a tree-lined gorge. Sergio glanced at the sat-nav again. It had picked up the route and indicated that it would soon come to a dead end.

"Can you see where we are?" he asked Hanna.

She consulted the map before comparing it to the image on her phone. "Yes, got it. The buildings are showing up, too."

Minutes later, the track dwindled into thick vegetation. Sergio braked and peered at Hanna's phone, zooming in on the image.

"Look, that's the way," he said, pointing to their location. "There's a narrow path that goes to a clearing. After that, there seems to be a more definite track that leads to the quarry. Probably a road at one time. You okay with that?"

Hanna nodded, feeling the adrenaline kick in.

"Ready to go?"

Another nod.

"Good luck, both of you," said Ceri, taking her place behind the wheel. "I'll be waiting."

"You go first, I'll follow behind you. See you back here. Remember, any problems, call me or call the police, or both. Good luck and stay safe." Sergio squeezed her hands.

Hanna's eyes had misted over now she was faced with the enormity of the task ahead.

"Thank you both," she whispered, struggling to pull on her backpack over the bulletproof vest. "See you later."

She set off resolutely down the path, clasping her phone with clammy hands. She had to concentrate hard to keep her balance along the stony path, and was grateful for Ceri's light hiking boots. The going was tough, brambles tearing at her hands as she passed, overgrown vegetation masking loose rocks along the way. She stumbled onwards, determined to see it through, the wound on her leg throbbing and slowing her down.

The straps of her backpack kept sliding off the bulletproof vest and she was constantly having to adjust them. This time, at least, she'd remembered to bring Orsina, Eva's battered old teddy. She carried on with mounting trepidation, startled by all the different sounds that surrounded her. Birds shrieking, insects buzzing, loud snuffling noises – she remembered reading that there were wild pigs in this area – all seemed amplified and menacing in her mind.

Soon she reached a clearing, after which the path dipped to the base of the quarry. From here, she had a clear view of the cluster of ramshackle buildings ahead. As she watched, a 4x4 with blacked-out windows drove up and stopped outside. Four men wearing balaclavas got out, one pulling a small wriggling figure out of the back seat. It was Eva! Hanna's heart soared. The kidnappers had kept to their word. She set off again, quickening her pace, filled with renewed vigour despite the pain coming from her leg.

The men disappeared into the main building with Eva, just as Sergio had predicted. Reaching the base of the quarry, she realised how exposed and vulnerable she would be crossing the area. The thought filled her with fear but she couldn't back out now; she had to go on for Eva's sake. The police presence gave her some reassurance and spurred her on. She continued at a brisk rate, breaking into a painful jog in her desperation to retrieve her daughter.

As she approached the outer perimeter of the buildings,

another 4x4 suddenly raced in, sending clouds of dust and stones flying in all directions. It skidded to a halt some way from the main building and five men wearing sunglasses got out. Three of them approached the building, holding something she couldn't make out, while the other two stood guard outside.

Hanna watched from the cover of one of the outer buildings, unsure what to do. Then she started running towards the main building. Her leg had become more painful now, blood seeping through the bandage, slowing her down.

The next minute, several shots rang out, reverberating around the rock face of the old quarry. The three men moved stealthily towards the building, guns in hand. It was all happening so fast, yet for Hanna it was like watching a film in slow motion. Then a loud volley split the air. An urgent exchange of gunshots.

Two of the masked men emerged from the building and made a dash for their 4x4, accelerating away at speed, under a hail of gunfire.

The men in the second party cautiously entered the building. Minutes later, they emerged, dragging Eva with them. As they piled back into their car, Hanna heard Eva cry out. Her words were unclear but Hanna thought she heard "*Babbo*". She stared intently at the men, feeling sick as she recognised the unmistakeable profile of the person sitting next to the driver. It was Luciano.

Chapter Forty-Seven

Sicily, Wednesday 6th December, 2017

Four uniformed policemen emerged from their hiding places, yelling to each other and brandishing guns, trying to shoot at the tyres of the second 4x4, but the vehicle sped off in a cloud of dust.

Hanna sank to her knees with an anguished animal-like howl, her hands over her ears to shut out the deafening cracks of the gunshots echoing around the quarry. Sergio ran over to her from an adjoining building.

"Hanna, are you hurt?" he asked, taking her in his arms, making soothing noises and stroking her hair.

"I'd have got to her if it hadn't been for this damned leg," she sobbed, shaking uncontrollably.

Three of the policeman ran off to the main building, weapons in hand, while the older one came bounding over to them.

"You must be Hanna. I'm Vincenzo, Sergio's father. Are you okay? You're not hurt, are you?" he asked in a concerned voice.

Hanna took a couple of gulps and managed to shake her head. Vincenzo turned to his son and there was a rapid angry exchange in Italian. Hanna didn't grasp what was being said; she was lost in her own world. Once again, her hopes had been dashed. She was beyond despair.

A shout came from the main building, and Vincenzo excused himself and ran over to join his colleagues. Minutes later, he emerged grim-faced and strode over to them. He took Sergio aside and had a frantic, whispered conversation with him.

The blood drained from Sergio's face as he looked at his father incredulously. Pulling himself together, he turned to Hanna and said in a shaky voice, "Hanna, sorry, but I need to go back to the main building with my dad. Will you be okay here on your own for a minute? The kidnappers and their attackers have gone, so there's no imminent danger. We won't be long."

Hanna wondered what else could have happened. Something was wrong. Very wrong. She nodded, remaining on her knees as if rooted to the spot, too weak to move, her vision blurred by tears.

The two men returned to the main building together. Hanna didn't know how long they were in there; time for her had stood still. The shock was starting to wear off now. She couldn't believe what had just happened. None of it seemed to make any sense. She could only hope and pray that Eva hadn't been hurt in any way. What the hell was going on?

Her despair was turning to anger. What was it going to take to get Eva back? What was Luciano's part in this? She wiped her eyes and looked up to see Sergio coming back. He was ashen-faced.

"What is it? What's happened?" she asked, struggling to form the words, her mouth dry.

"It's…it's…my brother Pino. He was one of the masked men. He's been shot. He's dead."

The next thing Hanna remembered was being escorted into the back of an unmarked police car with Sergio, his father in the passenger seat. A young police officer drove back to their car, stopping only briefly to speak to Ceri and tell her what had happened.

They resumed their journey, Ceri following on behind. Few words were exchanged, apart from Sergio giving their address to the driver who nodded and punched it into his sat-nav. The tension in the car reminded Hanna of the journey on the way up, except this was different – one of desolation and loss. She fretted about what their next steps would be; she still needed to get Eva back as quickly as possible, but now Sergio was facing his own personal hell. At some point of the journey she must have dozed off. When she awoke, they were pulling up outside the apartment.

The police officer took his leave. Wearily, the three of them made their way up the stairs to the apartment. Ceri had just arrived and she greeted Vincenzo and hugged Sergio.

"I'm so sorry that this has happened," she said quietly. "What a terrible shock. You must both be devastated. I really don't know what else to say. Can I do anything? Bring you anything?"

"A stiff drink, maybe. Ceri, Dad and I need to talk in private. We'll go into the lounge, if that's okay?"

"Of course, go ahead. I'll bring you that drink. Hanna and I can talk in the kitchen."

Sergio and his father disappeared into the lounge. The two friends went into the kitchen where Hanna slumped onto a chair. Ceri took a bottle of brandy out of a kitchen cupboard and poured a generous measure into four tumblers. She took two through to the lounge and handed one to Hanna when she returned to the kitchen. . "Here, drink this. It'll help to settle your nerves."

This is becoming a habit, thought Hanna, taking a sip.

"Are you up to talking about it?" asked Ceri, "The police officer only told me the bit about the shooting, nothing else. Did Eva get hurt?"

"No, no, she's fine. At least, I think she is. But I really don't feel like talking about it right now. I just need to be on my own for a while. If you don't mind, I'll take my drink and go and have a lie down. Can you wake me if there's any news?"

Ceri squeezed her shoulder. "Will do, don't worry. We can talk later when you're ready. There's no hurry."

"Thanks for being so understanding," said Hanna, making her way on unsteady feet to her room, drink in hand.

Hanna woke shortly after 9pm. Ceri hadn't woken her; she

must have let her sleep through deliberately. Images of the day's events came flooding back. She was in no fit state to try and make sense of them. She lacked the energy and couldn't think straight. Would this nightmare never end? She forced herself to get up.

The kitchen was empty. No sign of Ceri. She found Sergio in the lounge, his head in his hands, the half-empty bottle of brandy by his side.

He looked up as she came in. "How are you feeling?" he asked, slurring his words slightly.

"I can't begin to describe how I feel. None of it is positive. More to the point, how are you feeling?"

"Numb, shocked, resigned, slightly pissed." He attempted a smile but couldn't quite manage it. "Ceri's driven my dad home. We offered to put him up overnight, but he wanted to break the news to Mum in person. I've had too much to drink, so Ceri offered. She should be back any minute."

Hanna sat on the sofa next to him. "Want to talk about it?" she asked.

"No," he replied, tears in his eyes. Hanna put her arm around his shoulders; her turn to comfort him.

The act of kindness was too much for Sergio to bear, and he buried his face in her shoulder and wept silently. They stayed that way for what seemed an age, both stricken with grief in different ways, until the key turned in the lock, signalling Ceri's return. They sprang apart as if a spell had been broken just before Ceri appeared in the doorway.

"How was Dad?" asked Sergio.

Ceri shrugged. "Distraught, wondering how he was going to break the news to your mum."

"Did you see her?"

"Only briefly to say hello. She could tell that something had happened. I left them to it. Thought it best."

Sergio nodded. "I'll call them tomorrow and check they're okay."

"Hanna, are you feeling any better?" Ceri asked. "I didn't wake you. Thought you needed the rest."

"A bit better, thanks. Just wondering what we should do

next. Hope I've got the strength to keep fighting to get Eva back."

"Don't worry, you will. Enough's happened for one day. You're probably not hungry but we all need to eat something. I'm going to rustle up a *frittata,* then I think we all need to get some sleep. We can talk in the morning," said Ceri.

Chapter Forty-Eight

Sicily, Thursday 7th December, 2017

Hanna was finishing off her account of the previous day's drama when Sergio staggered bleary-eyed into the kitchen.

"Morning, *amore*. How are you feeling?" Ceri asked.

"Rough," he replied in a gruff voice, his brows knitted. "I need to call the paper and let them know I won't be in today."

"I've already done it," said Ceri. "Told them you'd had a family emergency. I didn't specify what."

"Thank God for that," he muttered, flopping onto a chair. He reached for the coffee pot on the table and filled an espresso cup, downing the contents in one go. "And how are you this morning, Hanna?"

Hanna shrugged. "Devastated, mystified. I was just telling Ceri about Luciano whisking Eva away. God knows what's going on and where we go from here. I'm beginning to think that we're never going to get Eva back." Her words sounded flat. Inside, she felt hollow, deeply depressed at the lack of progress in getting her daughter back.

"We came so close, it's just a matter of time," said Sergio. "Let me come round a bit and we can talk it through. I need to call my parents first to make sure they're okay and discuss the arrangements we need to make for Pino."

Hanna nodded, mindful of his distress. "Go ahead. We'll discuss it later."

Sergio picked up his mobile phone and slipped out onto the balcony to make the call.

"How are they?" Ceri asked when Sergio returned to the kitchen after calling his parents.

"As well as can be expected," he replied, sinking wearily into a chair.

"Does your father know why Pino was there with the kidnappers?" asked Hanna.

"He was obviously one of them. I've never talked much about Pino and there's a good reason for that," he admitted, rubbing his eyes and refilling his cup with coffee. "Pino was always trouble, even as a boy. First, it was just juvenile scrapes, but then he fell into bad company in his teens and got into more criminal activity and became involved in a mafia clan. My father did everything he could to bring him back into line, but nothing he did had any effect. Pino brought shame on the family and became the black sheep. He left home at seventeen and went his own way. He didn't really keep in touch with us any more. We tried to contact him from time to time but it was difficult. We lived in separate worlds."

He shrugged. "As you can imagine, it was difficult for Dad being in the police, to have a son like Pino. My brother was too deeply involved by then, and it's not a life you can turn your back on even if you want to – you know too much and would always remain a threat. But Pino showed no inclination to change direction; he seemed to relish the excitement and the danger. And it was lucrative, of course.

"He must have risen through the ranks to quite a key position. That in itself is quite unusual for someone with family links to the police and the media. He must have denounced his family or lied about his background. And remember, we saw him in the background of one of the videos? God knows what he was doing there. Maybe getting information for a rival clan.

"Dad tried to track his activities over the years, though I'm not sure what he'd have done had Pino been arrested or jailed, or what effect that would have had on his own career. I hadn't spoken or seen Pino for quite some time. We never really got on, not even as kids. We were always so different.

228

But he's still my brother, my own flesh and blood," his voice broke slightly, "and now he's dead…"

When Sergio paused, overcome with emotion, Ceri went to him and put her arms around him. "I knew you had a brother and I've always wondered why you didn't talk about him," she said. "I didn't like to ask; I thought you'd tell me about it in your own time. It's just so awful that it's in such circumstances."

He wiped his eyes with the back of his hands. "Dad's going to take care of the funeral arrangements so we can concentrate on Eva."

Hanna had been listening quietly, wondering what would happen now about getting Eva back but not wanting to intrude on his private grief.

"I can't make out what's going on. We thought that Luciano had been behind the kidnapping but that's obviously not the case. Any ideas?"

Sergio sighed deeply, trying to recover his composure. "I can only assume it's to do with warring clans and their claims for territory. Pino's clan must have been looking for some way to muscle in on Luciano and somehow learned that you'd left Sicily with information on his business dealings. They managed to track you down, God knows how, ahead of Luciano, and kidnapped Eva as a lever to get their hands on the information. It looks as though they had every intention of handing Eva back once this happened. Until Luciano and co intercepted them."

"I suppose it depends on Luciano's motives: whether he wanted to give the opposing clan a lesson, or whether he wanted to get Eva back, or both," Hanna said, wondering whether she had ever really known her husband at all. "What can we do now? Should we get the police involved officially?"

"I think there's more to it than just getting Eva back," Sergio replied. "I think we should sit tight for a day or two and see what happens. If he wants something from you, he's bound to get in touch soon."

Hanna's heart sank. More waiting. But at least she could

be reassured that Luciano wouldn't harm his own daughter. Or could she? Was Eva just being used as a pawn between feuding clans? A lump formed in her chest at the implications of this worrying thought.

Chapter Forty-Nine

Sicily, Friday 8th December, 2017

The following morning passed with no further news of Eva or any contact from Luciano. Hanna was frantic with worry, imagining all sorts of possible scenarios. She tried to console herself with the thought that Luciano wouldn't harm his own daughter. But with no news, she couldn't even be sure if Eva was even still with him.

Back in the lounge at the Cefalu apartment, she constantly checked her phone for any messages. She felt shattered, having only been able to sleep in snatches. Unable to face going over the shoot-out again, she sent Rhys a quick text update, promising she'd call him as soon as she had some good news. Sergio hadn't gone into work again. He, too, was glued to his phone.

"Sergio, I'm really worried that Luciano's not been in touch," said Hanna, her mounting anxiety showing in her tone of voice. "What if he was wounded at the quarry? He might be in hospital, or worse. What would happen to Eva then? What if he doesn't have my new number? How will he contact me? And what if he doesn't get in touch? What then? And what," she added in a whisper, "if he no longer has her?"

"Getting hold of your number wouldn't be a problem for Luciano," said Sergio wearily. "Let's give it until the end of the day. If we haven't heard anything by then, we'll get the police involved officially. They may already have enough on Luciano to warrant closer investigation of his business dealings. This may be the excuse they need to question him more closely."

"But I can't jeopardise Eva's safety and risk her getting mixed up in any turf wars between clans. Maybe I should contact Luciano directly."

"No!" said Sergio firmly. "He's taken Eva for a reason, and he knows you'll do everything you can to get her back. Besides, you know too much about his activities. He'll want to make sure that you no longer pose a risk to him."

"Christ, Sergio, you make it sound so damn final," said Hanna, feeling a sudden knot of fear in her stomach. "If I'm in any danger, shouldn't we be involving the police anyway?"

Sergio shrugged. "These things are always… delicate. It's hard to know which way to play them for the best."

Hanna felt her face flush with anger at this vague non-commmital response, but said nothing. *Was she doing the right thing listening to him and following his advice?* she wondered? *Could he be trusted? Did she have any other option?*

She was grateful to Sergio and Ceri for their support and insight, but it was hard to think straight. At times, she felt she might be better off handling it on her own. *Don't be stupid*, she chastised herself, *what do I know about dealing with such people?* Her thoughts were interrupted by Ceri bringing in a tray of coffee.

"Anything happened, any news of Eva?" she asked, looking at both of them in turn. She must have sensed the tense atmosphere.

"No, nothing. We were just talking," mumbled Sergio.

"How's your dad getting on with the funeral arrangements?" Ceri asked, changing the subject as she poured the coffee.

"It's all sorted for next Friday. A quiet affair in a small village church in the hills outside Palermo, just the immediate family. Dad tried to track down any other family that Pino may have had, but couldn't find anyone. There's no sign of any wife or partner, or any children. No friends or associates either. Either they don't exist or have gone to ground, afraid of any repercussions. It's as if he's been disowned, or never existed."

"I could come with you to the funeral if you'd like," said Ceri tentatively.

"Thanks for the offer, *cara,* but it's better if I go on my own," Sergio replied. "Just in case."

Just in case of what? thought Hanna. *Was he expecting trouble at the funeral?*

"Fine, whatever you think best," Ceri replied. "By the way, I'll need to pop out and do some shopping later. We're short of milk and bread and need something for dinner tonight."

"I'll go," Hanna offered, jumping up, grateful for the chance to escape from the apartment and get some time to herself.

"Are you sure you'll be okay on your own?" asked Ceri doubtfully.

"Course I will. Just let me know what we need."

"Okay, I'll make a list. You can take the car if you want."

"The shop's only round the corner, isn't it? The fresh air will do me good." She grabbed her jacket from the rack in the hall and followed Ceri into the kitchen.

Hanna stepped out into the shadow of the street, glad to flee the confines of the apartment for a while. Her joints ached through lack of exercise, her leg still hurting intermittently. Her head throbbed with fear and frustration. She headed for Corso Ruggero, the main thoroughfare in the historic town centre, now bathed in sunlight and busy with afternoon shoppers. She stopped momentarily to admire the Norman Cathedral towering above the pretty little square below fringed with cafés and restaurants. It brought back memories of happier times, when life with Luciano had been so blissful and intoxicating. How things had changed.

She turned off towards the seafront, down a narrow residential street, the mirror-image of the street where she had lived with Luciano. Two and three-storey buildings in muted colours, their balconies strewn with washing pegged out to dry, scooters parked in neat rows, people spilling out of bars and cafés, deep in animated conversation, others hurrying home laden with shopping bags, stopping to greet acquaintances en route. *Normal life*, she thought with a twinge of envy. She checked her phone: still no messages.

After stopping off at the fishmongers to buy some fresh mackerel for dinner, Hanna headed to the little *alimentari* round the corner from the apartment to pick up the basics that Ceri had asked for. She quickly found everything she needed, paid, loaded her shopping into bags, and left the shop.

Brakes screeched behind her. As she turned, two burly men in balaclavas sprang from a dark saloon and hurtled towards her. She screamed, dropped the bags, their contents spilling across the street. She started to run, pain throbbing in her leg, but the masked men quickly overpowered her. They bundled her into the back of the car which sped off towards the seafront. Hanna quivered as one of the men clamped a sweet-smelling rag over her mouth. She became increasingly dizzy and drowsy. Her head drooped…

Chapter Fifty

Sicily, Friday 8th December, 2017

The sun flickers through the trees, bathing the garden in patchy spring warmth. Eva totters across the grass in pursuit of a squirrel, gurgling with delight, her arms outstretched. I keep a watchful eye on her, laughing at her antics. The toddler stops suddenly as she spies a greater prize. She stoops down clumsily to pick some early daisies before waddling back with her booty, chuckling. "Guarda, Mammina, these are for you!" she says, holding out the little posy. Luciano comes out of the house and gathers us both into his arms for a big bear hug and...

Hanna came to with a jolt, her breathing shallow and irregular. Her head felt like a lead weight. What the hell was happening? Where was she? She tried to stretch her neck but any movement was restricted by the bulky men sitting either side of her. The car was approaching a large stone house that seemed vaguely familiar. Unable to focus properly and think straight, several minutes passed before a series of brief flashbacks slowly brought her back to reality. She remembered shopping, the car, the men snatching her from the street – it was all coming back now.

The car came to a halt outside the house and the men bundled her out of the vehicle and up the steps to the front door. She still felt woozy and found putting one foot in front of the other a challenge. The two men ended up half pushing, half carrying her through the front door and into a sitting room, before dumping her in an armchair and taking their leave.

Hanna felt as if she'd been coshed over the head, so intense were the waves of pain, her eyes only producing blurred images. Slowly she raised her head, her vision clearing. Sitting opposite her was Luciano, glaring at her coldly. His eyes burned with a ferocity that she'd never seen before.

"You've caused me no end of trouble, Hanna. Not only did you have the audacity to take my daughter away from me but you also stole information about my business dealings. Just what did you think would happen? That I'd let you get away with it?"

Hanna gulped. "I… er, was scared… for Eva. After the three silver bullets…"

"But you left without any warning and didn't give me a chance to explain or work things out. I can understand that your first consideration was for Eva's safety. I completely get that. But you have to understand that this is a life that you can't just turn your back on, even if you wanted to. Too many people are involved, including my family and several influential people in high places. Then there are my enemies, people who want what I have created. If I turn my back on all this, I'd be finished, ruined, or dead. I'm too old and set in my ways to start up somewhere anew. Besides, they'd find me…" He paused briefly.

"The silver bullets raised the stakes but I'd have dealt with it. I'd have done anything to protect you and Eva, you know that." His tone was softening, almost apologetic now.

But his words filled Hanna with fury. "Christ, Luciano, they were a death threat! Just how would you have 'dealt' with that, for fuck's sake? And I didn't have a clue about the true nature of your business dealings. You never mentioned anything. I accepted what you told me. The award-winning family winery. I took it all at face value. How stupid was I? Quite the naïve little English girl. You really played me for a fool." She shook her head and laughed bitterly.

"I thought you'd be shocked by the truth and I'd lose

you…"

"And I wouldn't be shocked to find out by accident and once we'd had a death threat?" Hanna rose to her feet in anger. She felt light-headed and her leg had begun to throb.

"Sit down, Hanna," he said calmly. "I'm truly sorry it's come to this. We need to talk about Eva. And the future."

"Where is she? What have you done with her? Is she here? Is she okay?" Hanna looked around wildly. Now that the woolly feeling in her head was clearing and she was able to focus again, she suddenly realised that this was *her* house, where she had lived with Luciano when Eva was a baby.

"Don't worry, she's fine," he replied. "She's somewhere safe and will be returned to you shortly. Once I have assurances that you won't hand over the information you have on me."

"How do you know about that?" Hanna asked, realising she needed to be calm rather than angry.

He shrugged. "I couldn't rely solely on the encryption to protect the files. I had hidden cameras installed around the house for security purposes. I saw you copy the files."

"And how did the rival gang know I had the information?"

"Remember Silvia, the cleaner we used to have? We caught her on camera rifling through my office. She must have been working for them. I can only assume that she'd been spying on us all along and must have seen you copy the files off my computer."

"Really? I wouldn't have thought that of her. She was such a quiet little woman."

Hanna shook her head, amazed at how gullible she'd been throughout her relationship with Luciano. Had she realised that something wasn't quite right but chosen to ignore it?

"And did you know where Eva and I had gone when we left Sicily?" she asked.

"Of course. My people were keeping an eye out for you. It took a while to track you down. We have contacts on Anglesey because of the ferry route to Ireland. We use it for another arm of the business."

Hanna shuddered, wondering who the contacts might have

been. Ottavio's father, perhaps, who she'd seen at nursery, or the men who'd followed her? It didn't matter now but it was chilling to think that she and Eva had never really been safe in Wales.

"But Pino and his associates beat me to it before I could intervene, and they kidnapped Eva," continued Luciano. "Even without that, you and I would have needed to sort this out eventually. I couldn't afford to run the risk of you ruining me. I knew you'd always want to protect Eva at any cost, whatever happened. And I know how strongly you felt about the refugee situation."

He shrugged, his dark eyes sorrowful. Hanna felt a lump in her throat, but was unsure why. Was it a sense of loss, or did she still harbour some feelings for Luciano and what they'd had together, despite all his lies?

"I'm really sorry that it had to come to this, Hanna. But this is who I am. I can't change and you won't accept me as I am. Maybe I should have been honest with you from the start but I didn't want to scare you off. But it's about survival, Hanna – mine, yours, and Eva's."

Hanna sat back in the chair, her head spinning, trying to take all this in. She had been an idiot, burying her head in the sand instead of dealing with the situation straight away. Why hadn't she acted sooner? Maybe at some point she'd still had some feelings for him, or blind hope that things could return to their previous state. But not any more.

"If your people were keeping an eye on me, how come Eva was kidnapped? What was all that about? And what happened at the quarry? Two men got killed, for Christ's sake. One of them was Sergio's brother, you must know that?"

Luciano nodded. "We have a long-standing feud with the clan that Pino was involved with. They wanted to take over our business interests. We'd had clashes with them in the past but nothing serious. Things changed with the migrant situation. They smelt an opportunity to make big money. At the same time, they were coming under pressure from immigrant gangs who also wanted a piece of the action. The kidnapping was a way to get their hands on my computer files so they could blackmail me or turn me in. God knows how they managed to track you down in Wales. We underestimated them; they must be more intelligent than we thought."

Hanna saw red again. "This is the life of your daughter you're talking about so glibly," she yelled. "It's not just a business transaction. Don't you have any feelings, any scruples at all?"

Luciano sighed. "Of course, I do, *cara.* Why do you think we arranged to snatch her back?"

"To save your own skin, more like. You've used her like a bargaining chip."

"While we were snatching Eva back, I had another group of associates retrieving the information from the other clan's headquarters. So I didn't use her as a bargaining chip, it was a question of honour."

Hanna sprang to her feet. "Honour? Don't make me laugh! What's honour got to do with anything? Honour among thieves? Honour be damned. I've had enough of this. Tell me what you want and hand over Eva. Now."

"I can't do that. Hand over Eva, I mean. Not until I have your assurance that you won't release any information you have on me. Ever. I know you must have a copy of the computer files. I need them back. "

"And what happens if I don't agree? What then?"

He shrugged, and looked at her coldly. "Then I can't guarantee Eva's safety in the future."

Hanna sat down heavily as the words sank in. Was he really threatening his own daughter? How low could he get? Her thoughts turned to the two men shot in the quarry and Luciano's part in the misery of the many hundreds of people being trafficked into the country. She shuddered, taking time to prepare her response.

Eventually, she said, "I can hand over my copy of the files to you and guarantee that I won't reveal their contents to the authorities or the media. But they may already have their own information on you. We can go and get the memory stick straight away. But I need you to hand over Eva immediately afterwards. And I need you to promise that you'll leave Eva and me alone in the future."

Luciano stared at her intently, as if weighing up her words.

Chapter Fifty-One

Sicily, Friday 8th December, 2017

"You've got yourself a deal," said Luciano, after what seemed to Hanna like an age.

"So, how do you want to play it?" Hanna asked, conscious that for the first time she felt she was gaining control of the situation and even had the upper hand. As long as she remained cool and didn't allow her emotions to get the better of her.

All she had to do was surrender the memory stick and promise Luciano that she wouldn't grass on him. She'd get Eva back and they'd live happily ever after. Or would they? It sounded too good to be true. And it didn't resolve her moral dilemma. She didn't know if she could live with herself, knowing that Luciano was free to profit from the plight of many more migrants trying to flee their native lands. And could he be trusted to keep his word? She couldn't be sure until she got Eva back, so the sooner this happened, the better.

"We can do it today and I'll arrange for Sergio to meet us somewhere with the memory stick, but you'll have to collect Eva and hand her over at the same time. Or we can meet on our own tomorrow."

Luciano gave her a strange look and said almost wistfully, "You've changed so much, Hanna, since we first met. You're like a different person, no longer my little Hanna of old. So much stronger."

Hanna looked at him coldly, realising for the first time

how little remained of their former mad, passionate love for each other. "I've had to be. Not much choice really when you find out that your husband's involved in people trafficking, you get a death threat, and then your daughter's kidnapped. Those things tend to change your perspective on life."

"*Infatti.* I'm so sorry that things have come to this," he said with a faint smile. "I'd give anything for—"

"*Basta!* Enough!" Hanna interrupted him. "It's neither the time nor the place for wallowing in false sentimentality. What's it to be, today or tomorrow?"

Her tone seemed to jolt Luciano back to his previous mode. "Tomorrow would be better. I have to collect Eva and I don't want Sergio involved more than necessary. Although no doubt he and Ceri have been helping you all the way along. I just hope that he's not been sharing the information with his father. Although I expect they've got other things on their mind at the minute."

This callous reference to Pino's death and imminent funeral horrified Hanna. Was this the real Luciano, a man so totally lacking in compassion for his adversaries? And how could he switch from man to monster so easily? Truly terrifying. Hanna realised that she and Eva weren't yet out of danger and she needed to conclude this as quickly as possible. She couldn't rule out the possibility that he would have both her and Eva killed if need be. The very thought made her feel nauseous, sending her head into a spin and her stomach churning. But she needed to maintain her show of strength. She was so near now, so close to getting Eva back.

"You do realise that there's a police investigation underway into all the trafficking on the island. It's been going on for some time and has nothing to do with me or Sergio." She maintained eye contact with Luciano, looking at him coolly.

"I'm well aware of that but I'd know if they had anything on me," Luciano replied arrogantly. "We've got people on the inside. I'd get the heads-up first if they did."

"So, back to tomorrow. We need to arrange a time and a venue."

"How about the entrance to La Rocca at 2pm?"

"That's fine. I'll see you there with the memory stick. No tricks, Luciano. All I want is to get Eva back safely and get the hell away from here. What you do is your own concern."

A pained expression flashed across Luciano's face before he regained his composure. Hanna hoped that he'd got the message that she wanted him to play no part in their lives.

"I'll get my men to drive you home."

"Was it really necessary to grab me off the street and knock me out?"

Luciano shrugged. "I needed to get you alone, unprepared, and on my own terms and territory, no wires. Here, you'd better have your mobile back. We took it off you on the way over here."

Hanna snatched the phone off him angrily and checked the screen. A string of missed messages from Ceri and Sergio, as expected, desperate to know where she was and if she was okay.

"See you tomorrow then, with Eva," she said.

"*A domani*," Luciano agreed. "And no games, Hanna. Don't take me for a fool."

The steely glint in his eyes made it clear that there would be serious consequences and no allowances made.

Not even for his wife and daughter.

The man instructed to accompany Hanna back to Cefalu drove confidently down the winding country lanes, making no attempt at conversation. She sank into the plush back seat of the car, feeling drained. Her show of strength had surprised even herself. Perhaps Luciano was right; perhaps she was a different person now. A wave of relief, quickly followed by one of fear, washed over her as she replayed the encounter in her mind. She had, for the first time, had a glimpse of the true Luciano – the complete opposite of the man she had known and loved. She couldn't wait for this ordeal to end, and for her and Eva to be able to leave this situation behind them for good.

She sent a quick text to Ceri and Sergio to confirm she

was okay and on her way home, telling them she would explain everything later.

Back in the apartment, Sergio bombarded Hanna with questions about what had happened, while she struggled to summon up the energy to give coherent answers.

Ceri looked at her sympathetically. "Go easy on her, will you?" she told Sergio. "She's been through a lot."

"Yeah, we've been pretty traumatised, too, wondering where the hell you'd disappeared to," he replied, running his fingers through his hair. "We thought you'd been kidnapped as well."

"Why don't you save the questions and let her tell us in her own words?" suggested Ceri.

"Thanks, that'd be much better," said Hanna gratefully. "It was turning into an interrogation."

Sergio opened his mouth to speak, but must have thought better of it and quickly closed it again. He nodded and they both proceeded to listen to Hanna's account of her encounter with Luciano without interrupting.

"So, there you have it," said Hanna, when she'd finished.

"Luciano really is a piece of work," said Ceri, wide-eyed. "Do you think he can be trusted to keep his word?"

"I guess he needs me to keep mine, too. He made it pretty clear that the consequences to not doing so would be dire."

"That man's bloody dangerous!" Sergio exploded. "He needs locking up. He's already responsible for murdering my brother. Now he's threatening his own wife and daughter."

"That's as may be, Sergio, but you have to promise me not to intercept tomorrow's meeting. I *have* to get Eva back at all costs. What you and your father do afterwards is your own affair but I can't get involved. And you can't use any of the information on the memory stick as evidence. If you do, he'll come after me and Eva. "

"But you're his—" Ceri tried to interrupt.

Hanna shook her head sadly. "It won't make any difference, I'm afraid. Promise me, Sergio."

Sergio exhaled loudly, punching his fist into the palm of

his other hand in frustration, clearly unhappy. Ceri looked at him pleadingly.

"Okay, okay, you win," he said, throwing his hamds up in the air in a gesture of defeat. "I wouldn't want to jeopardise your safety in any way. But the investigations into his business dealings will continue independently. *Va bene?*"

"Just make sure that Eva and I are well out of the way first before any action is taken against him," said Hanna firmly.

"We will, don't worry," said Sergio. "But rest assured that we're going to nail him as soon as we can. He's not going to get away with profiteering from human misery any longer than necessary."

But he will *get away with it*, thought Hanna. Even if the authorities managed to gather enough evidence against him without the memory stick, he'd no doubt have some clever lawyer to manipulate the system and get him off or negotiate some lesser charge. But she and Eva would be far away by then, away from his clutches. If all went to plan.

Chapter Fifty-Two

Sicily, Saturday 9th December, 2017

The next morning, they gathered in the kitchen as usual to finalise the arrangements for what Hanna hoped would be the conclusion of this whole trauma. She had mulled over the previous day's events before going to sleep, trying to decide whether she could trust Luciano to keep his side of the deal and return Eva to her safe and sound. She was still his daughter, after all. Surely he must have feelings for his child and want the best for her? Hanna wasn't so sure but she had to remain optimistic. What she couldn't understand was how he could contemplate giving up his own daughter so easily. Was his business more important than Eva? But then, maybe the choice wasn't his to make.

She chose not to share any of these thoughts with Sergio. He had been so wound up the day before. Maybe he was intent on seeking revenge for the death of his estranged brother. He hadn't spoken much or revealed his feelings about it, except for the bare details of the funeral arrangements. She remembered what Luciano had said about not wanting Sergio involved more than necessary.

"Strange place for the the handover," said Ceri. "There'll be people around even at this time of the year."

"That should make it safer," said Sergio. "We'll be able to park on the bottom road to the entrance so you won't have far to make it back to the car with Eva. I'll get my father to arrange back-up. Covertly. Just in case."

"As long as they stay out of sight and let the handover go

ahead as planned. Absolutely no intervention, no arrests, and no shooting," Hannah told him. "I can't risk Luciano getting wind of a set-up and escaping before he gets the chance to hand Eva over, or of her getting caught up in any crossfire. They're to stay undercover and are there purely in case something goes wrong. Understood?"

Sergio nodded. "*Chiaro.* Are you happy for me to drive you up there?"

Hanna considered this in light of Luciano's words. What harm could there be if he acted merely as the driver? If anything did go wrong, Sergio'd be able to get them out of there much faster than if she were driving or Ceri. Then there was also the police presence. Hanna felt her stomach lurch at the thought, the palms of her hands clammy. She glanced at the clock on the wall. Nearly 11am. At least this time they didn't have far to go.

"That should be fine but stay in the car. I'll go up there on my own as instructed," she answered. "What time do we need to leave?"

"I reckon about 1.15pm. That'll give plenty of time to park up and for you to get to the park entrance. You don't want to be late."

"Where's the memory stick?" she asked.

Sergio got up and opened a ceramic pot on the window ledge. "Here," he said, putting it in front of her on the kitchen table. "It's the only copy."

She frowned. "And your friend at the paper who decrypted it? Will he have made any copies?"

"Don't worry about Pietro, he knows better than to get involved more than he needs to. He's seen what happens to people who do," Sergio assured her. "I've asked him to delete all trace of it."

"Okay. If all goes to plan and I get Eva back, I'll want us to get away from Sicily as soon as we can. Ceri, can you see if you can get us on the next flight to the UK? It can be direct to Manchester this time."

"I'm on it," said Ceri, reaching for her laptop. "You go and get your stuff ready."

Hanna picked up the memory stick and made her way back to her room, feeling light-headed and unsteady on her feet. For all her bravado in front of Luciano, inside she felt like a shadow of her former self, an empy husk, as if her life here had been a lie. It *had* been a lie. She must have even lied to herself, only seeing what she'd wanted to see.

Throwing the windows open, she took in a few deep breaths of the crisp wintry air and leant against the wooden frame, gazing down at the street below, full of hustle and bustle. People going about their daily lives. Normal lives. Would she and Eva ever get back to some sort of normality, to peace and calm, far away from threats and violence? She sighed, opened the wardrobe door and began to pack her bag.

"I've managed to get you seats on a lunchtime flight to Manchester tomorrow from Catania," said Ceri when Hanna returned to the kitchen. "You're lucky – the flights only run twice a week at this time of year."

"Great. Let's just hope we'll need them." Hanna gave a tight smile.

"How are you feeling?" asked Ceri, rubbing her arm gently. "It's been a hell of an ordeal for you."

"More so for Eva. She didn't deserve this, poor little thing. But it's not over yet. It all feels a bit surreal, as if it's not really happening. I feel a bit spaced-out, truth be told."

"You probably haven't had much sleep over the last few days. Is there anything that would help, a couple of aspirin maybe?"

"No, I'm fine. Maybe a coffee and a quick bite to eat before we go, that might help." The kitchen clock showed it was now 12.30pm.

"Okay," said Ceri. "I'll make us a quick sandwich."

Sergio appeared from the balcony, clutching his mobile phone. "Just checked things with my dad. The same team as before will be in place in good time. They're under orders not to intervene unless there's trouble. If all goes to plan, you hand over the memory stick and come back to the car with Eva. Don't run, just be quick about it."

"No problem," said Hanna, her body tensing in preparation for what she hoped would be the final confrontation with Luciano. "What happens if Luciano doesn't show up, or he hasn't got Eva with him?"

"Then he hasn't kept his side of the deal and we get the police involved," Sergio replied firmly.

Hanna desperately hoped that it wouldn't come to that.

Hanna left Sergio in the car parked in Via Pitrè and walked back to the entrance of the La Rocca park. A few people were waiting to go in while others trickled out. No sign of Luciano and Eva as yet, but it was still early: 1.50pm. There was still time for them to arrive. She looked cautiously around to see if she could spot any sign of the police presence, but they were keeping well hidden.

She moved a short way away from the ticket machines and the tourist information board to a position that offered a good vantage point of the whole area. After a few minutes, she noticed Luciano approaching on foot, clutching Eva tightly by the hand.

Hanna's heart skipped a beat. Her precious little daughter, at last! She resisted the urge to run towards her, not wanting to jeopardise the situation. It would all happen soon enough. The toddler was dragging her feet and wailing, clearly unhappy. It was only when they got nearer that Eva spotted Hanna and wriggled from Luciano's grasp, yelling: "*Mamma, Mamma!* Where have you been? Why did you leave me?"

Hanna scooped the little girl up in her arms, tears of joy flowing down her cheeks. "Sorry, sweetheart. I'm here now and everything's going to be okay."

Eva tried to throw her chubby little arms round Hanna's neck but they wouldn't quite reach. "Don't cry, *Mammina.* I've been a very good girl, haven't I, *Babbo?"*

Luciano nodded. "And now you get to go home with Mummy, just like I told you," he said, a weak smile playing on his lips. But Hanna could see from his stony eyes how detached he really was.

Turning to Hanna, he asked, "You have the memory

stick?"

She balanced Eva on her hip while she reached into the pocket of her jacket and handed it over. Luciano whipped out a tablet from a small leather bag he was carrying and rested it on a nearby wooden fence. He proceeded to switch it on, waited for it to power up, then inserted the memory stick to make sure that everything was as expected.

Eva started to wriggle in Hanna's arms. "Can we go now?" she asked, tugging impatiently at Hanna's sleeve.

"In a few minutes, pumpkin. Shall we go and get an ice cream? Would you like that?" The process was taking some time and her arms were aching. She put Eva down but held firmly to her hand.

Eva's eyes lit up. Ice cream was one of her favourite treats. "Oooh, yes, please!

It was then that Hanna noticed Eva's unkempt appearance: her hair hung in greasy plugs, her clothes were stained, and her face smeared with dirt. "Just as soon as Daddy's finished," she said, eager for this to be over and done with.

Eva's face became petulant. "But I want to go now."

Hanna bent down and hugged her tightly. "Only good little girls get ice cream, remember?"

"Okay, okay, promise I'll be good!"

A lump caught in Hanna's throat as Eva hopped from one foot to another in excitement, her face breaking into a smile. She seemed to be in remarkably good spirits, considering everything she'd been through.

As Luciano stared intently at the screen, his face clouded over. "Something's wrong," he said. "The files won't open."

Chapter Fifty-Three

Sicily, Saturday 9th – Sunday 10th December, 2017

Luciano fiddled with the tablet, staring intently at the screen as he tried to bring the memory stick to life. Hanna couldn't believe it. She tightened her grip on Eva, getting ready to run.

A few tense minutes passed. Luciano's frown lifted. "It's okay, it's opened now. Just let me check everything's here…"

"Can we go now?" wailed Eva, hopping from one foot to another.

"In a minute, Eva. Won't be long now," Hanna assured her, trying to sound calm despite the churning feeling in her stomach.

Several more minutes passed as Luciano continued to scrutinise the contents of the memory stick.

"Everything seems to be in place," he declared finally, pocketing the memory stick and shutting the tablet down before putting it back in his bag.

Hanna relaxed her grip on Eva.

"Remember our agreement. Don't breach it. Take care of Eva for me. *Addio, bambolina.*" He planted a kiss on the top of Eva's head, turned on his heel, and walked away without a backward glance.

Hanna remained rooted to the spot for several minutes, stunned by Luciano's curt and icy dismissal. How could he turn his back on them so easily? He obviously put business before his own wife and daughter. Again, the thought occurred to her that maybe he had no choice.

Eva's constant tugging on her sleeve and plaintive chant of

"*Gelato, gelato!*" brought her back to the moment. Grabbing her daughter's hand, she steered her in the direction of the car, hurrying her along in case Luciano were to change his mind and come after them. She glanced behind them but the street was quiet. It was only when they reached the car that she relaxed slightly, getting in the backseat next to Eva.

The little girl pounced on Orsina, her old teddy, starting a one-side garbled conversation in her curious mixture of Italian and English, all thoughts of ice cream forgotten. Hanna marvelled at her daughter's abillity to bounce back after such a nightmare.

Sergio glanced in the mirror and smiled. "How did it go? Any problems?"

"Not really, once the memory stick opened. Everything went like clockwork otherwise. No tricks, nothing," Hanna replied, still smarting from Luciano's dismissal but overjoyed to have Eva back with her once more. She stroked the little girl's hair, noticing it left an oily residue on her hand. "Bath for you, young lady, first thing we do when we get home."

Eva chattered on happily, oblivious to Hanna's comment. *Back to normal in no time at all*, thought Hanna, saying a silent prayer of thanks to whichever god or patron saint had been protecting her daughter.

Sergio put the car into gear and drove off. The traffic was sparse at that time of day due to the afternoon siesta and they soon arrived back at the apartment. Eva skipped up the stairs ahead of them, seeming none the worse for her ordeal. Hanna could only hope that she hadn't suffered any lasting damage as a result. She didn't appear to have been hurt physically but there was no knowing what effect the whole episode could have on her mentally. But, Hanna tried to console herself, children often have an amazing propensity to take even horrendous events in their stride.

Ceri was waiting for them at the front door. Eva flew past her like a whirlwind before finally coming to a halt and allowing Auntie Ceri to envelope her in a big hug.

"Come and see what's waiting for you," said Ceri, taking her by the hand and leading her into the kitchen. There, sitting on the table, was a magnificent cake in the shape of a hedgehog.

Eva clapped her hands together in delight, chanting excitedly, "*Torta buona, torta buona, tutta per me!* Yummy, yummy cake, all for me!"

Sergio cut a large slice, dividing it into bite-sized pieces and handing them to her on a paper napkin. She used both hands to cram as many pieces into her mouth as possible, leaving a sticky brown mess around her mouth, behaviour that would have sent Hanna into orbit on any other occasion. But in these circumstances, she just laughed indulgently and watched Eva finish off the piece of cake and then wash it down with a tumbler of fizzy orange.

Hanna wondered if she had been fed properly during her time away. She seemed hungry but it could just be high spirits; she certainly didn't seem to be emaciated, just a bit grubby. *And tired*, she thought, as the toddler tried to hide a massive yawn.

"Okay," Hanna said, "let's get those mucky clothes off and get you in the bath. Then you can have your tea and go to bed."

Eva's face dropped and her mouth opened about to protest.

"And no buts," Hanna added firmly. "That's just the way it is. We've got a long journey ahead of us tomorrow and we need to be up early. Alright?"

Eva nodded. She looked sleepy now, her eyelids drooping, no sign of her previous energy. Without another word, she let Hanna carry her into the bathroom and undress her while the bathwater was running. Soaping her gently with a sponge, Hanna looked for any tell-tale signs of abuse: cuts, bruises, or worse. To her relief, none were visible, at least not to the human eye. If there were any mental or emotional scars, they would manifest themselves in time. She would need to keep a close eye on her daughter's behaviour in the coming days and weeks.

For now, Eva was struggling just to keep her eyes open. Usually bathtime became one big game and could last a while, the water often going cold in the process. Not this time. Hanna had just managed to get her out of the bath, towel her dry, and put on a pair of clean pyjamas before she fell into a sound sleep.

Hanna laid her gently on the bed, surrounding her with pillows, before kissing her on the forehead. She gazed at the little tot from the doorway for several minutes, hardly believing her eyes, before tiptoeing out of the room.

She sent a quick text to Rhys to let him know that Eva was safely back with her and they'd both be on the next flight home.

The four of them left the apartment shortly after nine the following morning. They made a good start, managing to miss most of the rush hour traffic, but it was still a good two-hour drive to Catania airport. Eva had slept through the night, grumbled at being woken up, then fallen asleep again lying across Hanna's lap in the back of the car. Hanna had slept fitfully during the night, conscious of the little warm body snuggled up next to her, snoring softly. It was as if she was afraid to sleep more deeply lest Eva should disappear again.

Now they were finally on their way home, having made the pact with Luciano, Hanna felt more at peace and able to relax. But she wouldn't feel truly safe until she and Eva were far away from this cursed island.

Hanna managed to doze off from time to time, lulled by the warmth of the car and the drone of the engine. Whenever she woke, she was conscious of Ceri and Sergio sitting in companionable silence – Sergio concentrating on the road ahead, Ceri watching the changing landscape out of the car window.

They had spoken little since Eva's return, focusing instead on her immediate needs and making arrangements to get the pair of them out of the country as quickly as possible. Hanna didn't know how she could ever repay Ceri and Sergio for all their support and help, even if at times she had doubted their motives. Sometimes, she'd even doubted herself; she certainly blamed herself for not protecting Eva enough.

By the time Sergio pulled up outside Departures, Hanna's

head was throbbing from all her pent-up emotions and the stuffy atmosphere of the car.

"C'mon, sleepy head, time to wake up," said Hanna, gently shaking Eva.

The little tot rubbed her eyes and slowly unfurled herself from Hanna's lap. Hanna got out of the car, struggling to straighten up, her back and joints stiff from being in the same position for so long. Eva tumbled out, clutching Orsina protectively to her chest.

"You see to Eva. I'll get your bag," said Ceri, going round to the boot.

"I'll park up. You go and check in. I'll see you at the desk," said Sergio, putting the car into gear before driving off.

Eva was looking around, confused. "Where are we?" she asked.

Hanna realised that she'd not had a chance to explain to the little girl what their long day would entail. She bent down and said, "It's okay, sweetie. We're at the airport and we'll be getting on a plane that will take us home. C'mon, we need to go and check in."

Eva clutched Orsina even closer to her chest as Hanna led her into the busy departure hall and over to the check-in desk for the Manchester flight. The queue was short and moving steadily forward. By the time Sergio caught up with them, Hanna had handed over her luggage and collected their boarding passes. They proceeded towards the security gate, an awkward silence between them.

"Well, this it it," said Hanna. "I can't begin to thank you both for everything you've done. I wouldn't have got Eva back safely without you. I… really…don't know what to say." Tears welled in her eyes and her voice broke with emotion.

"We're just glad that it ended well and you're both safe," said Ceri, hugging her tightly.

"And the situation's been resolved," added Sergio. "You won't be in danger any more. Rest assured that Luciano will get everything that's coming to him. And soon."

Hanna wondered how he could be so sure, or if he was just trying to reassure her.

"Thank God for that. As long as we keep our side of the bargain," she said gravely.

Sergio nodded and smiled. "Of course. Take care of yourselves. We'll come and visit you."

"I'd like that," said Hanna, breaking into a teary smile. She scooped Eva up into her arms. "We're going to be okay now, aren't we, poppet?"

"Is *Babbo* coming, too?" the little girl asked shyly.

Hanna stared at her, struggling to find a suitable response. "Err... no, it's just you and me now, pumpkin. Best buddies for ever, okay?" She held out her little finger and Eva giggled softly, hooking her own little finger around her mum's.

A tricky situation averted. For the moment.

"We'd better go. Don't want to miss the plane," said Hanna.

A final hug all round, then Hanna and Eva moved towards the waiting security guard, Eva waving to Ceri and Sergio all the way.

At last, they were on their way home.

Together.

Chapter Fifty-Four

Sicily, Sunday 10th December, 2017

Hanna continued to marvel at Eva's ability to bounce back to her normal self. One minute she was running around the airport concourse at full pelt, next she was chattering away non-stop to the flight attendants as they boarded the plane, then she fell asleep, curled up in a ball on her seat. Hanna smiled as she watched the little girl's chest rise and fall, her dark lashes glued tightly shut, twitching from time to time in her dreams. No evidence of any after-effects from her ordeal so far. Maybe not knowing the the true extent of the danger she'd been facing made it easier to shrug off. Only time would tell.

She slipped on her headphones and settled back in her seat, searching the radio channels to find some easy listening that would help her relax. After wading through heavy rock, political debates,and commercial pop, she finally found an Italian station playing light classical music that suited her mood. It had the desired effect and she was on the verge of nodding off when the hourly news came on. She listened through a hazy fog. The last item made her sit bolt upright:

"In Sicily earlier today, police made a number of high-profile arrests in connection with people-trafficking operations. This follows a lengthy undercover investigation to stem the flow of illegal immmigrants into Sicily from North Africa. Those arrested include Trapani judge Edouardo Giacalone, Mario Culotta, mayor of Alcatezza, parish priest

Agosto Bartolomeo from Mandragone, Michele and Luciano Cortazzo, award-winning wine producers from Alcudi, and rival clan boss Giuseppe Spadaro. The police are confident that they have sufficient evidence to secure convictions. Further arrests are expected in the next few days."

Hanna smiled to herself. Sergio must have known these arrests were imminent. And without her divulging any information from the memory stick. Her conscience was clear. She and Eva were safe. Countless more migrants would be saved from falling into the clutches of the traffickers.

She realised that Luciano and his father could still avoid conviction, thanks to their top-level connections and a wily lawyer. And Giulio, Lorenzo's younger brother, hadn't been arrested. But she and Eva were free to create a future far away from this world of organised crime. She looked down at her sleeping daughter and settled back into her seat again with a sigh of satisfaction.

The plane landed smoothly and taxied to a halt on the runway at Manchester airport. Hanna thought even the dull grey buildings looked a little brighter than usual in the pallid wintry sunlight as she looked through the window. Eva was grizzly from having been woken from a deep sleep a few minutes before, and Hanna grinned at her pouting face. Things were getting back to normal. She waited patiently for the passengers in front of them to collect their belongings and make their way slowly towards the front exit.

As she gathered up their things, Hanna noticed that Orsina was missing.

"Eva, I can't see Orsina anywhere. Has she fallen on the floor?"

Eva scowled and started to hunt for the missing toy. After a quick search, she held up the elusive bear in triumph, declaring in a loud voice, "Here she is, *Mammina*! I was sitting on her. She's a bit, err…"

"Squashed," Hanna said, laughing, helping her daughter out with the right word.

Orsina was completely scrunched up; Eva must have fallen asleep on top of her. Hanna adjusted the toy's furry limbs and knocked the stuffing back into position. "See? No harm done. Keep tight hold of her, though. We don't want to lose her again, do we?"

Eva shook her head in a slow exaggerated way as Hanna slipped her handbag onto her shoulder and held out her hand. "C'mon, munchkin, time to go. "

The little girl scrambled over the double seat and took her hand, following her dutifully off the plane and onto a moving walkway on the other side. This proved fascinating, and Eva kept trying to wriggle out of Hanna's grip so she could run up and down it. But Hanna kept tight hold of her and had problems tearing her away when the walkway came to an end.

The resourceful little girl started to sing, performing little pirouettes along the airport's cavernous corridor, much to the amusement of their fellow passengers. Hanna indulged her attention-seeking antics for a little while longer before hurrying them on, through passport control and on to the baggage claim area.

Collecting her bag off the carousel, she bowed to pressure from Eva to get a trolley. She knew what was going to happen: Eva hopped onto it straight away, taking a seat with her back resting against the bag, her legs splayed out in front of her as Hanna pushed the trolley into the arrivals hall.

A sea of faces, eagerly waiting to collect family and friends, greeted them. A voice rising above the crowd, an arm waving frantically in the air: "Hanna! Eva! Over here!"

A tall figure emerging from the swarm of people, a dog barking excitedly at his heels, tail wagging furiously.

"Welcome home, girls," said Rhys, his arms held open wide in welcome.

Hanna smiled. All that mattered now was Eva.

And the future.

Fantastic Books
Great Authors

darkstroke is
an imprint of
Crooked Cat Books

- Gripping Thrillers
- Cosy Mysteries
- Romantic Chick-Lit
- Fascinating Historicals
- Exciting Fantasy
- Young Adult and Children's
  Adventures
- Non-Fiction

Discover us online
www.darkstroke.com

Find us on instagram:
www.instagram.com/darkstrokebooks

Printed in Poland
by Amazon Fulfillment
Poland Sp. z o.o., Wrocław

49738362R00157